CALLINGS

CALLINGS

Lucy Rushton

Copyright © 2022 by Lucy Rushton

Published by Lucy Rushton

FIRST EDITION

Book design by Publishing Push

ISBNs
Paperback: 978-1-80227-844-6
eBook: 978-1-80227-845-3

In memory of my grandparents, who ventured forth to Burma - and with gratitude to my father, who opened my mind to the adventure of being.

"... *what we are, or what we can be, does not come ready made.*"
Tim Ingold, Being Alive

Table of Contents

1

July 1928

Ada

There's a ship on a disc of ocean, under a dome of sky. It has traced a line across the glistening surface and a trail of smoke draws a more diffuse line behind it, staining the sky with sepia.

The travellers, carried steadily forward each day, feel suspended, held in a glass globe, wound round with weeks of sunrises and sunsets.

This is a ship that carries cargoes as well as passengers. When it docks, each new kind of foreignness is a proof of progress, and the scents of timber and grain give a thread of connection to solid earth.

Ada sits at the side of the promenade deck in an upright canvas chair that one of the stewards has placed against the rail for her. She has folded her hands on the rail and rests her chin on them, letting the glint of the water weave curving traces between her half-closed eyelids. The throb of the engines awakens a tremor of nausea and a stab of pain in her ankle. She sits back but the ship is turning and the sunlight is pushing under the brim of her hat. She unhooks her cane and limps into the lounge.

It is her birthday. She is twenty-three. It is a relief to let this day pass without notice in the anonymity of being a solitary passenger.

Just a word or two with Miss Pinker across the narrow cabin when they slip their feet from under their sheets in the morning; there'll be a brief good night when it's time to lift them up again at night.

Miss Pinker is so much older than she is and passes the time playing bridge. If they pass during the day, Miss Pinker usually asks, '*All right dear?*' and moves on.

Ada has taken to sitting in the library alcove of the general lounge. The "library" is represented by two narrow glass-fronted bookcases and a rack of out-of-date magazines. The chairs are heavy and not often occupied and she can move with confidence between them even if the ship is rolling. The one she most often chooses to sit in has a high back and wings. She holds a magazine open in front of her. She has learnt to find the most unexceptional page with no picture and only a very small heading or two in case, as has happened, someone approaches and claims a shared enthusiasm for crochet or baking or impressionist paintings. As she sits, images of the past four months flit through her head. She shies away from some, puzzles over others. Now she is nowhere, not even in between, because she won't let herself think ahead to what comes next.

She often skips meals and lies on her bed staring up at the off-white shades of the dimpled steel ceiling, the mighty girder that passes through the cabin, the rows of plump rivets. The all-pervasive thrum of the engines sometimes seems to fill her head, like the cavernous beating sounds of thousands of rivets being pounded into place.

She knows that all is not well. She knows that if she were her own friend or relative, a sister, say, she would be concerned, watching herself.

The only thing she will admit to is her ankle. She can't hide it – still swollen where it meets the shoe and with purple weals running up the side of her leg where the poor young Sub-Assistant Surgeon had tried to correct the set of it. And she can't yet do without the cane because of sudden crippling stabbings. But she accepts the pain of it. It has to hurt to heal, the doctor had said. And she knows she deserves it. It gives her a sense of rightness. At least something went right. She is being punished.

On the eleventh day of the voyage she gets up late and reluctantly. Miss Pinker will already be at breakfast. The ship is rolling today. She stands holding the corners of the washbasin, riding the movement, confronting her image in the mirror. At first she checks her hair – a plait pinned into a bun, with the usual frizzy halo - but then catches her own eye. She has always thought her eyes look too pale, too indefinite. Unlike her hair her lashes are straight, projecting like sunshades, like the awnings over shop windows, wound out to protect the goods from the glare of the sun. What did Frank see? He had actually said, *I love your eyes*. He did say that, didn't he? Her nights have been so full of dreams lately she sometimes can't tell which floating strands of memory attach to reality, and which do not.

She goes to the library but a man is sitting in her usual chair – not leaning back between the wings but bolt upright. He isn't reading. His hands are resting on his knees and he breathes slowly and steadily, apparently quite unaware of his surroundings. His hair, dark auburn, is a thick fuzz all over his head except where his freckled scalp is just starting to emerge at the top.

She retreats, a quick turn into the ladies' lounge, through some ornate double doors. Her cane catches on a side table and she lurches against the chair he is sitting in. He leaps to his feet and offers an arm.

"It's you," he says. "The empty place."

She recognises him from her table in the dining saloon but cannot remember his name.

"Bernard Callandar," he says helpfully. "And you are Miss Henry."

She nods.

"But you wear a wedding ring," he adds.

"Oh," she says, and covers her left hand with her right. "Well, I'm afraid he's dead."

She hears her own words, and grimaces as they ring round her head. She looks away and limps to the door that opens onto the deck.

Some days later, Ada sidles along the rail. There's a line of cloud low in the sky – damp air steamed upwards by land. It reminds her that the days are slipping by, the lines of latitude passing under them. The milky, silky nothingness of sea and sky will give way to solid shapes, places, people. She will have to arrive.

Her left hand rests on the rail at the wrist. It dangles a little. On her fourth finger is the silver ring Frank placed there when they married. It is made from silver mined from a mountain Frank pointed out to her, worked by a local silversmith. It has a bubbling pattern of clouds impressed with a curved blade into its gleaming surface. She remembers her astonishment when Frank pulled it, gleaming, from his shirt pocket to lay onto the prayer book Andrew Sinclair held; transformed from the rough, black thing that it was in the silversmith's tongs, a dark shadow that lay across her finger when she tried it for size. Her finger now hangs clear of the others, clear of the rail. She can feel the ring very slightly loose but still held above the knuckle. With her other forefinger she scratches a little itch in the sweaty place between the fingers. She watches as the ring flies backwards against the movement of the ship and hits the water with a tiny silent white splash. She lays her head on her hands. Now, at last, there's a flutter in her abdomen that she cannot ignore.

In bed that night she lies on her side and runs a hand down her flank. There is a rising firmness a hand's breadth below her ribs, an unexpected curve pressing up into her hand. This isn't to do with illness or being troubled. This is a new, solid reality. She brings her hand round to the front, cupping her belly and waiting until there is a tiny movement under her palm.

She remembers Lydia's baby, who only took one breath, and was left as a stiffening bundle in Ada's arms while everybody strove to save his mother. She remembers, long before that, her own mother stretched white and limp on the big old bed, rolling her head and saying, "*I knew it wouldn't go right.*"

She has gone to bed early, weary of the weight of her foot, but has not been able to sleep. With her back turned, she listens to Miss Pinker going through her bedtime routine, fidgeting for a while and then starting to snore very gently. Now that she is safely alone, Ada rolls over and sees a shaft of moonlight striking through the porthole by Miss Pinker's head. There's a bundled silhouette of pillow and shoulder outlined by blueish light. It must be a full moon, catching the ship in the band it lays across the sea. Ada pushes herself upright, slips a skirt and blouse from the rods in the wardrobe, gets into them and quietly closes the cabin door behind her. When she emerges onto the deck there are still a few small groups of people smoking, drinking or playing cards. She stands alone by the rail and there, sure enough, is the path of the moon, diminishing saucers of light lifting and shuffling across the surface of the sea. Riding above it is the face of the moon, sleek but dimpled and familiar. She has stared at it so many times - from the riverboat crossing the Irrawaddy, from the veranda of the Crossroads Hut on the edge of the mission compound, from the hill-top bungalow at the Valley Station. Long before that, she used to watch moonlight glinting on the tiles of the roof over the workshop at home, and again filling the spaces between the stag-headed oaks at the back of Meredith Hall missionary college. Countless times she has seen it transform the sleeping face of her sister, from something soft, careless and inexpressive to a sculpted landscape of curves and certainties. Now the comfort she has been used to taking from the cool touch of the light that also touches Louise, and home, must be brushed aside. Louise and home are all ashes. She snorts out a breath and lets the cold knowledge enter her in a deep and permanent way.

When she first received the news, in the middle of March, it was not to be believed. Arriving back at the mission hot and dusty from a journey, she had snatched up her father's letter with the usual eagerness for anything from home, tucked it into a pocket with a feeling of riches in store. She was alone in her room when she finally opened it. He had tried to express the awful message in plain words, but words, on frail paper, could not batter their way through the weight of normal expectations.

It began comfortably enough.

February 1928

My dear Ada,

I hope that you are keeping well. I regret that you are so far away.

Then came the first warning stab:

I have terrible news to tell you. I do not know how to write it or how you will be able to bear it unless you have forgotten us all being so far away.

That raised a protest in her. Of course she has not forgotten. How unkind to make the accusation. The rest had to be read in a rush of dread.

Two days ago I had a funeral to see to and was out the whole evening. Your mother and Louise remained indoors. Your mother has not been well lately. We had her to the doctor but he just said she needed company, or a little job, but how was she to get out with Louise to care for. She has been taking sherry of an evening, more than she should.

A fire started in the workshop. As you can imagine it took fast, with all the shavings and timber. The house is gone, the hearse, all the business. Your mother was in the back hallway between the parlour and the workshop. Poor Louise was in the rocking chair. They are gone, both of them. It will have been very quick. The funeral is to be tomorrow. You cannot be here so there is no point in delay. I am so sorry to bring you such terrible news. I miss you, my girl, most painfully.

Your father

She couldn't tell anyone about the letter. To hear herself speak the words would begin to create a credible story.

She had sat all night on the hard edge of her narrow bed in the bamboo hut just beyond the edge of the mission compound, staying awake to protect herself from waking to the realization that everything had changed. It must have been her drawn face and lack of appetite that drew the attention of her colleagues. Eventually Diana took her aside and asked her if something was disturbing her.

"My sister," she managed to say. "My sister has died in a fire."

Diana drew her into her husband's study to pray with her, and they sat knee to knee while she asked God's blessing on Ada's parents and especially asking for strength for her mother who must be struggling to bear the loss of the child she had had to nurture so tenderly. Anger exploded silently in Ada, descending as a bitter, gritty ash of guilt.

"Both of them," she now told her. "Both my mother and my sister, both gone."

Now she could see the outline of everything, her whole ruined family, but especially the blackened bone tracery of Louise's vaporised body.

Frank returned from his trip to the regional capital and as soon as he sought her out Ada handed him the letter to read.

She told him she could not marry him. She was unfit to marry. And that was when he took hold of her upper arms, as if to brace her up, and told her that she would be strong now, she had his strength as well as her own to keep her steady. She must keep on steadily, they would marry as planned and then they would take a furlough together and she would see her father again. Guilt was just a manifestation of shock.

His talk was bracing but his touch became softer. He held her against his chest and stroked her hair. She couldn't pull away from his warmth and closeness and so she stopped insisting that she couldn't get married.

Now, all these months later, she tries to steer her memory away from Frank, his astonishing closeness, his confidence. She's sitting in her chair in the ship's library watching what she thinks is the island of Crete inching past the window when she hears heavy intakes of breath together with shuffling and bumping. She stands and sees Bernard Callandar by one of the tables at the other end of the saloon attempting to spread out a long sheet of paper, which keeps springing back into its roll. He greets her distractedly.

"Can I help?" she says.

"A thumb here and another one there," he says.

She pins the paper to the table with her thumbs.

"What is it? A building?"

"It's a dream. A dream of beautiful death." He startles her with a wide, toothy smile.

She can see it's a plan with buildings arranged round a garden with paths and bulgy trees.

"Where is it?"

"Portobello. Do you know where that is?"

"London?"

"No, Edinburgh. Near Edinburgh."

"Is that the sea?"

"Yes. It's a garden by the sea with a great sprawling building in it. It has been passed to me by my godmother who trusts that I will do something worthy with it."

"So, beautiful death ...?"

"Have you been with someone who's dying?" She sees him remembering that she's a widow but he carries on. "Someone who's clinging on, frightened, not wanting to make a scene, in pain, ashamed, unable to accept what's happening? We need places where a person can venture forth, let go, fall asleep, surrounded by people who accept that it is an inevitable part of life."

"My father is an undertaker and coffin maker. He sends people on their way, gives them a good send off."

He narrows his eyes. "That's good. But it's the bit before that we need to take care of."

"Are you a doctor?"

"I am." He sounds surprised. "I qualified, but apart from training, I've never practised. I chose to travel."

"I hope your plan succeeds," she says primly.

"It will. You may come to hear of the Pavilion at Portobello."

The distant deep booming of the ship's engines has ceased and instead there are sharp land noises – shouts, clattering of ramps, a motorcycle engine revving. Ada joins the torrent of passengers spilling off the ship, scarcely noticing the moment when she passes from the ship to the shore. Long-legged Bernard has her case under one arm as well as his own, and is slipping through the crowd ahead of her. Eventually he eddies off to one side and looks for her. They shake hands solemnly and she takes her case, assuring him that she has made an arrangement and will be met. But this is not so, and she stands there watching after him.

There's a call she doesn't hear because she's not listening. She limps forward, looking at the line of leather-bound cases and battened trunks. Porters are constantly plucking out bags and cases and the line of luggage starts to clear.

A familiar figure with her blonde hair framed by a neat straw hat darts forward, waving and calling: "Ada! Ada, turn this way!"

"Edith! What are you doing here? Are you meeting someone?"

Edith holds out both her hands.

"Dear Ada, I am so, so sorry. I only got the *Messenger* with the prayer request last Thursday and then I didn't read it at once."

"What *Messenger*? What are you saying?"

"About Frank's illness. Are you going straight to see him? But I forget, you are bereaved. There's your father, too."

"Edith, Frank's funeral must have been weeks ago. They sent me a letter from the mission when I was in Rangoon waiting for the ship."

"Has he died? I'm so sorry. Dr Grover went to Devon on Monday last week to offer support to his mother and say a prayer with him but I had not heard anything since."

"He was in Devon? But they told me he was dead! You mean he came home? He is still alive?"

She clasps the finger where her wedding ring should be.

"Did you not know? He's been at his mother's house and I thought you would be there as soon as you could. I checked with Henderson's and found out you were definitely on this boat.

"I've borrowed the car," says Edith. "Because Papa works in London so much, and needs to get to Chester station, so he's trained Mother and me to drive him. And the rest of the time, it's at Mother's disposal."

She organizes a porter for the trunk. In the car Ada watches Edith's hands on the controls and is silent. Edith asks questions about the voyage, and passes comments on the weather and the Cheshire countryside. They arrive at Pockleton Court, a wide red-brick house with startling black and white timbered gables. Edith drives round to a yard at the back and leads Ada round the house and into a cool, tiled hall. On a polished walnut table is a telephone and a silver salver. Edith pauses, then puts her arm around Ada's shoulders.

"You will want to make a call to Frank's home in Devonshire. He arrived there, Ada, but he was terribly sick. Something more than malaria, apparently. Nobody could contact you, I suppose, but now we must find out how he is ... I will call the office for the number and have it here for you when you have unpacked a little.

"You'll have to excuse the room. We didn't know how well you could get about," she explains as she shows her into a little room with a high window. "This is a spare, spare room; used to be a housekeeper's sitting room or something. We thought it would do for a night or two and it saves you going upstairs."

There's a vase with blue-green hydrangeas and a light green satin counterpane on the bed.

"We won't bring the trunk in unless you really need it. I'll have it put in the boot-room. It can stay here until you are ready to have it sent somewhere."

When Ada emerges from her room she sees Edith sitting by the hall table, her hand still on the telephone receiver.

"Oh my dear, you have had this sad news once and now you must have it all over again. I spoke to the mission office in Chester and they gave me the bad news. He died ten days ago and the funeral was yesterday. You must use the telephone as if it were your own. You will want to call your mother-in-law and your father, perhaps, if that's possible. I will leave you to it, but come and find me in the drawing room when you have finished. That door there."

Ada sits by the telephone. There is something Frank needed to know but picking up the telephone won't help.

When she joins Edith in the drawing room, Mrs Chancellor is there too. She is tall and pale and rather beautiful in a grey dress, with deep-set eyes and smooth cheeks. She holds Ada's hand in both of hers.

"I'm so pleased to meet you my dear, and so sorry to hear of your bereavement. It can come upon us so suddenly, can't it?"

They move to sit in front of the fireplace where there's a billow of some more pale hydrangeas.

"So, Edith will have told you about her new job. I'm so pleased she's not going off to some dangerous place after all. What courage you all must have. We so nearly lost Edith when she was a child and she has always been rather fragile."

Ada looks questioningly at Edith.

"You wouldn't have known, would you, that Dr Grover needed a research assistant, with all his talk of 'my schema' and 'my book, so nearly published'. But he finds it hard to settle to polishing his writing with all his other responsibilities. I had the useful experience of editing for Papa's publishing house, so Dr Grover took me on."

When they were training together, Ada used to worry about Edith going to the field, with her high-pitched, breathy voice and her secret, and justified, fear of having an asthmatic attack. *What a relief for you,* thinks Ada. *Not having to leave your family's claims on you flapping like apron strings in a breeze.* Not having to insist on an irresistible necessity that sometimes, in private moments, seemed to have melted away to nothing.

The bus from Peterborough swings slowly into the market square at Upham and comes to a halt. Ada waits for the driver to hand down her case and then has to stop herself setting off for Hatton Street and her old home. She knows that her father is staying in an annexe to Mr Darby's house. Mr Darby was another of the churchwardens alongside her father. Ada remembers picking apples in a long strip of orchard beside his house. Just along London Road, round the corner into Weaver Street.

The front door to Mr Darby's house is up a few steps. Through a window of what looks like a workshop at the side, Ada can see a stack of saucepans and dishes. She pauses. There's the cream-coloured enamel milk pan and the pale-blue china water jug, objects snatched from the wreckage of her past. The door at the side is in two parts, a stable door. She knocks.

She hears movement and her father appears.

"It is you, my dear girl."

His embrace is stiff and convulsive. His clothes are unfamiliar and Ada steps back to make sure that it is indeed her father.

"So you are hurt," he says, looking at her ankle. "Come and sit down. He waves a hand. This is what we have now. Just remnants, scraps."

Ada thinks there is a smell of smoke, of sooty dampness. Is it clinging to his hair, or is it just part of this shabby room and all that is in it? The room is long and narrow, with a work-bench that evidently now serves as a kitchen table with a hotplate at the far end. The electric cable hangs down from a hook twisted into a rafter. Further along is a bed that just fits across the width of the room.

Opposite the work-bench there's a garden seat with a folded blanket on it.

"Sit down, child, sit down."

He sits first. She sets down the coat she has been carrying under her arm.

"We will eat at the hotel," he says. "For tonight, you can have a room upstairs. Mr Darby has had it made ready and his niece will come over to keep you company. I'll just take your case up now."

Waiting for him to return, Ada sees that there is a small cylindrical iron stove with a flue pipe pushed through a tin panel in the window. Even so, she would not wish her father to still be here in the winter.

The contrast with Edith's parents' house could not be greater. But Ada sees that there is a certain resemblance between this shed and the hut at the crossroads she had been sharing with Ivy until a few months ago. There's just room to move between the items of furniture. Every joint in the structure leaves a crack where creatures undoubtedly settle and leave traces.

She misses the well-made shelves and cupboard doors from the old house on Hatton street. Every surface here is occupied by a jumble of small necessities. There, her mother used to place a single ornament – a glass vase with bubbles in the base, a porcelain garland of flowers in grey and yellow, a little inlaid box with a few screws and farthings inside – at the centre of any horizontal surface. Did her father manage to rescue anything at all from the house? That hairbrush, is that the one he had before? Or the little round mirror leaning against a window-pane? Does that look somewhat scorched and smoky?

Her father's hair is unkempt, unoiled and wispy. He looks older, which doesn't surprise her. He always had a bit of a stoop but in a way that suggested a readiness to bend over the bench with a plane or a saw. Now he just looks weighed down. She looks away.

"Where are they?" she asks. "Can I go there?"

"The churchyard, of course, the churchyard. There's no stone yet. I waited for you."

He reaches for his coat, hanging on a hook on the wall.

"It's a nice spot, not too far from the path."

She walks by his side through the streets which should feel familiar but don't. He keeps talking, giving her glimpses of the funeral, as if his interest had been only professional, observing the trimmings and the order of service.

"We can get a nice piece of granite but I wanted you to choose, dark or light. What do you think, now, dark or light? Not pink. Your mother never liked those meaty pink ones."

At the churchyard there's an earthy mound three places from the path with two small wooden cross-shaped markers. There are clumps of decaying flowers, transparent petals lying on the bare soil. She can see it has rained a lot since the mound was created so that sharp little stones have risen through the soil making a spiky surface. One grave for two people. Together again, as they were before Louise was born, in the time before Ada can remember. She doesn't ask how much of them was left, if he saw. If he has secret knowledge of a black outline with the meaning of a human, like an x-ray.

She doesn't know what she feels, only that this is a first step in an unavoidable sequence of steps she must take.

She turns to see her father still standing on the path watching her.

"I'll bring flowers tomorrow," she says.

"That'll be nice," he says, nodding. "We can still get some nice lilies from Manson's, or there are always chrysanthemums."

His tone is comfortable, the soothing professional adviser. It fills her with ice.

To get away from him she strides into the church and kneels in the pew near the front where the two of them always sat. He hovers in the side aisle, as if he is waiting to pass the plate, as he always did. After mentally mouthing a few words she pulls herself up.

As they walk back to Mr Darby's house he suddenly says, "You are with child, are you not?"

She says nothing.

"Well are you?"

"I am."

He stops and stares through a gap in the houses.

"How could you? We trusted you to go away, we believed you were doing good work. And you let us all down. Like some shop girl. When will it come?"

She tells him her best guess.

"You will ruin us both," he says, with bitterness. "I am promised an alms-house. That's why I'm staying in this hovel just until it is ready. Alms-houses are only for respectable people. I am not yet sixty so they already have to stretch a point. And now this."

He herds her through the gate and round to the door of the annexe.

Her throat is full of words of explanation – how she was married and that she abandoned her husband. That she thought he was dead, that she now knows he wasn't, but that now he definitely is. That he never knew that he would soon be a father. That she failed to care for him through a terrible illness. That she has never met his family, her child's family. She shuts her mouth firmly.

They eat a grim meal in a badly lit dining room attended by two waiters.

On their return, Ada hobbles straight up the steps and knocks on Mr Darby's door. A woman of about Ada's age opens the door and introduces herself as Ruth Murray. Ada hopes that keeping company doesn't mean they have to sit and make conversation. To her relief, Ruth shows her straight to her room, points to the bathroom door opposite, and wishes her goodnight.

She lies down and tumbles into sleep. She doesn't wake until Ruth Murray taps on the door and says: "I'm off now. My uncle's through the back in the breakfast room but of course your father is expecting to give you breakfast."

Ada finds she has woken with a plan. Her father offers her a breakfast of jaggedly cut bread, marmalade and a pot of tea. He keeps the milk bottle outside the door under a can but pours a little into a pink jug with a gold rim that Vera kept for best. Ada sees that a chip of gold has come off the spout.

"I can't look after you now," he says, as if they have been wearily arguing all night. "You see the state I am in."

"I don't want to depend on you," she says. "I have to manage for myself. I'm sure I can manage."

"That's what we said about your mother. We were sure she could manage. But she couldn't. Your mother needed you. You see now how right I was about that."

"She needed ... she needed a different life. I'm going now. I know where I'm going next. I hope you get your alms-house soon, before the winter. Do you need money?"

His face tightens: "It wasn't the bank that burned down. You keep your money. You're going to need it."

Ada's words to her father that she knows where she's going next are an exaggeration, but her plan works beautifully. She visits Dr Horton, who has known her since childhood. He refrains from expressing shock at her apparent situation. He makes a telephone call to a colleague in Ely. Mrs Parry, a widowed midwife, is prepared to take her as a lodger if she pays her way. Ada has accumulated salary, not having had anything to spend money on while abroad and so, by the middle of the day she is on a train to Ely.

At first when she arrives at White Cottage Ada wonders if she should be shame-faced or will have to answer difficult questions but soon realises that Jennifer Parry relishes it when a young woman comes to her to finish a pregnancy. She enjoys the company; she revels in the adventure of it, and she feels her own strength as she takes charge of the final stages. The process is full of its own familiar magic for her and she asks few questions.

Ada doesn't know how to make the time pass. She wants to write to her father. He must want to know that she is well and unafraid. Eventually, after sitting in front of the empty page she changes the F for Father into an E for Edith and writes a confession to her friend. The second time she writes, she puts a Poste Restante address at the top of the page and, sure enough, finds a reply at the Post Office when she enquires.

One afternoon when Ada and Mrs Parry have walked gently down and up the path beside the sloping meadow that stretches between the cathedral and the river, past the placid brown and white cows with maps on their flanks, Mrs Parry tells Ada that Dr Horton has sent her a letter. He has found a place for the baby if it is still her intention to have it adopted. An accountant and his wife who yearn for a baby to bring up. They live on the other side of the country, in Wells, in Somerset, which may make it easier for Ada. Mrs Parry herself could take the baby to them. She has done it before for other mothers. Ada can pick the moment.

They finish their walk in silence apart from the munching of the cows and the subdued chatter of a file of choirboys scurrying to evensong.

The two women spend Christmas quietly together in the little house. They attend services in the cathedral. Ada is by this time waddling a little and feeling that her pelvis may give way with every step. Her coat will no longer button over her belly so she has to hold it closed. She sighs as she heaves herself up and down in the pew. Jennifer Parry taps her on the knee.

"I've booked a donkey to get you home," she whispers.

Ada suppresses a giggle and feels a wave of gratitude. The "donkey" turns out to be a lift in the passenger seat of a friendly plumber's van while his tiny wife tucks herself amongst the copper pipes in the back. When she gets back to White Cottage Ada feels to the bottom of an inner pocket of her suitcase. She pulls out a small heavy object wrapped in a headscarf. She has no wrapping paper so she makes a little parcel by tearing a strip off a length of deep blue cotton fabric she had bought from a market stall when she and Frank were looking for wedding clothes.

On Christmas morning, while Jennifer minds the toast in the kitchen, Ada puts the parcel beside her plate. The fabric looks bright and exotic and Jennifer exclaims at once when she sees it. She unrolls the cloth and a grey jade amulet tumbles onto the table. It is in the shape of a hand with a bracelet of beads around the wrist. Cradled in the palm is a child and in the child's arms is a baby. Frank had been reluctant for Ada to buy it. *It's one of their protective things,* he said. *Magic. We shouldn't be seen to countenance it.* But Ada, whose arms still held the memory of the stiff little corpse of Lydia's baby, was drawn to it at once - the tender kink of the finger joints to enclose the infants, the plump perfection of the child's leg, the mostly hidden head of the tiny baby turning its face into the nearest shoulder; she could not put it down. So to cover Ada's purchase, Frank bought another piece, a tangle of fruit and vines carved from a piece of multi-coloured jade, like a faded and trampled autumn leaf, Ada thought.

Jennifer strokes the cloudy stone and cradles it in her own hand.

"You can't mean this for me," she says.

"Who better?" says Ada. "This is what you do. Protecting us, getting us through it. I want you to be able to help me."

She finds herself suddenly sobbing and would have left the table except that Jennifer has laid an arm across her shoulders.

"You mustn't think like that. It's an adventure, but everyone on earth was born. Look at them all!" She nods towards the front window and the street where dark figures pass the net curtains.

She returns to her place and takes up the amulet.

"This colour, it's just like clouds. Heavy clouds on one of those days that just won't lighten up. When I lost my Mervyn we seemed to have a whole month of days like that. It was terrible that he was dying, terrible for him of course, and it took so long. But all I could think of in those last days was the fact that there was no child. I thought there would be and then there wasn't." She closes her hand round the stone. "This is lovely, Ada, a lovely thing. It's so kind of you to gift it to me."

Ada shrugs. "I can't keep it, can I?"

After another week Ada wakes in the night and is aware of a pain in her back. She knows it has been there for some time, pushing its way through her sleep. She has become used to the clenchings and slackenings of her body over the last few weeks. Practising, Jennifer calls it. This is different, more penetrating and although it stops from time to time it feels as though the interludes are somehow accidental and the pain, still some distance away, is the deep reality coming ever closer. After a while Ada remembers that the coming and going matters and she gropes for the torch her father gave her when she set off for Burma. She starts to watch the face of her little alarm clock. Sixteen minutes. Fifteen. She heaves herself up and staggers to Jennifer's door. Instantly awake, Jennifer picks up the pile of sheets and towels she has kept ready.

"You see if you can get those spread on the bed, rubber one first, while I just get dressed and put the water on. It's curtain up!"

They work hard for the rest of the night and then, "Just this one," says Jennifer. "And that should be it."

In the shock of it all being over Ada hears a voice, an angry cry, a reply to the gush of air that has just hit new lungs. There is someone else in the room. There's another cry and then some gentler creakings and grunts.

"She's not pleased to be out in the cold," Jennifer says, "but she's looking just fine. Lovely and pink."

"A girl."

The visiting nurse, Nurse Best, summoned by a message via the milkman, holds the baby and murmurs to her while Jennifer delivers the afterbirth. Ada can see her looking over her shoulder at Nurse Best and shaking her head. She almost calls out, *Bring her to me!* She remembers Lydia, flat on a white bed in a room that smelt of new palm matting and blood, while she herself held a newly delivered baby, turning away from the anxious attendants and their patient as if to protect the infant from the panic surrounding the mother. Or was it to protect the mother from the dread fact of a dead child?

"Well done," Jennifer is saying with a hand on her shoulder. "Very well done."

Ada believes this is as much for her resolution in letting the nurse slip from the room with the baby in her arms as for her courage during the birth.

After the turbulence of the night, Ada sleeps but not for long. Jennifer left the rubber sheet in place but put a fresh cotton one over it. The feeling of one sheet sliding over the other takes Ada back to the bed she used to share with Louise. Before she opens her eyes, she reaches out an arm, checking for the warmth of another person.

There is a cup of cold tea on the bedside table and behind it a contraption, a glass bottle with a tube and a rubber bulb. They had talked about feeding the baby and on this Jennifer was almost stern. Ada must make sure the baby has breast milk to start with but it may be best if she uses the pump. She doesn't have to cuddle the child if it will make everything more difficult. Jennifer is happy to keep her in her own room and see to the feeds, so long as Ada draws milk at intervals.

Jennifer has arranged for the registrar to come to the house to register the birth. Ada is ready with a name. She knew she would have to do this. Frances Louise. The new person is, for the next few days at least, Frances Louise Mann.

When those days have passed, she crosses the country to her new name, which Ada doesn't know.

2

January 1948

Ivy

Ivy is constantly aware that this is not her house. These are not her things. She lifts them, dusts round them, replaces them and has done so for almost twenty years. They are not what she would choose, though she does not have a clear idea what she would have in a house that was hers.

It's not hers but she makes a difference to it. She has a special stick, strong and pointed, that just fits in the cracks between the slabs of the hall floor to poke out dirt. She knows how to gently wind the clock on a Sunday night so that it lasts precisely a week; take it too far and it sticks. She even knows about taking the inspection plate off the flue of the kitchen range to give it a bit of a rattle in between the sweep's visits.

There is something she loves and wishes was hers. On the bottom shelf of the dresser in the dining room there's a mahogany box with flat brass hooks that flip aside to release the lid. Inside is a set of wedding present cutlery, heavy, old-fashioned, meant for occasions and barely used. It's not so much the spoons and forks themselves that draw her as the dark blue velvet lining, the snug beds they lie in, precisely formed to hold them spaced just so and silent. She polishes them more often than is necessary in a house with no guests, merely for the pleasure of slotting each silver piece softly back in to its place.

Ivy is watering the big lemon geranium on the landing window-sill when a car pulls up outside. She leans from side to side and tugs the curtain back but the overgrown lilacs at the front of the house prevent her from seeing who is getting out.

It'll be somebody about those children, she thinks. *At last. Though I've got used to having them around.* There is another thought underneath. She pushes it down. Then comes the knock on the door.

Annie is down in the hall playing with the button tin – setting them all out along the top of the skirting board, across the bottom of the dresser, taking them visiting, sending them home again. Humming and hissing to herself, as is her habit.

She likes to open the door, though she isn't any use when she does. She just has a good stare. Before she gets to the bottom of the stairs Ivy can hear the voice of a woman, rather timid. Nobody official.

"I'm looking for Mrs Mann."

"Would that be old Mrs Mann?" Ivy asks, pulling back the door. All through these years, she thinks, I don't think I have ever told a lie. Not directly.

"Yes. No. I'm looking for my mother," she says gruffly, even angrily. A heavy emphasis on the last word suggests that the mother, when found, will be blamed for something.

Ivy could have shut the door then, but for some reason she doesn't. The girl on the doorstep looks terrified – thin, frowning, bracing herself for something. But there's something about her brows, her cheek-bones and jawline that make her immediately familiar.

Ivy's heart turns over. She lets her in.

She's lugging a case, heavy, sharp-cornered and awkward. Ivy wonders if the strain such a weight makes across her shoulders or the bruises it must leave on her shins in the course of her travels may account for her glowering expression.

"You look cold," Ivy says. "Come and have a cup of tea in the kitchen. Shut the door quickly, Annie, there's a good girl."

Following Ivy, the visitor lugs her suitcase down the passage to the kitchen. Ivy moves the kettle along the range so it starts to buzz.

Dark hair, a long rectangular sort of face and mauve patches under the eyes. Smooth skin with a couple of brown moles. Oh yes, Frank must have been her father. But she looks more like he was at the end, not in his prime. She wants to hear her speak, but not to hear what she might have to say. And not to say anything herself.

She keeps her back to her as she brews the tea, filling the big brown pot two thirds full, enough for the visitor and herself and one to take up to Mrs Mann. Then she thinks, *I'm just the housekeeper. Here I am in my flowery pinafore. It doesn't have to be difficult. I can keep the two of them apart.*

She points the visitor to a chair at the table. Annie stands a yard or so away, staring quite rudely. Ivy sends her to tidy up the buttons. The woman is young, just a girl, peering about her at everything. She opens her mouth and draws breath, about to ask something …

"You'll be wondering why we have children here," Ivy says quickly, knowing as she speaks that there's no reason why this girl should have any expectations.

"They're evacuees, but they got left behind, Annie and her brother. We think their family was bombed out; there were no relatives, so they're staying here until the authorities remember them. We think of it as doing our bit, you know.

"Old Mrs Mann, upstairs, she needs a lot of care now. I do all that. And with the children as well. It needs a lot of work – an old place like this. What's your name? Does she know about you?"

"Who? Mrs Mann? I don't know. I don't know anything about myself."

Well, what a foolish thing to say. And so snappish. Unless she has amnesia, in which case, how did she get here?

"You have a name, surely?"

"I'm Nancy Wilkin, but I don't know if that's my real name. I was adopted. Or sort of adopted."

"I see." Ivy's hands caress the fat curve of the teapot as she fits the cosy round it.

I'm not going to let her spoil this. I've been doing a good job here for all these years. I'm needed. I belong here. I do my bit for the church and people in the village. And the children - what would become of the children without me?

She's going to ask me. She's going to ask if I'm her mother. And when she does, I shall simply say no and leave it at that.

I've never felt more at home than I do here. I count for something. Growing up, I never counted for much at home. The boys mattered so much more. Out in the mission I felt I was pulling my weight but, oh, what a strange place it was to live. You always felt those bemused dark eyes on you. And success or failure, whether the others admitted it or not, it was all happening somewhere in the dark, in those mysterious hearts and minds.

How I yearned, there, for the sight of a bit of red brick, for the battered porcelain of a kitchen sink, for the comforting hug of a well-fitting new winter skirt as one slid into a polished pew.

Ivy riddles the range and takes the coal-scuttle to the back door. The young woman turns her head to follow her movements and Ivy feels relief when she's safely behind the door. She pauses to fit the past together in her mind. So Ada was pregnant when she left. She stole the child from Frank. And then abandoned it, evidently. He never knew. Meaning that poor Esme Mann upstairs doesn't know a thing about her.

Dennis comes home from school and seems pleased to see a new face. He gets out his little draughts board and ropes Nancy Wilkin in for a game. To Ivy's surprise, the girl doesn't refuse to play. In fact she sets the pieces into their starting positions with a firm clacking that suggests she will not be merciful.

Now he's asking, in his solemn way, all the questions Ivy refuses to ask. *Where are you from? Did you come by train?* Then he tells her, "We came by train, Annie and me. Are you an orphan?"

That catches her out. Yes. No. She glances towards Ivy. *She'll get no declarations from me*, thinks Ivy.

Now she is asking Dennis questions. Where is he from, then? Is *he* an orphan? She does look fleetingly sorry when he tells her.

Annie has crept up on the other side and is tugging the tortoiseshell comb out of her hair. The young woman keeps very still, as if avoiding catching the eye of a dangerous animal. But as she frowns over the draughts board, Ivy wonders how long it will take before she turns and snaps.

Ivy remembers the children in Burma sidling up and picking at things. A button or her watch-strap. As if they were no more significant than a leaf or a bit of bark. They'd even try fiddling with the mole on the side of her wrist. Now that was irritating.

Nancy sweeps up Dennis's last king with a glint of a smile. Dennis looks oddly pleased, as if he has hooked a fish.

Ivy sighs with frustration. She wants to tell this young woman to go away but she knows she cannot. It's bitter outside and the kitchen windows have darkened in the last few minutes. This is actually her home, though she doesn't seem to know it.

"Have you got somewhere to stay? I'm thinking we'd better put you up for the night."

Nancy looks as though she's critically considering the offer, one among several options.

"There isn't anywhere in the village, except the pub," says Ivy. "And you wouldn't want to stay there. Bring that up." She points at the case with the leather corners as she hurries past. She shows Nancy into a room where their breath crusts in the air. The bed is already made up.

"We'll put a water bottle in that," she says. "I made it up for Dennis months ago and he used it as a playroom before the winter, but they won't be separated, those two."

As they emerge onto the landing a voice calls from behind one of the doors, "Who's there?"

Ivy opens the door a little and says, "Have you got Annie in there? The little minx has disappeared."

But Annie is sitting in plain view on the bottom step of the stairs, apparently waiting to show Nancy that she has coloured threads wound round her finger.

Ivy makes the most fiddly supper she can think of – leek and carrot pie with a bit of bacon in it, stewed apples from the shrivelled stock that weren't really keepers and need a lot of trimming, and custard. She slams the knife into the board and twists the pastry unnecessarily. When it's ready she sets up the big wooden tray with a clean cloth and cutlery from a drawer in the dining room and adds a plate of steaming food. When she comes downstairs again they sit at the kitchen table. The children sit silent until she has said grace. She talks about the war, the weather, the village; encourages Dennis to talk about school.

Nancy Wilkin gazes at her, nods abruptly, lets Ivy lead the conversation where she wants. But it is as if she cannot believe she will not hear what she wants to hear, if she keeps listening with her dark brows drawn up at that questioning angle.

After supper, Dennis takes Annie up to bed. Ivy can hear him saying, "Face, hands, neck and ears Annie. Not my flannel, use your own!"

Ivy starts filling the pie dish with water. Behind the judder of the tap, Nancy blurts a question. Ivy doesn't quite hear. But she decides to drop the dish anyway.

Crawling across the cold flagstones, chasing the fragments with a brush, she makes up her mind.

The last bus comes through at eight. Exeter tonight, Bournemouth tomorrow. Who knows what after that?

A few hours later, Ivy slips into semi-consciousness.

Bournemouth, Bournemouth in the morning. I could swear the kitchen clock said ten to eight. Should have been good time. Must have stood in the cold for at least three quarters of an hour. Was so sure the bus had to come, had to finish its run. Drat the bus, slipped into a hedge somewhere.

Drat the boy. Little busybody, won't just sit back and be looked after. Insists on knowing everything about everything, checking all the doors at night. Couldn't call for him to unbolt the door. Couldn't bear that – questions, questions, the "pointing finger" like when we were children and Richard and Alan liked to cast the blame. Fault. It's your fault!

Whose fault? It is my fault.

3

January 1948

Nancy

Nancy wakes up from somewhere so deep and strange that she doesn't know if it is morning. She hears nothing and rolls over. By the time she wakes again there's a bright line around the heavy plaid curtains. She takes a moment to recall where she is. For two and a half weeks she has been homeless, picking her way back and forth across the country on a quest that was so suddenly thrust upon her that she still expects to wake up and find herself relieved of it. Her sleepy brain works through the hard facts.

Where am I? Homeless. The eighteenth day. In that village, Middlecombe, in a house called Moorside. My father's house. My real father, not my dead father. Except he's dead, too. But there is a grandmother, behind the door at the end of the landing. Why haven't I seen her? An invalid, but what can be wrong with her that I can't be introduced? And the other woman, Auntie Ivy – she doesn't want me here. Can she be my mother? Please not.

She had arrived just as dark was about to fall, with the high winter hedgerows scratching the sky on either side and her stomach rebelling against the combination of winding roads and the stale smell of old carpet and ashtrays in the car she had hired. Now she is here, she is full of doubt as to whether she should have come. She could leave the past alone, concentrate on finding a future...

She realises that this much daylight means it must be at least seven thirty. She opens up her nest in the blankets and dresses hastily in yesterday's clothes. When she finds her way to the kitchen it is unpleasantly cold. Frost flowers have crept half way up the window-panes. The range is barely warm to the touch and when she opens the fire door there's nothing but ash.

She hears a shrill protesting voice on the stairs: This can't be right. It's too bright! It's Dennis in his school shorts and pyjama top.

"Where's Auntie Ivy?"

He bustles across the kitchen tiles in his socks. He picks an iron pot from where it was set to dry at the end of the range and tips it up dramatically.

"No porridge! Where's the porridge?"

He's looking at her accusingly from under his fringe.

"But where's ... the lady who was here yesterday? Your Auntie Ivy? Doesn't she usually get up and start the fire?"

"She does," he says. "She starts the fire and makes the breakfast and takes Mrs Mann her cup of tea. You've got to get the kettle on!"

"Well, which is her room? Can you go and knock on her door?"

He comes back, his heels thudding on the stairs.

"Gone. Not there."

Nancy follows Dennis upstairs and peers through the bedroom doorway. The room is tidy, everything in it precisely arranged. The bed is undisturbed except that a corner of the counterpane is folded up as if someone has been hunting for something under the bed.

With Dennis snapping at her heels, Nancy gets the range going, heats some milk and porridge and tries to guess what else needs to be done. The battered metal alarm clock perched on the mantel above the range says ten to eight. Annie suddenly materialises in the kitchen, clutching a small, ragged satin cushion. She's wearing boy's pyjamas, still a little too big.

When they have all eaten porridge and Dennis has assembled what he needs for his satchel, they realise that the clock still says ten to eight. As Dennis sets off down the road, (Nancy has no idea how far he has to go), he turns and warns her, Annie won't talk to you, you know.

Annie stares and Nancy stares back, slightly offended. Then she and Annie step from one plainly necessary task to the next. Taking breakfast to the invalid upstairs is clearly important. Nancy is used to looking after invalids. There was a year with Dadda after his stroke and then, with only a few weeks' respite in between, the eight months of Mummy's decline.

Annie opens the door of Mrs Mann's room and skips across the floor. Mrs Mann hears her and lifts her head. "Is that my little angel?" Annie takes the pale, mottled hand and lays it to her cheek and then flits to the window where she drags the curtain open a little, revealing more frost flowers and thick trickles of ice. There's a whiff of paraffin and Nancy sees that the reason it is warmer here than in the rest of the house is a large ribbed radiator with a ring of blue flame behind glass. The old lady drags the covers to one side and swings her legs, rather startling, like two densely packed bolsters upholstered in a purplish damask, to the floor.

"I think we're a bit late this morning, aren't we, she says. Pass the gown."

Nancy sees that her eyes are three-quarters closed.

"It's not who you think it is," says Nancy. "I'm Nancy. I'm just helping out. For this morning." She takes the brocade dressing gown that is slung over the rail at the end of the bed and lays it across Mrs Mann's lap.

Mrs Mann hears this without too much surprise, but she mutters to herself.

Back in the kitchen, Nancy realises the range is sluggish and there's no coal left in the scuttle. She riddles until the ash compartment is choked and then hunts around and finds an ashy shovel and a pair of galoshes in the back hall. There must be a bucket or a heap for ashes and a coal store to replenish the scuttle. After a fight with the bolts, she opens the back door and finds herself in a cobbled yard with an outbuilding on one side. There's a tell-tale stain of black dust in the frozen puddle by the door of the outbuilding.

She opens the door. The coal shed is dark, its only window stacked up with tins and jars of nails. A few sheets of corrugated metal make a bunker for the coal on the left and there's a slatted compartment for logs in front of her. Piled up on the tumble of logs is a huge bundle of clothes. Nancy's eyes adjust. She recognises the olive-green skirt Ivy was wearing yesterday. Then she makes out the woman's curled figure, hunched up, arms around legs, leaning against the brickwork behind her.

"What? Whatever are you doing there?"

She cannot tell if Ivy is awake or even alive. Heart thumping, she puts a hand out and detects a tremor. Ivy is shivering. She shakes her arm. Her eyes are open but they refuse to meet Nancy's.

"It's so cold! Come on now, you've got to get indoors. You're freezing out here."

There's no reaction so she pulls at Ivy's legs, one at a time, until she has them over the edge of the railing, stiff and apparently useless.

"Missed the bus. Don't say…" mumbles Ivy, lolling her head as though she can't stay awake.

After heaving her upright, Nancy walks her indoors, leading the way backwards, pulling her off balance until she moves her legs. As she hitches her up the step to the back hall she finds her face pressing into the woman's neck, chilly where it should be warm. The kitchen is the only warm room, apart from old Mrs Mann's upstairs.

Nancy pushes Ivy onto a blanket box covered with a knitted rug that sits against the wall. The shivering is increasing in intensity. She rubs her limbs and thinks about running upstairs to ask Mrs Mann about a doctor.

Ivy mumbles again: *Don't tell her.* Again and again: *Don't tell her.*

She keeps mumbling as Nancy persuades her to sidle up the stairs, a step at a time, pushes her into her room and onto the bed where she immediately adopts a foetal position.

"You have to realise, I did right by him," says Ivy. She sounds drunk, pushing her words out through immobile jaws. "I'm the one who brought him back, helped him through his last weeks. Your father."

"My father?" Nancy stops tugging at the eiderdown and stoops to hear.

"Poor dear man. But he wasn't mine. It wasn't right. He didn't like me much. But what more could I have done? He didn't deserve to die like that. Not even forty. Do we get what we deserve? Or deserve what we get."

Most of the hairpins have fallen out of her plaits so that the tail of one of them sticks up like an old hemp rope that has given way.

"Shivering, can't stop shivering. Like Frank. When I brought him here, sweating and shaking. The driver kept complaining that he couldn't drive with someone kicking his seat so. I got into the back and held him. I held him when he needed it.

"She, Mrs Mann, Esme, was expecting us. I'd sent a telegram. Place was all lit up. Full of lights. She was eking out her sight then. We came through the door and I could tell she could hardly make us out. Moving her head like this. Side to side. Lost the centre. Looking for a son-shaped dark patch. Centre of her vision, that was the bit that was fading.

"The driver had caught on by then, realised I needed his help to get him out of the car. He wouldn't get rid of us if he didn't help. He even helped me to get him upstairs. She insisted on paying him and gave him a message to take to the doctor. She spent the next two days just sitting beside him. She was shocked. Thought she knew about malaria and such like.

"I had to find my way about, choose myself a room. That room you're in. I told no lies. Esme was sure who I was. The first time she called me Ada I said, 'Actually, everybody calls me Ivy.' And that was it.

"I was the one who held him when he needed it. I was the one. When we got in here and he was tucked into bed - the headboard hitting the wall, he was shaking so much - I looked at myself in the mirror, that great, grand dressing table, and I saw I had the imprint of one of his buttons on my cheek. A criss-cross from the woven leather. Stamped with his mark. But not really his.

"At the funeral, Esme introduced me to the neighbours as Frank's widow and so I was Mrs Mann from then on."

"Where was she?" asks Nancy at the first pause. *Where was my mother?*

"She left us," says Ivy clearly. "She turned her back. She was on another path altogether. You should have seen what I found." She nods, with satisfaction, it seems to Nancy. "It shocked me to my core," whispers Ivy.

Ivy looks warmer and more comfortable though she is still shaking uncontrollably. Nancy starts to feel there is no need for her to be sitting here in another woman's bedroom.

"Maybe you should sleep," she says and backs away. "I'll cook something. There are some eggs and potatoes I think."

Annie is on the landing, breathing on the window and drawing shapes.

Nancy takes her hand.

"Come on, it's cold up here."

She stokes up the range and opens the draught to boil the kettle. She fetches the stone bottle Ivy had given her to warm her bed, fills it and takes it back up to Ivy who has closed her eyes but takes and cuddles the bottle gratefully when Nancy offers it.

"I think I know what we can have for lunch," says Nancy to Annie who nods hopefully.

She cooks bubble and squeak with fried eggs. She sets a tray and takes it up for Mrs Mann thinking, as she does it, she's not Mrs Mann, she's Grandma, Granny, Grandmother. Her other grandmother, the one she knew, was Granny Hodge and not particularly friendly to her only grandchild. It suddenly dawns on Nancy that she probably thought of her as a little imposter. A substitute for the real one her parents never had. Granny Wilkin had died quite young and Nancy was always able to imagine that she would have been the gentle, indulgent type, sharing games and treats as grandmothers are supposed to.

She sets the lunch out carefully on the side table in the bedroom, with the napkin in its ring and the little cruet. She takes the water jug to the bathroom and fills it at the basin. She watches the old lady feeling her way across to her chair. She almost sits on the edge of the bed, ready to speak. But Mrs Mann says, *All right dear. Thank you.*

The next morning, Ivy successfully catches the early morning bus.

They have had very little further conversation after the torrent of confession as her frozen brain thawed. Ivy has stayed in her room, emerging briefly to send Nancy to get eggs and to take a note to the man who brings the logs. But when she has gone, Nancy finds a closely written note on the kitchen table with the doctor's name and address, the days of deliveries from the baker and the grocer, descriptions of keys for the different doors and the details of a bank account. There's no signature and no forwarding address.

Nancy continues to be shy of spending time in Mrs Mann's room. She empties the commode and replaces the tablecloth where the old lady eats at the table by the window, moving the tarnished little cruet and replacing it exactly in front of the place setting. She took up a feather duster once but Mrs Mann was asleep and Nancy crept away again. Dennis visits several times a day and adjusts the tuning of the huge radio set that hums by the bed. He draws the curtains when dusk is falling.

The day after Ivy's departure is a Saturday and Dennis doesn't have to hurry to school. Nancy tells him as she puts porridge on the table, "I shall be staying. I shall be looking after you for now." He looks relieved.

"Don't you have more things than just that case in your room?" he asks.

"I have nothing. When my mother who adopted me died, it all went to my cousin. The house and everything. There were no papers to say I was adopted. There was no will though we looked everywhere."

That was a wretched hunt. She had looked in and under all the furniture of her previous life, not yet aware of just how badly the lack of a will would affect her. She remembers returning to the brassy-haired solicitor empty-handed and seeing his shocked expression.

"I needed that will," says Nancy.

"What's a will?" asks Dennis.

"It's when you write down who should have your things when you die."

"If you can write. I could write for Annie to have my things but she can't write for me to have hers."

"Does she have much?"

"Not really. The buttons. She has some of the crayons and I have the others."

Later, sweeping the passageway, Nancy realises she doesn't have to ask herself what she should do next. It is plain as day what she must do. Who else will cook meals and light fires for Mrs Mann and the children? She puts energy into the task. This house has dark corners where fluff builds up. Mummy would have turned her voice up several notches if she saw such a thing, "You clean before you see the dirt, not after".

So far Dennis has been telling her what to do and Nancy finds she doesn't mind it. He oils the wheels of the household, as he has probably been doing ever since he came there.

But he does ask her questions she is not ready to answer.

Are you really a grown up?

What happened to your mum?

Where's your proper home?

I don't know, she wants to say. *I don't know, I don't know, I don't know.*

4

October 1947

Nancy

First there was the waiting while Mummy withdrew into that other place where her illness ruled. She, Nancy, had been alone beside this death, waiting, avoiding thoughts about afterwards. It wasn't like the year before when she and Mummy had shared the care of Dadda, even quietly planning for the time that was to come. This time "afterwards" was an empty space; it could not be visualised. She had been meticulous in her sickroom duties, following instructions, adding drops to water, helping her mother roll over periodically, straightening wrinkles in the bedclothes. She followed instructions because she didn't know what to do. Her anxiety built up as the doctor's visits approached, not because of what he might say but because he might be silently appalled at her inept nursing. She was sure that he would arrive to find stained sheets, or Mummy fidgeting crossly and helplessly. It sometimes felt as if Mummy was siding with her own wretched body, bringing ever nastier weapons of mess and pain to bear upon Nancy, so that she had to move through her tasks muttering to herself, *Poor Mummy, oh poor Mummy.*

The doctor wouldn't say what was happening. He managed to speak about how his patient was without giving any hint of an outcome. She was "a bit brighter", or "doing well with the new medicine". With part of her mind, Nancy knew what was due to happen. The treatment was all for the sake of comfort and a calm sickroom. But she wanted someone to say so, to give her permission to think it.

On one visit the doctor confounded Nancy's expectations of disapproval. He fumblingly squeezed her hand as she stood aside to let him leave the room and said, "You're doing well, my dear, very well under the circumstances". She was taken by surprise and her eyes met his for an instant before flicking away.

"Doctor Packer," she said, determined to map out the path in front of her. "Doctor Packer, you have always been our doctor; you must even have been there when I was born..." She had stumbled to a halt because that was a shockingly personal thing to imagine. She was so appalled she felt a choking in her throat that was almost a giggle, and that was even worse. "Tell me, please..."

He took a step towards the stairs.

"There is something I should tell you," he said. "Can we sit down for a moment?"

He descended the stairs and paused in the hall so that she could lead him into the living room.

"I don't believe your mother has spoken to you, has she?" he said.

"She was able to ask for water this morning," said Nancy. "And yesterday she asked for my father's picture."

She'd had to shuffle aside the little brown bottles, spoons and boxes to make room for the portrait of Dadda with his broad moustache and cheeks bunched up as though he was considering something carefully.

"Ah, yes." Doctor Packer nodded. "I think there is something she has wanted to say to you about you and her and your father."

"About us? But tell me, please, am I right in thinking she is not going to live? She cannot recover?"

The doctor looked flustered.

"Of course she cannot recover. She has a growth that is laying claim to most of her internal organs and I would think that she has no more than a few days now. He recovered himself. You must prepare yourself, my dear. And think, are there relatives you should summon? Is there anything she might have left undone?"

"Undone?" Nancy had wailed. "What can she do?"

"Well, a will, that sort of thing. That's what one thinks about at such a time. Affairs in order. But maybe you are right, it is too late. And it is not for me to intervene. Far from it." He stood up to go. "So you have the nurse coming back at night, do you not? You need the nurse. You will not be alone. Keep giving her sips of water. And send a message if you need more of the drops."

He shook her hand formally and departed.

The solicitor, Mr Oliver, was somewhat younger than the doctor, with pale popping eyes and a lick of brassy-yellow greased hair.

"It should all be very straightforward, Miss Wilkin, he had said leaning very slightly across the shiny width of his desk. Both their chairs creaked, as though they, too, were conducting a conversation. "There is just you, and although you are not yet of age, the estate will pass to you, under the guardianship of the executor, which, in the absence of a will, I may myself have to appoint, once we have established probate. A small problem is that I have been unable to find amongst your mother's papers your birth certificate. Would that be because she passed it to you? Do you have it amongst your own papers?"

"My papers?" said Nancy. "I have my ration book. I kept all our ration books because I did the shopping."

"There is one odd thing, in addition," said Mr Oliver. "I did find a birth certificate for another female infant, one Frances Louise Mann. Now would she be a relative of some kind?" He paused to read her face. "It is a delicate matter, but could it be that either of your parents had a previous - marriage? Another daughter not much older than yourself?"

"That is out of the question! My parents longed for a child for many years before they had me. Any previous marriage would have been over years before I was born."

"Well, it is important that we establish who this person is, if she still lives. It could possibly, in very particular circumstances, have a bearing on the transfer of the estate. I think it best if you give me a little time to research the matter. You can, in the meantime, continue to live in the house." Mr Oliver was staring at her thoughtfully, so she jumped to her feet.

The permission to continue living in her own house had been especially unsettling. And what particular circumstances did Mr Oliver have in mind? It seemed that he was permitted to think about her parents in ways that she could not.

She can hardly think about Mummy at all; she can only see the pinched, discontented mouth, the bony restless hands and the dull eyes of recent weeks.

To force aside that picture she makes herself think of a particular dress from long ago - rich blue with large mauve and white flowers, fitting neatly at the waist, with some kind of pleat or panel structure at either side of the bodice. At that stage Mummy's hair was shoulder length, still dark and wavy. There was lipstick and a social smile, as there always was with such a dress. But Nancy cannot conjure the eyes, cannot make them meet hers, or even hear the bright tone of her voice.

After returning from the solicitor's office she had slammed the door behind her and was standing in the dim light of the hall, puzzling about where important papers could be hidden. The knocker thundered on the door immediately behind her. She almost ran from the noise. But it was her house and her door, if only for the moment, so she turned and opened it. Dr Packer stood on the step with an envelope in his hand. With no medical routines to get through, he seemed nearly as awkward as she felt herself.

"Miss Wilkin, your certificate, that is to say, your mother's certificate, you will find you need it."

She had pulled herself together and ushered him in. She directed him into the front sitting room. "You did say, Doctor, that there was something you should tell me."

"Did I?" he said dubiously. She felt a surge of fury that gave her the strength to take charge of the situation. She offered to make a pot of tea.

"How kind," he said, and, alert to all kinds of secretiveness, she left him to recall his earlier half-revelation.

When she returned he had evidently braced himself for a speech.

"Miss Wilkin, there *is* something I should reveal. It seems Mr and Mrs Wilkin believed that you need never know, but we cannot see ahead to what the future holds and what encounters we may have, and in the end I believe the truth is healthier. I accepted responsibility for you as an infant, and I must fulfil that responsibility now."

His head drooped a little and he looked older than ever. Nancy's mind was racing to the unlikely conclusion that he was about to tell her he was her father. She was reassured when he started again:

"I know little about your birth, and you were not born here in Wells nor anywhere in Somerset. You were born in Upham in Norfolk, or somewhere near there. A good friend of mine had a practice there. It's just a little town. We, he and I, arranged your adoption. Your parents, Mr and Mrs Wilkin that is, had recently been to see me in distress at their persistent failure to conceive a child, and were delighted when I made the suggestion. Very, very happy. You must never think they thought less of you because you were not theirs. By birth, I mean. Do not think that."

His rather anxious denial gave her a question to ask herself later. But immediately she had to ask, "So who were my parents?"

"I have been searching for the correspondence. My friend, Dr Horton and I were both relatively young and not thinking of the time when we would not be there to answer questions, but I did, I believe, keep the correspondence. A search has not produced it, however. As I recall, your mother was the daughter of an undertaker. She had been abroad for some reason and returned some months before you were born. Of your father I know nothing. Maybe there is a birth certificate with his name on it."

"So it is me," she said. "I am Frances. Frances Louise Mann. The solicitor has the certificate. He didn't know who it could be."

"It is a shock for you," said Dr Packer, trying to be a doctor again. "You are already grieving and now you have to confront the reconstruction of all you thought was true about your birth and family. But it is my judgment that it is best you should know. I thought your parents would have told you. There may be others, you may have brothers, you see, and, while the chance is small, if you were to meet them, you know... It is best you should know. Close-breeding is a terrible thing. I thought the distance was a great advantage in your case, but people travel so much these days."

She had to force herself to follow the fanciful route of his concern. Could it really be that he was anxious in case she had a half-brother somewhere on the other side of England whom she might meet and marry and with whom she might breed monsters? But while his preposterous and grubby concerns and pompous interference annoyed her, even then she was aware that if this was the truth, she did want to know it.

She reached for his cup in a way that meant he had to give it up, and when he no longer had it in his hand he began to feel the need to gather himself and go. She bolted the door when he left and sat on the stairs. She ended that day a different person, with a different name. Mary-Ann Wilkin, usually known as Nancy, was a disguise for this other person. Not the child of John and Martha Wilkin. The child of, even the disgrace of, Miss Mann of Upham. The certificate must hold the key. She heard the loud ticking of the sitting room clock and leapt up, because if she hurried, she might catch Mr Oliver still at his office.

Mr Oliver was with a client, and she had to ask his assistant if he wouldn't mind looking through the box of papers from the bureau. The certificate was a short one, an official copy of the original, and had no details of the parents. The date on it was the 31st December, just over a month before the day she had learned to celebrate as her birthday.

Back at home she searched out Dadda's copy of *The Open Road* and leafed through it to find Norfolk. Upham was only just inside the county boundary, but a long way from Somerset nonetheless.

All that was a few days before the funeral. Whatever feelings she had expected to have during the funeral were pushed aside.

Mr Oliver attended the funeral. Nancy avoided him, irritated by his habit of never finishing sentences where he did not like the ending. But as she was standing by the grave waiting for the people to stop watching her and go, he came up to her holding out his gloved hand.

"Would you be able to attend me in my office before four o'clock? I wouldn't ask, but it is rather, er... And could you bring... I take it your cousin Mr Norman Hodge is here? Could you both attend? It is rather, er..."

Cousin Norman was there, with his recently acquired wife and mother-in-law. They had approached

Nancy before the service with expressions of appalled solemnity. She felt immediately reprimanded for the trace of a polite smile that had lifted her face for an instant. She felt disapproved of for the white spots on the black chiffon scarf she wore to keep her wool collar from chafing her face.

She had to go up to Norman and explain about Mr Oliver's urgency. It presumably meant good news for Norman and his wife. He looked doleful. Nancy had not often seen him as an adult. He was the little boy she remembered by smell, who, although older than her, had wet the short trousers of a nasty little tweed suit at a family event when they were about six and eight.

Fortunately she had chosen not to invite people back to the house, but had let the vicar's wife organize some tables in the church rooms. Mr Oliver had evidently expected that she would have spent at least some time pointing out sandwiches and sugar lumps to the guests but she was relieved not to have to face people – her brusque employer, her two school friends – when she no longer knew who she was. As she and Norman were shown in to his office Mr Oliver was bending behind his desk pulling his shoes back on and his jacket was thrown over the back of his chair.

When he was properly dressed he began.

"Miss Wilkin, Mr Hodge. I should normally be expected to read a will at this juncture. But, while there was a will to read when your father, that is Mr Wilkin, died, this time, I am certain, there is none. He left all to your mother, with the exception of a single charitable bequest, and she, I am sure, intended to leave all to you, her only daughter.

"But, as I must explain, that is not what she has done. That is to say, in dying intestate she would have left it all to a surviving daughter, if…"

"If I was really her daughter?"

"Indeed."

"But they adopted me."

He paused, digesting the fact that she knew.

"At the time you were adopted there was not actually any formal procedure. The mother gave you up, you were given a new name, and that was all there was to it. There was not actually anything for the law to recognise, nothing for us to get a grip on."

Norman was frowning deeply. Then it dawned on her. He could not believe his luck. He could barely restrain his face into a suitable expression.

"So it is not mine. None of it? I am not the next of kin?"

"In the eyes of the law there is nothing that makes you anything other than a…"

"Stranger," she finished for him.

By the time they left the office Norman had, with apparently good grace, agreed that she should be allowed to continue to live in the house for at least three months, should be allowed to take personal effects belonging to her and Mr and Mrs Wilkin, and that he would make a gift to her to start her in her new life, of £500. He even tried to put a fatherly arm around her shoulder as they left the building. Once she had seen him heading back towards the church and his allocation of sandwiches, she went home. Three months was the length of time Mummy had been bedridden. It was just twice the length of their longest ever holiday, at Barmouth before the war. Three months was no time at all.

Back in the house she did not turn the light on. She was to have a new life. She did not want to look at the old life.

It was a bit like when Britain joined the war. Everything was suddenly measured by different rulers and scales. You had to make new judgments about what mattered. Then, Dadda, the accountant with such confidence when it came to knowing what things were worth, had turned off the radio and said, "This is when we have to remember what we're protecting. There'll be a price to pay." And then he'd filled his pipe and tapped it with a finger and added, "But some'll be pleased when the prices all go up."

She tried to imagine his voice saying something reassuring: *You've got a good enough head for figures; you'll make your way. Use the bit of book-keeping I taught you.*

When she got home after the funeral and the visit to the lawyer's office, Nancy had sat on the stair wondering what good it could do her to dwell on what she was losing. Could she forget it all, all the life she had ever known? She thought of her friend, Penny, crying the night before she and her family moved away, dragged unwillingly to Birmingham where she was to work in a factory that made pillowcases. Penny had sent one terse postcard: *Dear Nancy, Don't come visiting, there's no room anyway. Yrs ever, P. PS The job's awful. You don't want to buy linen from Sewards.*

The funeral had been only ten days before Christmas. She spent her time emptying drawers and cupboards, picking out the few items that still seemed to belong to her, and then stuffing everything back in again. After a few days, when the story had got about, she had to keep answering the door to kind neighbours eager to invite her to spend the festive season with them. She declined as many as she could. Mrs Rogers, probably her mother's closest friend, was particularly pressing. Nancy gave way and went there for her Christmas dinner and received a shower of gifts appropriate to her new nomadic status – a travelling alarm clock, a manicure set in a small leather case, a tin of barley sugar and a satin pouch which, Mrs Rogers explained, would help her to pack her smaller items of clothing. Then, on the 2nd January, she set out.

She had the name of the town and the name of Dr Horton. She knew that her grandfather was probably an undertaker. There would not be many of those in a small market town. The clerk at the railway station had leafed through his timetables and constructed a journey of many parts for her.

She kept the list of train times and changes tucked into her glove. The last change was at Ely just as darkness fell. After that, the dimly lit carriage stitched its way through a flat landscape with gleams of water, drifts of frost by the hedgerows and very occasional lighted windows. When the train slowed, she felt reluctant to stir but the helpful guard was shifting her suitcase and making sure she knew she had arrived.

Quite clearly her first task would be to find a place to stay.

The room at The Bell smelt of worn fabrics, cold wallpaper and a hint of stale beer, but the sheets were encouragingly white and crisp. There was a washstand with a ewer and basin, and she wondered whether she needed to use it. But the proprietor returned, after a moment, with a towel on her arm, and she directed her to the bathroom at the end of the landing. Baths by arrangement, if you don't mind, she said as she left. The towel was thin and small, and did not encourage the idea of a bath. Nancy drew the curtains and sat on the bed.

Supper was a stew of butter beans with small nuggets of lamb in it and over-boiled potatoes. Being waited upon, with thick crockery and a flimsy napkin, made her feel she must be ill or incapacitated. After she had brought her plate of stew, the waitress asked her, with a giggle, "Will you be wanting a sherry with that?" For all her inexperience, Nancy knew the sherry should have come first, and was a blatant attempt to add something to the bill as an afterthought. But she felt in need of warmth and comfort, so she accepted. When the waitress brought a plate of treacle tart and thin custard she said, "I need to find somebody. Would you know, or should I ask someone else? It's someone in the town."

The waitress grinned and shrugged, but carried the query off to the kitchen. The landlady came to clear the table.

"Who is it you want, then?"

"He was the undertaker here, maybe still is. Mann, Mr Mann?"

"No one of that name. We've had two undertakers in this town. There was Henry, who's now retired, and there's the Cuthbertsons. We always went with Mr Henry, but then he got burnt out, and lost his lovely carriage. He wasn't much better than a carpenter after that and I don't believe he's still working. The Cuthbertsons are a bit new-fangled; they have the motor hearse, of course, and I suppose that's become the proper way to do a funeral. You're not needing a funeral are you, miss?"

"No, no, I'm looking for someone. Someone quite old, in his seventies, perhaps."

"If he has to be in his seventies, that'd be Mr Henry. I'll just go and ask in the bar, but I think he was living at the almshouses in the little yard off Crown Street. He had a lot of misfortune, but I think he ended up there."

She bustled away towards the sound of the bar. Just as Nancy was starting up the stairs she came past again.

"That's right, dear, the almshouses. You go and ask there tomorrow."

As she cleared breakfast, the landlady paused.

"It was a sad story, Mr Henry's family. Perhaps you know all about it. You know, the fire and all."

"The fire?"

"His house and workshop, the lovely hearse, his wife and daughter, all lost in one night. They never knew how it started."

"His wife and daughter? They died in the fire?"

"He was out in one of the villages arranging a funeral, and when he came back all was ablaze and it was too late for anything. There was so much oil and lacquer and shavings and the like in the workshop; it went up like a firework."

She shrugged and the kitchen door swung behind her. His daughter. Lost.

The almshouses took up three sides of the cobbled yard, with pointed arches over the doorways and mullioned windows. A man with a broom accosted her.

"Are you wanting one of the gentlemen, Miss?"

"Mr Henry?" she said. The man frowned.

"Ah now that's sad. We had to move Mr Henry on, poor old boy. He wasn't managing on his own. He was over at Lynn, St James's for a time."

"St James's? Is that a church?"

"The hospital, my beauty. He was in the hospital. But he died during the War."

An elderly woman with a basket entered the courtyard.

"Now here's someone as knew him. Young lady came looking for Timothy Henry," he calls out to the woman.

"Morning Andrew. You're a bit too late to find him here, Miss, I'm sorry to say." Nancy felt accused.

"I didn't know he wasn't well. I didn't know anything about him."

The old woman looked suddenly curious.

"So, you'd be ... You wouldn't be Ada's child would you?" Her voice changes. "Fifteen, twenty years it must be since she came back from abroad."

Nancy stared.

"Ada. That was the name of the daughter? I think Mr Henry was my grandfather."

The woman exchanged a glance with Andrew.

"I think you'd better come to my house and we'll have a chat about it."

As Nancy followed her, the woman told her that her name was Susan Sands and she used to live next door to the Henrys. She was very good friends with Vera, Ada's mother, and after the fire she had tried to keep a bit of an eye on Timothy. But he couldn't get back to his old life, not at all. He got a place in the alms-houses and at first everybody thought he was just struggling with being on his own and having lost the business and everything. But after a few years it was clear that he was losing track of what was what. Putting the clean plates and cups in the oven instead of the cupboard, that sort of thing. Leaving the front door wide open all night. And when Ada came to visit, which she did just the twice that Susan knew of, he kicked up no end of a fuss and said he didn't know her.

By this time they had arrived in front of a small house at the end of a terrace set back behind a grassy bank. Beyond it was a roughly cobbled space and then a taller, wood-clad building like a barn or a warehouse.

Susan nodded towards the cobbled area.

"That's where it was, the Henrys' place. You can see a bit of the shape of it, how it was built round the yard, with the workshop on one side. But all that building is new.

"Come in, darlin' and I'll make you a cup of tea. Shut that door tight so we don't get the draught. What name do you go by?"

"Nancy Wilkin."

"What's that, properly? Is that from Ann?"

"Mary-Ann."

"Ooh, very nice." Susan studied her for a moment. "You don't look much like her. So where are you staying?"

"The Bell. It was near the station."

"Yes, well, it's got that to be said for it. Look, my girl, you could come and stop in my back room if you don't want anything fancy. Just a night or two."

So Nancy had stayed a night or two. Susan chattered about the family but said she didn't know where Ada lived now. She thought it was in the north somewhere, probably Scotland. It's not surprising, Susan suggested, that she wanted to be a good distance away from all her previous connections. Susan thought she was nursing, and, thinking about it, she'd be good at that. She had been so good at looking after her sister. Until she'd left altogether. After some effort Susan remembered the name of the missionary college Ada had gone to.

"I'll know it if I hear it. It's like a girl's name, Marilyn House, Margaret House. Over near Wales. Meredith. That's it. Meredith Hall.

"Timothy didn't take kindly when he knew you were on the way. All that training, all those prayers and donations from the church people, and then Ada went and got herself into trouble. It's not what you expect. But I felt a bit sorry for her. Those Sunday School girls, they don't have the foresight to keep a man in his place, give him a slap if necessary. And then they stick them in the middle of nowhere and expect them to manage. At least you didn't turn out brown!"

Nancy took a cup of cocoa to bed and spent the first part of the night facing up to the fact that she was her mother's downfall. Her mother must have hated her, feeling her growing and becoming more and more of a problem. She must ask Susan Sands how old Ada would have been. She couldn't have been much more than twenty if she'd just finished college. Her own age.

"A man came here once looking for her," said Susan. "Could he have been your father? I was having a cup of tea with your grandpa as I did most days but

I could see it was a bit ticklish – he didn't take to him – so I got myself out of the way. But there was a bit of shouting and I couldn't help but hear. *You left her with a baby and you didn't even have the decency to marry her!* Timothy was saying. And this man said, *You don't understand; it wasn't me - of course I didn't marry her!* And Timothy, by then he was already losing a bit of control, he knew he was losing it, and he shouted, *Don't you tell me what I don't understand!* Hammer and tongs it was. He scuttled off soon after, the poor man, but I don't think he can have been your father from what he said.

"Poor Timothy, he was such a courteous man, before all the misfortune. But he shouted after that visitor, all down the street, *That little baby... she'll be better off with her new people and without the likes of you! And good riddance!*"

The morning she set off again, Nancy made a small detour on her way to the station. She searched the rows of stones in the churchyard until she found a speckled grey stone: Vera Isabella Henry 1888 – 1928, then a dash beneath and Louise Ruby Henry 1911 – 1928. There's another dash under Louise's name and space for another below it. But, oddly, no mention of Timothy.

Nancy worried that the college would be ashamed of Ada, the missionary who got into trouble; very likely they wouldn't be able or willing to tell her anything about her. But it was the only link she had to follow.

The journey to Shropshire took most of a day, with four trains and a bus. Inevitably it was dark by the time the bus deposited her at the foot of the drive. Very few lights showed. Of course, the students would have returned to their families for the Christmas holiday.

There was an old iron bell-pull overgrown with ivy, and below it a white china doorbell marked "Press" set into the door-frame. She pressed and heard nothing. The bay window to her left revealed a dark and empty room. But soon a swish and a rattle announced someone behind the door.

"Yes?"

The woman had her arm raised to hold back a heavy curtain.

Nancy's explanation seemed clumsy to her own ears and, she thought, unlikely to meet a helpful response.

But the woman pulled the curtain back a little further and said, "Step inside," brushing past her to close the door.

The hall was white-painted and there was a noticeboard with fluttering notices on one side. The woman who had answered the door squeaked briskly along the shiny floor and disappeared through a door. Nancy hovered uncertainly until the woman came back.

"You can have a minute. She's busy, you know. She should be left to get on." She waved her through the door. "Left along the main passageway to the end. The Principal's office."

Nancy tapped on the door and a high voice called, "Thank you, Mrs Dodge." And then, "Come on down this end or you'll freeze".

The room was large with tall shuttered windows set into two walls. Angled in a corner was a wide brick fireplace with a small fire.

The Principal peered round the wing of an armchair. She appeared to be a small woman weighed down with a quilt across her knees.

"Excuse me staying put, but I've just got cosy. Now you'll need the other quilt, so you sit there."

She pointed to a smaller armchair with a brown quilt folded on the seat.

Her pale hair was escaping from whatever arrangement kept it up. Her glasses had slipped low on her nose, but that seemed to be her intention as she gazed at Nancy over them.

"Now. Is it that you have come to talk through a vocation? We do have to strike while the iron is hot in that case. At least for a first chat about it, so you could be ready for next year."

"It's something else. It's to do with my mother. She was here, before I was born of course, and I wanted to find out."

She was still fidgeting with the quilt, so she made herself keep still and explain properly. The Principal was attentive, an easy audience really.

"She was a student here? And did she go to the field?"

"She did, but she came back, and then I was born and I don't know where she is now. Or where she has been."

"Ah, so you were parted when you were young?"

"I've never known her."

"And her name?"

"Ada ... " The Principal's voice chimed with hers.

"...Henry. Of course. I can see the resemblance."

"Do I look like her? Someone said not."

"Not like her. Like your father."

It startled Nancy to hear her speak so confidently about her father. So there was no mystery about him.

"Miss Chancellor?" Mrs Dodge reappeared at the door. "Am I to do a supper for two?"

"If you could, Mrs Dodge. Sorry it's a bit unexpected."

She forestalled Nancy's apology with a shake of the head. When Mrs Dodge had left the room she said, "She looks after me a bit too carefully, really. And I do let her take the reins rather."

As they ate a supper of oxtail soup with macaroni in it, Miss Chancellor told Nancy that she had only met Nancy's father once, many years ago. He had come to the college to demonstrate the use of a magic lantern. His name was Frank - Frank Mann.

"I saw his picture, often, in the magazine of the Society. I noticed especially his obituary. And your mother wrote me letters, lots of letters, so to some extent I saw him as she saw him. As she got to know him."

Miss Chancellor swiftly turned the conversation to the different parts of the world where the college had sent missionaries – Africa, the Arctic and, of course, south-east Asia.

"It's rather wonderful to receive news from so many exciting places. We keep scrap-books and albums as a record of it all. She nodded to a stack of large bound books on one of the bookcases. I've got a file for almost everyone. One day I shall get round to writing some of their stories. But just now, while I'm Acting Principal and while I've got this book on the go, I never seem to have a minute."

After supper Miss Chancellor led her up the stairs, wide with shining brass stair rods, and along passageways until she threw open a heavy varnished door. A gold lettered plaque on the door read "Kings".

"The girls have all gone home for Christmas. We'll have to pick one of the rooms for you, so it may as well be this one. It's just as it was. I shared this room with your mother when we were students."

The next morning Nancy didn't see Miss Chancellor at breakfast. Mrs Dodge brought milky tea, toast and bitter, watery marmalade to a table beside a radiator in a broad passageway just outside the vast dining hall. She didn't say anything about what Miss Chancellor might be doing. But later, as Nancy walked about the grounds, she heard footsteps behind her.

"Forgive me, please. I had letters to deal with. There's something I should have said. I was worried that you might have taken off. Chased away by Mrs Dodge, who is determined that I should finish my book before the start of the new term."

The path was awkward for two. If Nancy stopped, she blocked Miss Chancellor's way. If she walked on, she turned her back. The grass on either side was crisped with frost.

"Let's see if Mrs Dodge can manage tea and a biscuit," said Miss Chancellor.

They sat again in her huge, glacial study.

"I should have told you that I do have some idea where she is. The awkward thing is, how can I know if she would like me to tell you? We send a card at Christmas, that's all. She has left a lot behind her.

"What I can tell you is where your father lived. It is possible that your grandmother is still alive. I had a letter from her a few years ago, asking if I knew anything of you, or if I could tell her how to find you. I had forgotten the details, but I looked it out from Ada's old file last night. She would very much like to meet you. You will be all she has left of your father."

She seemed to be holding the letter protectively so that Nancy couldn't see it. She glimpsed large careful lettering, done in pencil – if she had not been told otherwise, she would have guessed it was a child's letter.

"We were close, Ada and I, for the two years of our training. We wrote such letters when she was away. I had yearned to be called to the field, or thought I did. So I tried to live it through her. And then when she met Frank, she had so much she wanted to say, thinking it all through. But when it all went wrong, she stopped writing. She wrote a few times when she was expecting you. I would have wished to be with her in her difficulties but she was hiding herself away. I wished it even more when I heard you were on the way. We had decided, one evening before our training ended, that we would be godmothers for each other's daughters. And in the end she never asked me."

Her gaze crossed the room but seemed to miss Nancy and drift off through the window.

There was a thud of feet and Mrs Dodge thrust the door open.

"Bullocks are on the lawn again, Miss!"

Mrs Dodge disappeared as fast as she had arrived. Miss Chancellor unwrapped herself and hurried to the door, still holding the quilt.

"Mrs Dodge? Can't we telephone? You don't have to chase after them yourself! Please take care!"

Her voice receded down the corridor. Nancy stood up and leaned over the side table. The letter was dated November 1945, a little over two years ago.

She heard voices beyond the bay window and could see Miss Chancellor standing on the frosty lawn like a chess piece, wrapped in her quilt. She read on, guiltily:

Moorside,
Middlecombe,
Devon
November 1945

Dear Miss Chancellor,

I hope you will forgive me writing, and the manner of it. I am blind and depend on others to write my letters. My present amanuensis is just 8 years old and I am unable to make a judgment about his capacity for the task.

I am the mother of Frank Mann, whose acquaintance you may have made in the course of your work in training for mission. I have learned that he died in ignorance of a very material fact, that he had a child, a daughter, whose existence was, for whatever reason, kept from him and from me. I understand that this child was adopted and will most likely have lived her life in total ignorance of her origins.

I have many hours to spend in solitary reflection but am unable to understand why the child was abandoned to strangers. Why her father and his family were kept in ignorance of her is a little easier to understand, though not to forgive.

I am troubling you because I have reason to believe, from things Frank told me, that you were intimate with the woman who was to be the mother of his child and may have received from her the explanation I have not been given. I am near the end of my life and this is a loose end I am loth to leave untrimmed.

Sincerely yours,
Esme F. Mann

Nancy sat down briefly, muttering the address to herself: Moorside, Middlecombe, Moorside, Middlecombe. But above that rhythmic undertone there were phrases that screamed. *Died in ignorance. Abandoned to strangers. Near the end of my life.*

She dropped the letter, left her quilt in a heap round her chair and hurried upstairs, back to the room called Kings, to pack her case once again.

5

January 1948

Nancy

Having zig-zagged across the country, from Somerset to Norfolk, from Norfolk to Shropshire, Nancy has to think carefully to remember where she is. Devon. Not far from Dartmoor. Or in the middle of it, probably. Those dark hills are probably moor. She leans against the wall, staring out of the window of the bedroom she has slept in for two nights. She is looking over the slates of the outbuildings, past the stubby chimney of the tiny cottage attached to the side of the house and the stove-pipe of the washhouse that is now the woodshed. There's a gate to an overgrown patch of land, clogged with twiggy growth. She thinks a stream runs along the edge of that patch, hidden by nettles until it curves round to the road and runs under it. Beyond, there's a sloping green field with boulders in it. And then the dark hills.

She hears a crash downstairs. She knows there is no one else here to respond. The anger she has felt since the moment her past was taken away from her bubbles to the surface. She pushes away from the wall and heads downstairs to see what has happened.

A glass jar is shattered on the flags of the hall and a puddle of water is forming rectangular canals in the cracks. It's Annie's jar of rosehips. She likes to put rosehips into water, shake them into a furious maelstrom and then watch as the clear bubbles and scarlet berries race to the surface.

As she sweeps up the splinters and softening berries with the hearth brush, Nancy catches sight of Annie's tear-stained face, and Dennis intently tearing a piece of paper into ever-smaller pieces, and the darkening window reflecting nothing cheering. She thinks of winter afternoons when hail and sleet attacked her as she walked home from school. Days when the seven times table seemed impossibly out of reach and friendships were unbearably complicated. Mummy used to tell her not to feel sorry for herself. That's what weaklings do. There's always something you can do, or blessings you can count. But then a few minutes later she would be called into the kitchen for drop scones glazed with butter, or triangles of cinnamon toast. She drags the log basket outside and fills it, picking wood chips and fragments of bark from the floor of the shed to act as kindling. She sets a fire in the sitting room grate, patiently coaxing flames and then piling on an absurdly generous amount of logs. The children sit on the sofa and watch intently, as though something even more exciting will rise from the flames. Annie starts each time there's a crackle and, as if she'd complained, Dennis says, "Don't do that. It's lovely. It's a lovely fire."

"Toast," says Nancy. "Is there a toasting fork?"

Dennis doesn't like not having an answer.

"There are the spears," he says, pointing to a display on the wall.

Nancy untwists the wire that holds the two spear heads, weighs them in her hand and decides they will do if she wraps cloths around the sockets so that they can serve as handles.

After a few slices of toast spread with old, toffeeish jam, they get adventurous and try spiking apples on the spears. There's an exciting sizzling as juice dribbles onto the logs, but the result is disappointing and difficult to eat – sooty and rather too much like unsweetened stewed apple. They speculate about what else may have been spiked on the spears and Dennis grabs the tin of crayons to start work on a hunting scene.

Nancy looks round the room – wallpaper with a brown ferny pattern, dark bookshelves with glass fronts and large, dull-looking books, faded landscape prints in dark frames, bits of unnecessary furniture made of carved and pierced wood – and she realizes that by far the most interesting and appealing things in the room are the children, leaning together to share out the crayons. Her heart swells with pity for them, abandoned in this house where they don't belong, making the best of things, watching out for each other.

They are careful with their crayons, shading lightly, sharpening carefully and devastated if a lead gets broken. But they are voracious users of paper. Nancy has already given them all that she can find, including the brown paper that wrapped the sheets back from the laundry. Annie found a tissue paper pattern for a panelled skirt, in a packet jammed down behind the log basket but it was frustrating as it tore at every touch. Nancy remembers there was a notebook in the drawer of the chest in her room. Maybe that can be spared, though the pages are rather small. She runs upstairs, rummages under her few clothes and flicks through the notebook to see if there are blank pages to satisfy the children's need. It is filled with small, faded handwriting in pencil. But at the bottom of the drawer there is a drawer-liner printed with very faded sprigs. Inhaling the scent of lavender and wood, she takes it downstairs. Dennis receives the huge sheet of paper with popping eyes and eager exclamations. He lays it across the writing table, plain side up, and sets to work, directing Annie to do some clouds and sky at one edge. She sniffs at the paper and does some M-shapes for birds. Nancy sees Dennis's forehead wrinkling as he registers that the birds are flying upside down, sees him take breath to utter a reprimand and then suppress it. His frown relaxes and his head tilts to one side.

After they have eaten and she's taken and removed the tray upstairs, after the children have washed and gone to bed and she has closed the door on their shadowy shapes, already retreating into the privacy of sleep by the steady flame of the little night-light, she withdraws to her own room.

The notebook has a scuffed, water-stained cover of soft grey paper. At the back, someone has been making calculations – columns of pounds, shillings and pence on page after page. The other end is also written in pencil, sometimes quite faint, but Nancy can make out the first paragraph.

Before you were born - I can't remember before you were born. Perhaps I can. I remember Mother saying, "You won't be the only pebble on the beach when we've got the new baby. You'll have to look after yourself then, be the big sister.

Nancy lets out her breath. It is not addressed to her, not a message from a mother to her child. She reads on.

I didn't know what she meant. I hadn't noticed I was alone. And then, as I held you and talked to you and moved you about, I found out I had been. Now there were two of us. Like sticks bobbing along in the stream, touching, moving apart, touching again.

I thought Mother meant I would have to do all the things she wouldn't let me do. I'd be allowed to open the drawer with the knives in it, saw up the loaf of bread. I'd grate nutmeg in my milk and butter both sides of my bread.

I remember the day you were born, and the two days before it. I was staying at Auntie Susan's next door. I didn't know how long it was supposed to take; didn't know

I should be worrying. Auntie Susan said, "She's taking too long." I'd stayed two nights and she took up the sheets she'd put out for me and then had to flap open another pair the next night. And that wasn't how it should be.

So then Auntie Susan told me in the morning that I'd got a little sister, and that you were very poorly. I went home and up the stairs. Mother was in bed, very pale and sleepy. There was a nurse sitting in a chair by the window and that's where you were. She was holding you, concentrating on you. Mother said, "Go on, have a look, she's your sister." So I went round in front of the nurse. She told me to touch your hand. I couldn't see much of you but there were your fingers, dark red, in a bunch. My first sight of you. They were like the tentacles of sea anemones, bulging slightly at the end. I stroked them. I held your hand. You didn't grip but as I peered at your face I could see your nostrils and a little bubble blew out of one. I thought it was amazing, such a clever thing to do.

Then I was sent downstairs again. The nurse told me to run along, I couldn't be noisy in there. She stayed for weeks. It meant I had to sleep in the parlour on that hard little sofa. Just occasionally I heard your thin cry through the ceiling. But you didn't cry much.

All the life you ever knew was in that house. I hear the sound of it burning – the crackling of pine panels, the roaring of flames through the floorboards, curtains sizzling and then, in the workshop, the cans of oils and varnishes exploding and the beautiful etched glass panes of the hearse falling to the floor and shattering, its carved mouldings curling and cracking.

I pray there was smoke first, choking, blinding smoke. I pray that you slept in a blanket of sweet smoke.

Where have you gone, my darling? How did Father manage to give you a good send off with everything burnt to ash? He always said that. A good send off. It made Mother cross. What's the point of spending all that money on glazed hams and chicken sandwiches and silk linings and a fine pair of grey horses, she'd say. It's all too late. You can't make a difference now. It's much too late.

It's too late for you and Mother.

I asked him once, where do we send them? We send them off in their coffins. Where do they go?

All gone to ash. And your chair and the tablecloth with the tassels you used to swipe at as you jiggled in the chair. But you needed me to rock it. My feet on the rockers, my hands on the arms, my head hanging over yours. We'd rock until Mother complained about the noise. We made tracks in the floorboards. In the end she wrapped a ball of red string around the rockers to stop the clatter. I'd love it when my hair was loose and it would hang down and make a tickly cave and I'd rock us until you started to laugh.

We were dancing partners. They said you'd never walk, but you did, after a fashion. You just couldn't decide where to go. One foot on the rocker to tip you into my arms, the other leg braced to take your weight. And then off in a kind of polka to the kitchen table or the privy. Do you remember when I hugged you tight and waltzed you along the street? It was better than that wretched chair that rattled and juddered over the cobbles fit to loosen your teeth.

You outgrew your cot. You came in with me. We had a rubber sheet shifting about under us. What luxury it was when I went to college and had nothing but soft cotton under me. You twitched and flapped your arms, but I was used to it and how I missed your warmth when I went away.

And I miss the mornings when I woke before you and I could look into your calm face and see another life in it. I would whisper you some dreams. "We run and run for miles, over the hills and down until we come to a town with a tower, and we go up the tower ..." And then your eyes would open, dark and deep for an instant and then they'd slide away to the side. And then I'd heave you out and onto the pot. All the time I've been here, I've worried that Mother would forget, would not get to you in time. And now I should stop worrying.

Going to school made the first distance between us. I would come home at lunchtime, and there would be Mother on the doorstep with her hat and coat on, just needing to dash to catch the butcher or to pick up some apples from the stall. I never really knew what the other children did in the playground at dinner-time. I was never there. There was a temporary teacher once who stood me at the front because I was late back – but somebody must have said something because she didn't do it again. That might have been the first time I noticed I was special because of you.

Let me take your hands, Louie. We ride a horse together and gallop, we conduct a band, we wave from the deck of a ship. Goodbye, goodbye, goodbye.

I thought I knew what was good for you. But I wasn't always right. I took you for a walk beyond your strength. You sagged in my arms. I had to ask a stranger, I had to call out across the road, so he came and picked you up. You lolled in his arms, trailing snot on his waistcoat. When we got home Mother couldn't look at him she was so ashamed. I got a rap with the wooden spoon for that.

Bedtime. Sit here on the bed, Louie. Hands together now. "Now we lay us down to sleep, We pray the Lord our souls to keep. If we should die before we wake, We pray the Lord our souls to take. Aa-men."

Where do we go, Louie? Do you know? Were you always there?

How did I tear myself away?

Was it the church camp that started it? Was I eleven, and you about seven that first time? Father heard about the plan at a church meeting and told Mother at supper. Mother just stared at her plate. I thought she'd swallowed a fishbone. But she said, It's right she should go, she should go to something like that. Then after a bit she said, I can manage. I worried, wondered what I should do. I watched

Mother, I wanted her to make me believe it would be all right. I tried not to think what it would be like for you, with Mother in a flap, not noticing when you'd had enough of one thing and needed another.

I went. When I was sitting on the train, no chance to change my mind, I felt a panic, a clenching round my heart, but the strange thing was, it turned delicious, like a thrill. Miss Woodman came through the carriage, stuck her head into our compartment and said, This is it, girls! What a week we're going to have! And I found I was smiling.

I wasn't very good at all that, being with the other girls, saying the right thing, making sure they liked me. I'd annoyed the others just sitting down on the train: Did you bag the window seat? Well, you'll just have to sit in the middle then. I was even worse with boys, always in their way or not doing what they expected.

At night, from my bed by the door of the tent, where the upper part of the door flap hung open, I lay watching the stars and listening to the rustlings of the grass on the dunes. How I missed you, no anchoring weight beside me. Staring at the stars until I fell upwards, hanging there, alone.

Alone. Were you ever not alone? I remember I sat in a hollow at the crest of the dunes, with banks of sand and marram root fitting round me like a cool hug. The grass blades jangled and whispered in my ears. No one could see me. I couldn't hear anyone. I was running the finest trickling sand through my fingers. I watched my elbow getting buried as a little dune of blown sand built over it, first clumping between the hairs, just as it does between stems of marram. A bird, a gull, laid its shadow on me and then glided on.

The edge of the sea was coiling and unrolling, coiling and unrolling. I watched a sheen creep across the beach as a tide pool was refilling – just a glistening finger. Then the sun slipped a little lower and the tide crept a bit higher and there was a lovely golden rush stretching into new channels, like an opening hand reaching towards me. I wanted to tell you, Louise. I wanted to put that in your dreams.

That night Nancy falls asleep with tears on her pillow.

6

September 1925

Ada

Make a record, he said, *a record of your journey.*

So there will be twenty-eight records of twenty-eight journeys towards a vocation in twenty-eight dark blue hard-backed notebooks on the front of which someone has carefully pasted typed labels. Ada Henry, Meredith Hall, 1925 – 7. Which makes it seem as if I really will be here for two years.

We'll see, Father said. He was so reluctant at first. "It surprises me," he said, "why God would want you there. You have enough to do at home. Mother needs you." But then he did say, "If you really do have a calling, I suppose you have to follow it, however fanciful it seems."

It doesn't feel fanciful. I may be wrong, but it's not to do with being fanciful. Is it to do with being needed?

Perhaps he is afraid. It could take you anywhere, he says. I hope he's right. (Except I, too, am afraid.) He suspects me. Or he trusts me but doesn't trust the world out there. It was he who taught me to put pennies in the missionary box at the back of the church. He had made a nice box from some off-cuts of mahogany and I decorated it with a picture from a magazine of black children in a school under a tree in Africa. The seed of an idea. A mahogany seed. Where did that mahogany come from, I wonder?

Was I about fourteen when we went to that meeting to hear a missionary from Uganda speak? Cramming ourselves into a packed hall; we got the last two chairs. The dais looked just as it had done for the meeting Father sent me to about the school for mentally deficient and crippled - a lectern and three chairs and an aspidistra on a stand behind.

The missionary looked ordinary enough when the vicar led him out of a side door. But lots of people gasped, myself included, as the missionary was followed by a tall black man. How shy he must have felt. How will I feel if I take my astonishing white skin to a place where people are black?

We had a chance to stare during the solo from the Messiah - the pianist fumbling and dust hanging in the sunset light above the old piano. Charlotte Simms was the best in the choir, always reliable: *How beautiful are the feet of they that preach the gospel of peace.* Charlotte lowered her music and there was a pause. We call people black but I realised that no visible part of him was really black except perhaps his hair. Anyway, I saw that he was passing a finger over his cheek and I'm sure he was crying. Perhaps they didn't have such stirring music where he came from.

Mr Budd started his address with the calling of the disciples by Jesus, the simple carpenter from Nazareth in his country clothes and dusty sandals. I could appreciate that - a man who walked with humble feet in humble shoes, making knotty wood smooth as Father does, and not turning away from the stumblers and dribblers. Follow those footprints, said Mr Budd. And more than that, hold out your hand to bring others along with you. Here before you is Thomas. Thomas was in darkness. He has emerged from that darkness and I want you to rejoice with me about that. He took Thomas by the hand and made him stand. Thomas's lips suddenly parted in a beautiful smile and he started to speak. I was full of fear, he said. (A voice that was interestingly deep and high at the same time.) Always full of fear. I longed for peace.

I thought he might shed another tear. I know I was moved. But I hoped he would not cry, not in front of so many staring people.

Now hear the fruits of his conversion, said Mr Budd. He nodded at Thomas and Thomas went on: "I came to know my sins, all my very many sins. It was a sin to be fearful, but I did not know Lord Jesus would be my guide. Now I am filled with courage. I know what Jesus wants me to do. I go this way, I go that way, I come here because Jesus wants me to."

At the time I took that as a natural consequence of his contact with missionaries. But now it seems truly remarkable. Which of us really knows our sins? Which of us would go so far because Jesus wants us to? And yet that must be precisely why I am here – following where

Thomas led. Can I lay a hand on my chest as he did and say: *I know what Jesus wants me to do?*

Mr Budd told us that Thomas faced many challenges, surrounded as he was by Satan's followers who believe they can control evil forces. Thomas heard and understood in time. Oh, how they resist us, he said, some of these people, clinging to practices that spread harmful thoughts, that let Satan in. I remember his exact words. "Each of us, each of you, is travelling towards your end, towards death and judgement. We don't like to say it but it is so. What better work to do, my friends, than to support these conversions, lifting people like Thomas here out of their doubts and fears into a life of joyful confidence?"

Then he told us of course that this work could not be done for nothing. Missionaries needed salaries, homes, boots, and sun helmets and tickets on ocean-going ships. So I contributed two whole shillings from my savings jar and thought about the few pairs of socks, perhaps, that could be bought to help the work in Africa.

That evening meant something. But perhaps, too, a mouse has a place in the story. Maybe I started on this journey some years before.

I thought I saw a miracle. A resurrection, even. I thought I'd understood something. In our house we often spoke of death, who had died, who was about to die, what they needed in terms of furnishings and clothing. I sometimes planned my own funeral as other girls might picture the decor for their dolls' houses. But even so I did not think about what it meant to be dead. I was very young when I found the mouse, no more than eight.

The mouse had appeared among the wallflowers outside Auntie Susan's front window, shaken from the trap with an exclamation that made me look up from where I was playing jacks on the drain cover. I went and looked and found it lodged between two stems, its lovely tender white belly uppermost. Would it let me pick it up? Then I sneaked away with that special thing soft and stiff on my palm, and sat under the elder tree in the back yard to study it. The mouth was a little bit open – I could just see two goofy teeth and a dark red stain on the jaw as if it had guzzled a blackberry pie.

It's dead, I told myself. Like a dead person.

I said "Hoo!" loudly to see if it would move. The whiskers trembled but the eyes were like chips of coal.

I would have shown it to Father. He could have made a coffin. But Father had gone to the War. He was making coffins for soldiers. Then I thought of my hiding place in the roots of the elder tree where I kept things - the tiny wooden doll Mother put in the dustbin when one arm came off, and a glittery piece of green glass and one of Louise's baby teeth that we'd managed to stop her from swallowing.

I pulled out the wedge-shaped piece of brick – the space was about the size of a shoe – just right. I laid the mouse to rest, bloody side downwards, and thought how nice it looked. Its fur was sleek, shading from grey to yellow to white. Its staring eye was thoughtful. It looked as if it was just beginning to understand something somewhere deep inside. I pulled some pretty little heads off forget-me-nots and scattered the cloudy blue petals around it. Then I locked the bit of brick back into the niche where the elder root had grown to fit it.

I waited for a week. The first time I looked, nothing much had changed in the darkness except the petals had faded and the mouse looked duller and less appealing. There were ants bustling about its face.

The second time, the eye had sunk into the fur, the mouth was agape and the skin seemed to be pulling back from the teeth, which were bared in a savage grin.

I remember telling it, "I don't like you anymore."

I still went back for another look. That time – what had happened? At the first glimpse I nearly slammed the brick back into place. When I pulled it out again, I set it gently aside, ready to take in the wonder before my eyes.

The outline of the mouse could barely be seen, except the ears, which were crisply frosted with a white fuzz with tiny grey balls in amongst it. The rest of the body was lost in a cloud of spiky fur, longer and whiter and more erect than a living mouse ever wore. Some of the spikes were jewelled with minute greyish yellowish globes.

I stared for several minutes.

It's gone to heaven, I thought. Amen.

Carefully, carefully, I put back the brick. Reverentially.

I didn't tell anybody then. Perhaps I knew there'd be trouble about playing with a dead thing. But I did feel I had understood something. I now knew something the grown-ups knew and would talk about but couldn't explain. Even if I couldn't explain it either. But the best part was what happened afterwards.

Long after - a few days after my thirteenth birthday it would have been - I was fiddling with the silver charm bracelet Aunt Marion gave me. I liked stretching it out and gazing at all the charms she had chosen: a tiny house with a window and a door; a cockle shell; a swallow with outstretched wings; a mouse with its tail curled round in a loop; and finally, just before the padlock-shaped catch, was a thick little book with a hinge on its spine and a clip on the front. I loved that one because I could see it would actually be possible to put an even tinier treasure inside. I wondered, what could I have that would fit?

And then I remembered my old cache of treasures under the elder tree, guarded by the snarling mouse. I loved them once, the pearly tooth and the chip of glass. Both would be too big for the little book, I thought, but I wasn't sure.

The elder tree had gripped the bit of brick more closely so it was a struggle to get it out. On the floor of the cavity, laid out in order, was a very perfect set of tiny white bones. Rib after rib, like spoons in a drawer, the vertebrae like a finely twisted cable until the tail end where the gaps between them were wider and wider. The snarl had disappeared completely. Two big yellow teeth curved from the front of the upper jaw in an arc to almost meet the two projecting from the lower jaw, like the brass calliper Father uses to measure the wood he's shaping.

How glad I was that the cloud of inexplicable fluff had gone. How much more I preferred the revelation of tiny bones. They were precisely the bones needed for being a mouse with.

Did I start to feel it then, that there is resilient substance deep inside me, something to give me strength and direction, the tools for the work of my life? God knows my bones; God will know what to do with me. It must be right to try my strength.

Father and Mother very gradually got used to the idea that I might come here. Father has agreed to pay for my first year. He says if the college people decide they really want me and give me the scholarship for the second year, well, we'll see then. I can try out if there really is a place for me. But missionaries, he says, they're adventurers really. Who's to say if the church takes root in all these foreign places? So often, he thinks, it's a failure. They don't put those ones in the magazines and appeals. But his view is that a year at college will give me a good basis for the Sunday School and helping the young people at the church at home. That's no bad thing, he says.

When it was all decided, when the papers had been filled out and sent, I went into the workshop where he was sanding a plank. He didn't turn round but he started talking about when he was in France in the War: you saw all these people being moved around the world. "But everybody just longed for his own place. Longing, they were, for their bit of England wherever it was, where they could talk to the people in the shops and be remembered when they died. And, you know, my girl, there's always work to be done near at hand. Can you pass the linseed oil and the rag, girl?"

His arms were gliding along the plank, sandpaper hissing like the sea. Fixed to the wall in front of him were all his orderly rows of chisels, files and planes.

It's always like that with Father. If he gives you a glimpse of what's inside, it has to be smoothed over, covered up with everyday business.

The jar of golden oil had a piece of my old flowery nightdress stuffed in the top. I put it into his dusty hands. Just then the light caught the jar and his hands turned to gold.

Getting used to it must have been worse for Mother. But towards the end of August she arranged for Auntie Susan to mind Louise for a day so that she and I could go to Cambridge to buy what I would be needing for college.

I had my list. Mother never normally spends any money, but she seemed eager to do things properly.

We were looking at the raincoats and she said, have something you like, pick the one that suits you. There'll be all the other girls there and you want to look the part. She read my mind - she told me not to think about if it'll hand down. She doesn't wear a mac anyway, she said. You like the green one, don't you?

Do I? I said. And then I realised that, yes, I did like that one. It is dark forest green with a bit of gather between the shoulders and what I think are rather stylish turnings on the pockets. And the lining will make it warm.

And while I was arranging to pay for that, she drifted away to a display of scarves and drew her hands through them and she said, I'm going to get you a scarf to go with it, something that'll be nice and soft on your face.

She said it as though she thinks the world is going to be harsh to me. Perhaps it is. I'm not used to being watched, nor even accustomed to being a stranger or pushing myself forward.

We had lunch in the restaurant at Eaden Lilley's but Mother's enthusiasm for spending money was starting to fade. We had a leek soup with slices of bread on the side and then she waved the waiter away.

Then she said what was really on her mind: It's going to be very different without you – getting the shopping in and so on. And when Father has a funeral and all that running about, I'll have to ...

And I said, You'll get a bit of help, Mother. You can ask the Carr girls. Or Auntie Susan. As long as you're there at bedtime. It'll work out. It will work out.

That's what I was saying to myself all yesterday afternoon in time with the rattle of the train.

We had our first meeting with Dr Grover. Mrs Hart, whom I'd met at the interview, walked around ringing the bell, getting us all assembled. There are twenty-eight of us. We all stood about in the drawing room not knowing whether to sit down, not knowing whether to start chatting. Then a big voice from the doorway asked us to be seated and he strode up the aisle to a lectern near the fireplace. His voice sounded as if it should come from a taller man. He speaks with great authority, it seems to me.

We prayed together. We prayed for the miracle of true vocation and for the strength to fulfil it.

I tried to relax into a contemplative state on the dainty chair, but my mind was buzzing. I had irrelevant thoughts and had to pull my mind back. I was looking at the heels of the women in the row in front of me. Will one of these women become my friend? Will Edith Chancellor, who shares my room? I could hear Edith's rough breathing beside me. Is it anxiety, or some other emotion? Dr Grover's prayer took us through Jesus's baptism by the Holy Spirit and into the desert where he was tempted. I did try to bring my wandering mind to order and just about managed it in time for the blessing.

Then he explained to us about vocation. A calling. The sound of a voice heard by no one but ourselves. He pretended to be intently listening with his eyebrows raised and his head cocked. He's got this little iron-grey curl that falls onto his forehead when he moves.

This is what he said. I've got to keep this in mind because this is what I am not clear about.

We imagine ourselves praying on our knees at dusk. Then the call comes, like a clear distant voice.

Is that what I imagine it is like?

"My dear young ladies," he said, "I must disappoint you by announcing that, although hearing such a call would be possible, it is unlikely. Instead, we must, between us, assemble a myriad tiny pieces of evidence. Like detectives at a crime scene, we must let nothing go unobserved. We must use our daily prayer and periods of reflection; we must be open about our thoughts and feelings. My staff and I will assemble the evidence with the utmost precision and delicacy, and, by the time you leave here we will know that, if you are heading for a distant field of mission, it is in response to the guidance of God. Your part, dear ladies, is to shed your shyness and timidity, and to share with us the moments when our Heavenly Father touches your elbow, or your errant heart pulls you back."

I want to trust my heart. I want to have a heart that spies someone's need from across the room, across a clearing, and draws me over. Is that arrogant?

These notebooks, he assured us, will be read by no one but ourselves. But we are to write in them daily to ensure that we reflect every day on our progress and setbacks.

We sang a hymn, not very well – *Lift high the cross, the love of Christ proclaim, till all the world adore his sacred Name.* I think some of us knew different tunes.

I thought at first it would be difficult sharing a room with Edith. I arrived first and when Mrs Bugle took me up she told me which bed I was to take. They both have brown bedspreads and three grey blankets. We each have a chair and a rug and a little chest of drawers but there's only one writing table between us. Our window looks out to the back of the house. There's a dark wood rising up against the sky but in front of it is a lawn with beds of rose bushes and a litter of petals. It's all quite grand and spacious.

Edith is tall and has very smooth fair hair, and pink cheeks as though she's anxious. My first thought was, "She's scared of me!" But then she told me that she is simply not used to sharing a room. She's an only child. We'll just have to manage. I'm sure there's worse than sharing a decent sized room to worry about.

Our room is called Kings. All the rooms are named after books of the Old Testament. The other doors on our landing are Samuel and Chronicles.

I went along to the bathroom to get into my nightdress. When I came back she asked to borrow my dressing-gown. I should have had "dressing-gown" on my list of things to buy. I had to show Edith the awfulness of the hand-stitching where the material was too thick for the machine and the half-dozen places where the cord trim is coming off. I told her it is the worst thing I possess and I hope that wasn't a lie. But she still wants to borrow it. She says it's better than nothing. That did make us laugh. She's going to keep sharing it until hers comes in the post.

5th October 1925

We have started our studies. We had to choose today whether to specialize in pedagogy or nursing. I chose nursing. I think Mother would have liked me to try teaching. She was so careful at teaching me about apostrophes and using the subjunctive. But nursing is what comes more naturally to me. Surely it will be easier to offer people help with their ailments than to persuade them they need to be able to write! Curiously, Edith has chosen nursing because it is what she is least familiar with. We all have to do gardening because it is healthy and strengthening, as well as being a practical survival skill. I hadn't thought that scurvy would be one of the dangers we have to face! It seems I'll leave here knowing how to grow vegetables for the whole year round, not something I've tried before. The whole of a Shropshire year, anyway. Does anything grow in the Arctic?

We have prayers each morning and evening of course, and everybody has an individual "Progress" session each week in which either Dr Grover or Mrs Hart will be exploring our vocational progress, or guiding our reading. Most of our classroom time is to be taken up with Bible study. We've been given a printed guide (we're getting a first sight of Dr Grover's next published work) pointing out the typical role of each part of the Bible in a Christian's formation.

We'll have visiting lecturers who share their methods and experiences from the field. Towards the end of the year we are to start going out on deputations, first listening, and then contributing to the platform speeches at fund raising events.

In the first nursing lesson we did temperatures and aspirin. Next time it's foreign bodies in the ear. At least I can now authoritatively state that however pink her cheeks look, Edith's body is the right temperature and she assures me mine is, too.

Edith's dressing gown came in a parcel. I think I might ask if I can borrow it – lovely dove grey cotton velvet!

Roberta who's on our landing tapped on our door this morning. It was clear we were just getting ready to go out around the garden, putting our shoes on and finding scarves. So when she asked if we were off out and could she come with us we could hardly say no. It seems she had been longing for a chance to go for a walk with us because we're the ones she hasn't got to know yet. She's been organizing the window bay at the end of our landing with a sofa and a pile of magazines so it can be a "friendly place" for us all. You can tell she's been at boarding school. And I can tell that I am not likely to sit there waiting for company.

She said she was intending to visit an old friend who'd love to see her and it would be a case of the more the merrier if we went along. So we did. Roberta knows her way around this area. She's had holidays here since childhood and the lady she took us to see used to be housekeeper at the place they rented.

It's stopped now, but this morning the trees along the drive were thrashing in a powerful wind, and the leaves were rattling and letting go and whipping past our faces, but it was good to be out. As soon as we got level with the first row of houses in the village there was a voice calling from an upstairs window, "Well if it's not little Bobbie! And with some friends!"

She, Mrs Jones, said we weren't on any account to walk past so Roberta took us round to the back. Mrs Jones opened the door and it was as if a river of cats streamed out and started weaving round our legs. Edith sort of jumped and exclaimed, but Mrs Jones bustled us in to the dark and smoky room, and sat us in a row on a settle in front of the fire. She shook a stack of tins one by one until there was a thudding sound and she put a plate of rock cakes on a curly-legged stool in front of us. But Roberta said she was very sorry, she'd love to have one of her rock cakes again but we'd just had breakfast at college. I took that to be a warning.

Then I could feel that Edith was struggling with her breathing. It's the smoke, she whispered to me. She was starting to wheeze and scrabble at her chest so I tipped the cat off my lap and took her outside. I didn't want to offend Mrs Jones who just flapped her hand at each puff of smoke. That fireplace, she said, doesn't like the wind off the hill. She brought a stool out and Edith sank onto it and her head was dragging backwards with each breath. Mrs Jones kept fussing; should she bring a blanket? Should she get the doctor? Thankfully, Roberta took her back indoors and I found myself looking after Edith, almost as if she were Louise leaning against me, while the trees on the hill thrashed and hissed. There's plenty of air, I said. Just breathe, breathe. Her ribs were heaving and she kept doing little useless coughs, so I just kept breathing with her, my stomach against her back. Gradually I could feel her relaxing and the coughing stopped. I could tell it had frightened her. It had frightened us, too. Roberta was gabbling, telling her she was feeling better now, wasn't she, and she'd just run and fetch a car from the garage in the village to get us back to the Hall. While we waited for the car, Edith looked me in the eye and begged me not to tell anyone. She said it had been touch and go whether they'd have her here at the college. Of course I won't say. But I do wonder if it can be right for her to think of going into the field.

Yesterday evening when we came back up to Kings, Edith wanted to talk about what happened. She assures me she's not trying to deceive anybody. She says she's usually perfectly healthy. And she doesn't want her health to hold her back from doing what she can do. Whatever that is.

There's always something to hold a person back. Half of me wants a great adventure and half of me really doesn't. But I don't want to be like poor Mother. Angry. Sitting in the corner of a cage. Edith probably has two halves as well.

She told me this evening how she nearly died. She was about three. They kept her in hospital for months. Her parents despaired. So after she got better they kept telling her how precious she was. She grew up knowing that she was too special to die. But she says it made her think about it a lot. And it's made her feel she should live for some purpose. She needs to do something thankful with her life.

It must be different for you, she said. You have made a gift of your life already, spending nearly every moment caring for someone who needs you. And I said, no, no, she's just my sister, just part of being me. It's true. I wouldn't be myself if I hadn't been Louise's sister. It frightens me sometimes, that I am letting go of that part of my life.

This building echoes with chatter. There are always people around - always someone talking and expecting an answer. I've found a place to go, the patch of woodland behind the grounds. There's not really a path there but you can wind your way through the shrubbery. It's usually wet. Water trickles underfoot on most days, leaving pale drifts of grey sandy soil in half circles edged with small dark bits of tree debris. It's like a delicate design woven in silk. And there's a huge chestnut tree with bark with deep ripples, long slow waves up above and shorter, deeper twisty ones nearer the ground. I like to lean there and I look along the valley to see the very same trees and glimpses of fields and hedges every time I'm there. Its smell changes almost as if the wood knows my mood. One day it's sullen and stagnant, and then the next it's fresh and hopeful again.

Today I skipped chapel. I watched tiny gleaming beetles weaving their way through the miniature forest of mosses at the foot of a great thrumming living tree that reaches high into the invisible streams of air above. I cannot say why it seems important to crouch there and watch and listen. As important as being in church.

7ᵗʰ December 1925

Edith just asked me what she's like, my sister, but then she had to hurry off for her appointment with Mrs Hart.

What is she like, Louise? When she was small I always thought she was like a creature from deep under the sea. You could watch her and touch her but it was as if she was under water, as if she was being washed about by great currents and waves. That's what made her helpless. We could stand firm, somehow, while she got washed about.

When she was little we could play together – but I guess it was me playing with her, like a great big doll. We read the Pilgrim's Progress at Sunday School. I loved it. I can remember how the beginning sent a shiver down my spine.

'As I walked through the wilderness of this world I lighted on a certain place where was a den, and laid me down in that place to sleep; and, as I slept, I dreamed a dream. I dreamed, and behold I saw a man clothed with rags standing in a certain place, with his face from his own house, a book in his hand, and a great burden upon his back.'

Father's copy of the book had wonderful engravings. Louise and I would act out the pictures – me hoisting

Louise onto my back and staggering around. 'How am I to be rid of this burden? Rid me of this heavy burden'. I'd be sinking into the Slough of Despond and struggling, crying out, 'Woe is me I am undone!' And then I'd toss Louise onto the rocking chair and skip about saying 'I am glad and lightsome!' while Louise giggled in the chair. Or I'd do the fight with Apollyon for Louise to watch (or not, as she chose).

When it was time for bed, I'd undress her in the scullery, leaving her clothes for the wash-tub. "The billows go over your head!" I would say, pulling off a petticoat. "And the rest of your mortal garments, Louie." And then, flourishing the flannel to wash her face: "There appeared a HAND, with leaves from the Tree of Life".

Of course she's got older and heavier and now I think it frightens Mother and Father, her solidity. It worries me that Mother thinks of herself as rather frail, not strong enough for the task. Maybe that's one reason why I've come away. She's not difficult at all, Louise, she's very calm. And they, both of them, have to know they can manage. Now she's older I can see that it matters more to other people. I get glimpses of people thinking stupid thoughts about how she should have grown up, stood on her own two feet by now.

Of course I don't think that, but I can sometimes think she's a bit of a lump, always sitting between me and the world.

Edith makes me out to be a heroine as though I've given up a lot for her.

Perhaps. But at other times I remember my gratitude. This is the bit people don't understand. She helps me so much; she helps me to be me. I hardly knew until I came here. I miss her, our secret conversations, the stories I tell her. She doesn't understand a word I say. But she understands me. Better than my parents do. With them I talk about things that need to be done and things people have said and it all feels so distant. With Louise, it's direct, she knows it's me talking to her and she doesn't mind a bit what I'm saying or struggle to understand or make out meanings that I don't intend.

I think in a way Edith envies me. She's anxious to work out what she wants to be and do; what a worthwhile woman should be and do.

She says I'm good for her. Like syrup of figs.

That made me laugh. What she means is, the fact I'm here to talk to means she does the work she needs to do. She's used to talking to her mother, but she knows her so well and thinks she's so wonderful. With me she has to explain herself.

I told her she does need to explain herself. She says very strange things that need explaining.

It's almost Christmas. The mantelpieces are all dressed with holly and there's a tree at the end of the dining hall all wound round with red ribbons. I'll be home in a couple of days.

24ᵗʰ December 1925

The house looks small and dull. Mother came to the door with a potato peeler in one hand and a potato in the other, but perhaps she'd guessed it was me. Louise was hunched over in her rocking chair and the first thing I had to do was hitch her upright and set her in motion. It's funny that I had a foolish expectation that she would notice I was back. We had a cheerful supper.

It's Christmas Eve so we lit a little fire in the back parlour. Father brought us fragrant cedarwood shavings to put on the fire and it smelled wonderful. We only normally go in there if we've been cooking fish or onions and want to escape the worst of the smell in the living room. I fetched Louise through and we flopped together on the little sofa. Mother stood in the doorway and laughed.

"Just like when you were little – what a pair!"

Her laugh was the same as it's always been but it struck me now as a sad, mirthless laugh – just a dropped jaw and a spoken "Hah!"

She settled with her crochet in the fireside chair and I lay back and gazed at all the things that make it my home, illuminated by low winter light: the way the light falls on the polish on the wooden arms of the carver chair opposite Mother's chair, the textured fuzz of the fabric, very slightly different lengths for the different colours, on the sofa I was lying on, the lunar landscapes in the uneven plaster of the ceiling, the pattern of tiles within the fender. The little kick of Mother's hair above the middle of her forehead, from which an unhappy lock hangs down whenever her responsibilities overwhelm her. The efficient way her fingers work amongst the threads of the crochet. The warmth of Louise's leg lying alongside my own, twitching from time to time.

Am I really going to leave all this? At this moment everything feels so full of life and meaning, attached to memories of when I was tiny, when I was ten, full of the certainty of it all being here tomorrow, next year and the year after.

It got dark as we sat there. Winter darkness. Waiting for the coming of the gift of light. Mother sighed and put away her crochet. She asked if I'm staying awake for the midnight service. She assures me she won't mind at all if I go. Is that a way of saying how sad she is not to go herself? But she looks tired and says she'll go in the morning.

I'm glad to go, to stand with my fellow Christians and give thanks for Christ on earth. It lifts my heart. Is this what vocation feels like?

8th January 1926

We're to start going to the Royal County Hospital once every two weeks to observe the surgeons. Today we were shown the operating theatre and told how we have to behave. It's rather like a chapel, with dark-painted pews and we're to keep perfectly still and not distract anyone. It's a matter of life or death. We're not to lean over or ask any questions. Even the medical students who will be with us will not be allowed to ask questions. The table is brightly lit but we'll be at such a distance I am not confident we will gain very much from it.

Mr Bugle has sciatica so our gardening lesson was cancelled. We walked back past the drawing room door, which stood open. The second years were gathered in there. We could hear there was a visiting speaker, or else someone was practicing for deputations.

The speaker was on the low platform by the lectern with her head thrown back and her arms held forward. She looked as though she was about to strike a chord on a piano. She certainly had the audience's attention.

"It is such a blessing to be able to do this work. We can change the course of people's lives in such a deep way. It's like being a doctor. A person goes to a doctor with a pain, some cause of anguish. Or maybe they don't even know there's anything wrong. And the doctor has the special skill and knowledge. *We* have the privilege of living in a Christian country. *We* have the word of God at our fingertips, to guide us, to pass to others at their moment of need."

Her voice was rather hoarse. I couldn't tell if she was striving to project it or perhaps struggling with deep feeling. Pale blue eyes peering past her sharply pointed nose.

"The people we meet in the course of our work – how can they know what is wrong with them? How can they know that God waits for them to turn towards him? Their ignorance is like a cancer and it gets worse and worse the older they are, because God expects more of us as we get older and more experienced.

"I'm not very clever or very educated. I don't know all the science a doctor has to know. But I have carefully and humbly studied the book of instruction for human lives and I can pass that guidance on." She laid a hand on the Bible on the table beside her.

"At our headquarters in a little town near Rangoon we hold classes for the children. I only speak a little of their language and they speak even less of mine. But we have translations of Bible stories to read to them. The stories begin to get a grip on them. They begin to see right and wrong in them, especially as they get to know us and see our example.

"The viewpoint they are brought up with lets them drift along just taking things as they come. They see someone taking something that doesn't belong to him and it is as if they did not see it. They cannot seem to make judgments." She raised her brows and fixed her gaze sternly on those in the front row in a way that would have made me want to disagree.

Overhearing that ought to make it begin to seem real. But at present, the whole idea of mission seems like a story I tell Louise. Travelling to a faraway land where people carved from ebony bare their shining teeth in smiles and chant the Lord's Prayer under a blue, blue sky ...

I said so to Edith and she laughed at me. She says it's impossible; it'll never be simple. People are never what we want them to be. It's what makes the world feel so rough-edged and difficult.

At least the speaker we overheard has started to face up to the challenges of persuading people that we have good guidance to share with them.

I know Edith is beginning to wonder, to doubt that she should be training at all. She thinks she wants people to find what they are, not to make them be something she wants. To pick their own way.

12th February 1926

I saw someone die today. We were at the hospital and there was a long wait before they brought the patient in. Watching the surgery on our visits to the operating theatre, I have been amazed at what the human body can endure – the intrusion of cruel instruments and five or six bloody hands at a time. We've never been able to see the details or had much idea of the anatomy. One time I thought it must be the liver they were working on but as we were leaving one of the medical students overheard me and laughed because apparently it was simply an appendix. There's not much you can do with a liver.

Today there were so many of them around the table murmuring to each other. Someone in the row in front kicked the pew loudly and the chief surgeon looked up and glared, and then the anaesthetist said in a loud voice, "Can we *please* progress this procedure?" And then they bowed their heads to their work again; there was a bit more muttering and suddenly we heard the surgeon saying, "Can you record the time of death please, Sister," and that was that. A soul departed.

21ˢᵗ June 1926

Gerald Grey. Our supper is to be early because we have a visit from the renowned Gerald Grey. He has worked in Africa but what he is famous for is his success with inner city missions in London and Liverpool.

I saw him arrive - he is short and seems quite unassuming, with thick black hair like a cap on the top of his head. He shook hands with Dr Grover, smiling modestly beneath his thin moustache. What does he do, I wonder, to earn the reputation that has meant his name is mentioned with meaningful looks?

So, this evening we were packed into the chapel. It's too narrow really because it was originally a carriage house built against the garden wall. The benches were so packed together we'd had to take the kneelers away for this evening.

Gerald Grey has a way of speaking that forces you to lean forward and listen hard. His words seem to come out in sobs and whispers, full of passion. I felt he was expecting more from all of us than we were able to give. He was able to pray at length, entirely extemporised, on behalf of the unconverted people of the world, entangled in Satan's traps and devices. And just as we were all far off in our minds thinking of the people who needed us, he suddenly become focused on us, right there in front of him.

"Stand," he said, "and declare yourself. Send Satan scampering! That tremor in your breast, it means something! Don't ignore it."

His eyes were sweeping along the rows expectantly, piercingly.

"What attractive young women you are!" he suddenly shouted. "Don't think you are healthy. Don't trust in your youth and wellbeing. Death haunts this lovely, comfortable place with trees and flowers all around. When we let ourselves rest in the eager arms of nature, then we are sliding towards a darkness where no light shines. You are cripples, every one of you. Until you take that step towards Jesus. Until you say 'Yes!' to all that he offers."

Not one of us dared to move, or scarcely to breathe.

Then he was moaning, "Oh, let us leave our hard-hearted ways. Bring us nearer to your path, Lord, stepping in your footsteps ..."

That made me feel a bit steadier. Footsteps. Following, carefully taking one step at a time. But steady steps, not these passionate lurches. I'm not hard-hearted – I'm sure I'm not humble enough, but I'm not hard-hearted. And I wish people like him would refrain from trying to push my heart around with their moaning.

As we sat there in turmoil, we heard a chair scrape and someone stood up. It was Felicity. Her mouth moved, opened and shut, but no words came out. She was wringing her hands. He beckoned so that the others in the row moved their legs aside and bundled her to the end. Gerald Grey stepped forward to take her hands and whispered words of blessing over her shoulder.

I was just a row back from them. I could see a tremor in his half-closed eyelids and Felicity's transparent hair moving in his breath.

I wanted to tell her to pull away. But her face was turned aside as though she was listening to a piece of music, perfectly calm with her eyes closed. It was Gerald Grey who dropped her hands, turned away and walked back to the front. He scanned us all again, nodding encouragingly. Two more stood and received his whispered blessing. Then he called the three of them to the front to stand facing the rest of us. I expected them to look flustered, nervous, embarrassed. But all I could see was calm relief. Is that it? Have they heard their call?

22nd June 1926

How can he be so certain? Why do I have so little trust? Because that's the way it is, I suspect. Like Father, I am suspicious. Do I think they are making themselves feel called, forcing their own feelings? I'm not sure I should be here.

Edith has evidently been reflecting on this as well. She says perhaps not being certain is a gift in itself. "Not having the words, knowing that we are in the dark with just the odd glimpse of light. Maybe it's not that we have words of certainty to tell, but we set the example of searching."

So that makes mission the art of teaching people to stumble about in the dark! What about the Basis? All that belief?

They gave us the Basis at the start of this term. To be a member of the Scripture Pathway Missionary Society one must sign up to it, and we need to reflect on the ten beliefs one by one, to be sure that we are ready to sign when it comes to the Summation interview in the summer.

Edith says that the Basis is for us. It's not what we teach. It's our glimpse of light, where we can put our trust. But we can't expect converts to make sense of all of that.

One breath at a time, she says. When you are struggling to breathe you just have to trust there will be a next one. (I seem to remember telling her that!) If we believe in God's saving grace for as long as it takes to sign the Basis, that's enough, isn't it, enough to make a glimmer of light?

30th March 1927

Yesterday afternoon I was lying on my bed having another look at the little pink card with the ten statements of the Basis on it and I actually threw it across the room. The Grace of God as manifested... the essential Deity of our Lord Jesus Christ... the trustworthiness of the Canonical books... we are by nature dead in trespasses and sins... that the Lord Jesus Christ is the only Priest and Mediator... a sacrificial priesthood has no place. It's just words and more words!

I shocked Edith. She was putting a jar of flowers on the window-sill and nearly dropped them.

It's not that I don't believe. But I think we have to creep up silently on our beliefs and find them lurking in the bushes. Not shout them out loudly.

Words just give us something to disagree about. Written words are worst of all. Locked in place.

Edith thinks that's a good thing. A firm footing. I should think of the gospel writers getting it all down while it was fresh in everyone's memory. Making the first link in the chain that comes down to us. Words make all the connections it's possible to have with other people.

But to me words seem to be a feeble link to the real you, and the real universe, the bit behind the words.

We can love wordlessly. We don't need to say anything to make it happen. Come to that, I expect we can hate wordlessly.

Edith and I are quite different. "I think I'm made of words," is what she says. "My name, the promises I make, especially the promises I make to myself."

But to me it seems there's so much you can't pin down – fears and weaknesses, or even dishonesty. I sometimes think it's better just to listen to someone breathing. Less confusing than words. Or their heart beating. What could be lovelier?

15th May 1927

We're all getting wrought up about the Summations. So much hinges on one interview. It's quite unlike the written examinations in that there's very little we can do to prepare ourselves. It's designed to expose our personal and spiritual strengths and weaknesses, our readiness or otherwise for work in the field.

I bought a pair of shoes - stout walking shoes. It was probably a foolish expense but I wanted to give myself a sense of being ready to set off to the mission field. They're almost like boots, with high padded sides and deep ridges in the soles. Roberta caught sight of them and now she wants me to go for a hike with her on Pole Bank. She says it is a hill with a view to lift the spirits.

We went for our hike and it did lift my spirits. Roberta looked at my shoes and remarked that they're rather heavy. I might find I am sent somewhere tropical.

She said how exciting it is, not knowing. But then she admitted it is a bit of a strain. Not only do we not know where we are going but we don't know *if* we are going.

She warned me I might regret wearing the shoes today as it is quite a hike. Her footwear looked well worn-in - a scuffed pair of heavy-soled suede shoes and thick socks rolled several times round her ankles. New shoes can be unforgiving. I seem to have got away with it – no blisters, just a rather shiny pink patch on each heel.

I did wonder if I would be able to keep up. There was a skip in Roberta's step, and she can never seem to stop her stream of chat: how wonderful it is to get out, and we all get a bit crazy, shut up together, don't I think? And with the Summations hanging over us it's even worse. Ididn't need to say yes to everything she said, a grunt was enough. And actually it was all I could manage.

I did enjoy the exercise and the shoes felt pleasingly solid. But it was all uphill as we took a track up a sloping valley before zigzagging up a grassy bank between clumps of gorse. I was quite incapable of talking. Roberta seems to be able to swing along and her breathing is hardly altered when the ground gets steeper or she has to step up a ridge.

She's bothered about whether she gets Dr Grover or Mrs Hart for the Summation. Mrs Hart understands her best but then again, she wants to truly meet the challenge so it might be better to have Dr Grover. Not that she thinks Mrs Hart would be lenient or see a vocation where there is none ...

Though we all do have a vocation in a way, she says. No one can say we haven't. It just might not mean we are destined to go abroad.

Every time she paused and turned, she'd wait for me to catch up and then launch herself off again, probably with another set of questions: "What *do* you think God wants you to do with your life? I shouldn't ask, should I? I mean it's not easy to know the answer, is it?"

No, it's not.

Climbing a steep hill brings the earth close to your face – with the slabs and blocks of rock stacked up at an angle, small square stones chipped from the mountain, lichens and mosses finding crevices and filling them with colour, creeping plants that don't seem to mind being crushed filling all the cracks in the path. How lovely these tiny details are. Then when we paused, we straightened our backs to look back down into the tops of the trees in the valley we had been climbing out of.

Are you looking forward to the view? Roberta kept asking and telling me we would see for miles, especially on a day like this. Every time we paused she offered me the bottle of lemonade but each time I was too short of breath and so she tucked it away again.

I'd never have gone there on my own. Roberta told me how she'd ridden a horse up there on those childhood holidays. She's hoping she'll be able to ride in the field. But lots of SPMS people are being sent to the Arctic and she fears she'll have to trudge about in snowshoes. Or it might be me that does that. We tried swinging our legs wide in snowshoes for a few steps.

At the top there were billows of tussocky grasses and, beyond, a misty patchwork of fields and woods. The wind came at us in warm gusts. It felt as though we had joined a main thoroughfare of invisible travellers, whoever or whatever rides the wind.

Roberta took a dramatic breath and I was waiting for her commentary on the scenery. But at last she was quiet and found a rock to sit on.

We had a picnic of crumbled scones that they let us have because we would miss afternoon tea and Roberta had some dented apples at the bottom of her knapsack.

The wind was scented with sweetness like coconut. It probably came from the flowers on the gorse bushes on the side of the hill below us. All part of a rich smell of wildness, non-human things: plants and earth and rock.

And then a bird made a bubbling call. It made me hold my breath and wait for the lovely chain of sound to come again.

It's a curlew Roberta told me. I thought they were supposed to say 'Cur-lew'.

Why do they call? Across the empty moorland, telling us where they are and what they're doing. But it's not *for* us, is it.

The sun got lower and slanted across a slope of wispy golden grass in front of us, the stems bending in the wind but resisting and returning to vertical.

I believe at that moment I was praying – one of the truest prayers of my life. Just to say to God, 'Here I am. Here. Where have I been all this time?'

The wind strengthened and it became quite chilly so we got up to leave. We both spread our arms and leant forwards, testing the strength of the buffeting wind. It makes you feel like a child. A child with an uncle to romp with.

The timetable for the Summations has gone up. It'll be Dr Grover for me. If I can't convince him then, my chance of going to the field will fade away. Father will be both pleased and disappointed.

10th June 1927

What happened? Did I succeed? This is more or less how it went:

"Miss Henry, do take a seat. Mrs Hart and I will be making the decision together as to whether we can send you to do the work of Christ in one of the fields in which we are currently spreading the Word. But in this interview Mrs Hart will be taking notes and I will be asking the questions."

So I sat, wishing that Mrs Hart were not seated where I could not see her, behind me.

Dr Grover said, "Now, one of the most important questions we have to consider is whether the young women who pass before us have the requisite strength, both mental and physical, to address the very considerable challenges and difficulties of the mission field. We have been pleased to note that you appear to be healthy and strong and actually well able to look after yourself in practical ways. We understand you have spent a lot of your time before coming here looking after your poor, unfortunate, handicapped sister, and so you are accustomed to not putting your own needs first. This we see as a very hopeful starting place."

This was annoying but I was wise enough not to try to answer.

Then he said, "Now, your written examinations show that your knowledge of the Bible is reasonably thorough, as we would expect after two years of study here". (That must mean I've passed the written exams.) "But the question remains," he said, "are you one of those who picks favourite passages and books, rather than accepting a responsibility to submit to the discipline of the *whole* of this book of instruction?"

Is that what I do? Of course I have favourite passages, who doesn't? And this question was something of a surprise. The only hint we had been able to get from former students who visited was to make sure to prepare a particular Bible passage that you would use for teaching.

Book of instruction. It reminds me of the visiting missionary with the pointed nose insisting that the book she was patting would answer every query in an Indian's – is Rangoon in India? – troubled life.

This is how I see it, and it's clearer to me now than it was in the interview: it's the story of a journey through one misunderstanding after another. Ancient misunderstandings. But I don't think it tells me how to be a traveller, wisely choosing a course through the wilderness. It tips me into the flow of a great river, tossed like a bubble, sometimes shining clearly, sometimes caught in a swirl of silty confusion.

That was the picture in my mind, but I was uncertain that Dr Grover would take to that analogy.

He had me fixed in his gaze. So I said it rather carefully. "Taken as a whole," I said, "it is like a great river. It flows from the beginning, when people were first trying to understand. It shows where we have come from and where we are going. Flowing onwards from ancient times."

"A great river like a perpetual source, you mean?"

That seemed a helpful suggestion and he looked less dissatisfied than I expected.

"And what refreshment would you dip from this great source to guide potential converts?"

This was what I had prepared for. So I said that there would be many situations when we could start from 'Love thy neighbour'. And the story of the Good Samaritan. That being a story that would translate into the experience of just about everybody.

He seemed a bit grudging about that. He humphed. "You might have to explain where a Samaritan came from and what a Levite was, but our work is full of such demands.

"Now, Miss Henry, in my adult life, indeed from childhood, I have become accustomed to turning aside in prayer many times during the course of a day. Can you tell us if this is so for you?"

I do turn aside. All those moments when I lean against the chestnut tree, with the ripples of the bark pressing into my back, gazing through the hazels, along the valley, to the bright piece of hillside where the sheep make different patterns every day. Or listening to the voice of that curlew at the top of Pole Bank. But most likely Dr Grover will think such moments are self-indulgent daydreaming. When do my reflections turn into prayer?

Dr Grover again looked expectant. He has such sad, damp eyes reaching out over his eye bags. I do believe he wants me to pass, but maybe is not very hopeful.

"I ask for help," I told him. I do. I give thanks. Of course I do."

He interrupted. "What are your conversations with Jesus really like? That you are a little shy and private is something we have both observed. Are you truly ready to draw others along with you on your journey as Christ's foot soldier?"

"To tell you the truth…" I began. And was then furious with myself. What else would I tell them?

The picture in my mind was of his feet, Jesus's feet. His dusty sandals, his feet carrying him forward on the way he somehow knows he must go. And he knows it because he can hear what God is telling him. He doesn't have to pretend. He can hear.

I think I said, "I use the words we have been given, by Jesus himself and by others who have followed. I find it helpful."

Heavy, substantial words, with strength at their heart. Like bones left behind. Or the tools on Father's bench, all set out ready.

What I said then was, "People have been where I am before. I am a follower and I respect the strength of the words that people have tried and tested. Words are just like tools we can take up and use. But also they give us courage."

Did I really mean that? Knowing what comes next, where to go, that cannot come from the past. Take the next step, step forward with just enough courage. If it gives way, there's another step, harder, steeper, but it's probably there. Lean on the wind, take the next step, the next breath.

Thinking on my feet, I said to Dr Grover, "And the other thing is, I know that I have to stop and listen and recognize when I go wrong, when I mistake something. When I take difficult words and instead of facing up to the awkwardness of them, I carry them off in my own direction. So I have to remember the many times when I have made mistakes."

I was a bit cunning there. I know Dr Grover has a soft spot for an admission of weakness. But I am not sure it did me any good.

"As a disciple of our Lord, Miss Henry, it is appropriate to carry the responsibility with a due humility, aware that we all stumble, ready to admit our faults, but at the same time, we are bearers of a tremendous message of victory. How will you, Miss Henry, show and share your relief that your debt is paid? What may, on the one hand look like a seemly modesty, could also be the indication of complacency. Can we be sure that you do not take the Lord's acceptance of you for granted?"

I didn't like this. It's something that bothers me. If my debt is paid then will God and I ever need to see each other again? Surely God keeps giving, I keep taking, and that's acceptable. That is how we know each other. And, in the same way, I give what I can to others.

I was so disconcerted that I gave a really lame answer: "Oh, I give thanks every day. And I do what I can for others."

He just nodded.

Then he said, "Now this, Miss Henry, is the moment when we ask you to consider, can you truly adopt and put your signature to the Basis of our Society?"

He put before me a large printed sheet with the ten statements of the Basis on it. "I am going to ask you now," he said, "to confess which part of this you find has presented the greatest challenge".

The first line of each paragraph was printed black and bold and the answer jumped out at me. "**Belief that we are by nature dead** in trespasses and sins."

Dead. Stiff like every dead creature or person. Like that mouse from long ago. Dissolving into the ground, scattered upon the sea, dust to dust. What was borrowed, all given back. That's dead.

Dr Grover was staring at me and for a moment I couldn't think why. Then I realised tears had welled up. I didn't dare blink or look at him.

I pointed to paragraph 4. We are dead.

Why did it upset me so? A tear dropped onto the back of my hand. I thought I was going to collapse completely.

So I gabbled on. I said, "We are quickened and called by God's spirit working in us; it says that. We are, aren't we?" I said.

I must have sounded like a child. But that is what we can share. I am still confident that God is there somewhere. Somewhere between Louise's night-time breathing and the call of the curlew. Surely I can share that with people in other parts of the world when they're fearful of devils and emptiness.

He dismissed me and now I have to wait.

15th June 1927

They give us the limp, grey second copy. There's a crisp white top copy in one of the two stacks on Dr Grover's desk. Sheep and goats. The stack on the right will be rather higher than the stack on the left.

They take an age to get to the point. My strengths are trivial, unexceptional and surely outweighed by the burden of weaknesses they have noted.

They are concerned that although I have a caring spirit and a desire to bring others to the knowledge of Christ, I appear to have a humble expectation that they may be better able to care for themselves. I lack a sufficient sense of the great victory to be shared with those who are still struggling in darkness.

"We see, however, that you do have an appropriate sense of making your own life the message. You are not merely clinging to words, the words by which we attempt to transmit, in translation, the message Jesus gave us, but it appears to us that you devote yourself to the Word himself, deeply understanding that in his person, he was and is the Way, and that it is for each of us to show the outline of that way with our own lives. This, combined with your practical nature and general reliability, suggests to us that it will be appropriate to find you a place in the field of mission."

7

October 1927

Ada

The train comes to a gradual but screeching halt alongside a row of tin-roofed shacks. Ada and Mr Pavey, the missionary who came to meet her where the line branched, clamber down opposite a hoarding advertising Horlicks Malted Milk. Mr Pavey takes Ada's case and guides her to one end of the platform where a bullock cart is waiting behind a paling fence. The bullocks are handsome, milky-white dusted with grey, and seemingly placid. They appear to be controlled by rope threaded between their nostrils. The driver meets her eye and looks away, but greets Mr Pavey with urgent news and a hand on the arm.

"Sad news," says Mr Pavey to Ada, "Very sad news. Our colleague, Rachel, who is so very ill. She is not expected to survive until this evening. We should get back in case there is to be a funeral. We don't have the means to delay such things. We must press on." He lodges the suitcase in the cart. "Besides, we don't want to be in the jungle after dark."

When they have settled on the plank that spans the cart, the high wheels begin to roll, flicking up grit so that Ada draws herself into the middle of the bench. The bullocks cross from side to side of the rutted track, rocking the passengers against each other. The driver doesn't seem to have to do anything; he slumps, apparently asleep.

The mission compound looks, from a distance, more substantial than any of the villages they have passed on the way. It is on the plateau of a mostly bare slope, with jungle lapping up from the valley. A few tall trees suggest that this is a space hacked out of the original forest. There is one large shingle-roofed house with two storeys and verandas all round. It is raised somewhat off the ground but is not as leggy as the smaller building next to it, or the village houses a little way off. There is a series of tin-roofed shacks and then a larger building with a steep-pitched thatch roof and solid timber corner posts, but no side-walls. At one end is a beautifully carpentered arched door, by which Ada recognizes it as the partly built church. Beside the track is an area enclosed by bamboo palings, planted with rows of vegetables - jewel-like tomatoes, shrivelled-looking onions and some bright green leaves. Higher up the hill, two men in European sunhats are standing watching two turbaned men digging. When they notice the cart the white men hurry down towards the house.

Ada climbs down stiffly and is welcomed sombrely by a woman in a brown dress who enfolds both her hands in hers for a moment. "You are very welcome, my dear Miss Henry. I am Diana Sinclair. You must forgive our disarray – our friend and colleague called Home so suddenly."

Ada meets the light-brown eyes glinting with tears and finds herself blinking. She turns to take the hand of Andrew Sinclair, the leader of this mission station, and then that of Bill Hocknell who had been with him supervising the gravediggers. She is directed to a cane chair in a spacious room where a ceiling fan is working unevenly.

A cup of pale, milkless tea is placed on a small table next to her, with a sugar bowl beside it.

Andrew Sinclair puts a hand on her shoulder as if to stop her from drinking it. "Let us first say a word to ask God's blessing on your work here with us, and to thank him for your safe arrival among us." The others gather round and bow their heads. Ada wishes she was not the only one seated. She would stand if she wasn't aware that Andrew is still leaning slightly over her chair. As she stills herself for the prayer that is about to begin, she feels a wave of gratitude that she can stop travelling. Then she thinks of the funeral yet to come. They have to send Rachel Burstow on her way.

They stand on the hillside. The sky is yellowing. The heap of upturned soil combines the colours of spices - light ginger, darker cinnamon. Ada gazes at the feet around the grave - bare, dusty feet, the army boots of one of the missionaries and the canvas shoes of the rest, except Andrew, who wears polished brown leather shoes, with a tide-line of dust. The familiar words of the funeral service give their conditional promise - but Ada is confident on Rachel's behalf. She can only imagine her as the ideal missionary, dying in the course of a life of selfless service. Ada gazes down at the layers of earth in the side of the grave and her heart hovers uncomfortably. The screwed-up courage she had packed inside her as part of her preparations springs apart as she thinks that her journey home might, like Rachel's, end here in a hole, instead of taking her back to her parents, to Louise, and everything familiar. Suddenly she appreciates her parents' anxieties.

The rectangular coffin is lowered on bands of matting which are allowed to fall into the grave alongside it, being, Ada surmises, too rough to draw out without a struggle. Diana drops a flower - a gardenia, perhaps - and two Jinghpaw men start shovelling earth while the missionaries stand back. Andrew looks round the small group of stiff faces and appears to decide against announcing a hymn. But while he hesitates, a Jinghpaw woman starts a chant in her own language. After the first repetition Ada recognises something that could be "Hallelujah", and on the third she realises the jerky tune is a shrivelled version of something joyful they had sung at the Youth Camp when she was a child. Bird calls jangle in the valley. Tears slide down Diana's cheeks.

That evening there are eight of them round the table, eating a chicken stew with rice, while insects buzz around the lamp, and the generator drones in an outbuilding.

There are three other women besides Diana. There is Maud Bennett, the nurse who runs the little dispensary in the hut across the compound. Bill Hocknell's wife, Lydia, emerged from resting just in time for the funeral; she seems to be treated with special consideration and Ada surmises that she might be pregnant. When Ada is introduced to the third woman, Ivy Smith, she sees her tilt her head back to look along her pointed nose and reach out a hand in greeting, and realises she has seen her before. "You did a demonstration deputation at Meredith Hall," she tells her. "You won't have seen me. I was just passing the drawing room door. But I heard some of what you had to say."

Ivy Smith nods briskly. "Well, you made it here, then! Good for you!"

The next day after a breakfast of smoky toast with an aromatic mixed fruit jam and lots of tea, they gather outside to see Bill and Lydia set off for their station, further up the valley, across two ranges of hills. There is indeed a baby on the way but it is not expected until the middle of February and there has been an earnest discussion with Maud after which it was decided that the better climate further north, and the comforts of home, outweigh the disadvantage of making two journeys.

"It is so important that we show our trust in God," says Diana, "And you have such near converts now. This is not the moment to slacken our hold on his hand."

Ada thinks Lydia looks a little uncertain, gazing into the distance as Diana speaks. Bill pats her hand and says, "We'll be back in seven weeks, in good time for Christmas. I've got a good set of coolies so we can put you in a chair."

Four men, barefooted and turbaned, wearing dark skirts and, to Ada's surprise, with swords slung under their arms, stand ready to shoulder the poles lashed to a very ordinary cane chair. Lydia sits in it rather gingerly and is inevitably lurched about as they settle the poles on their shoulders. But then she manages to get her parasol up and finds the rope Bill has slung between the poles to rest her feet on, and looks quite comfortable.

"All right, my pet?" says Bill, from the saddle of his pony. "God bless!" he waves to the others and kicks his pony into the lead. They hear laughter as he calls farewells to two Jinghpaw men with a pig on a rope who step aside as they pass.

Having spent the night in a tiny room normally occupied by the Sinclairs' little boy, now Ada is to set off with Ivy to go to the house they are to share, which is a little way beyond the sketchy fence that marks the edge of the mission compound. Ada understands that she is to take Rachel's place, which Ivy has been making ready for her. Her work is to be closely supervised by Diana and Andrew at the headquarters and she will start by helping Maud in the dispensary.

At first the track is good enough for a cart. It passes along the side of the slope, with glimpses of a river gliding below them. Then they take a well-worn path uphill. "This is awful in the wet season," says Ivy. "The sensible thing is to go round by the road, but it's longer." She steps over a band of glistening ants. "You don't mind insects, do you? You're in the wrong country if you do!"

Ada has been swatting at flying insects of all sorts since they set out. Is Ivy mocking her?

They pick their way across a stream that appears from the bushes on their right. Ka Pa, employed as table-boy and cook for the Crossroads House, as the hut is grandly known, is carrying Ada's case on his head. Ivy has a small haversack, the buckles of which jingle cheerfully, and Ada has her overnight bag and waterproof in a bundle under her arm.

Ada's new home, when they get to it, is a hut on stilts, an adapted version of the village houses around it. Where they have thatch, it has corrugated iron sheets. The matting walls are interrupted by unglazed windows covered with fine mesh. A wide ladder constructed of lengths of tree trunk leads up to the veranda.

The ladder is the most solid part of the house. The floor of the upper storey is made of springy bamboos covered in mats. Ada feels insecure and reaches for the walls. Two corners, front and back, are divided off as bedrooms with split bamboo doors. The other back corner is a kitchen and store area, opening onto a rear veranda. In fact most of the cooking is done outside. Ka Pa uses a hearth constructed underneath the veranda. In the central part of the house is a sitting area and a dining table. Ivy flicks her hand towards it.

"It looks nice, but it's so bouncy we hardly use it. It's easier to sit on the veranda. You did know you would be more or less camping, didn't you?" She frowns at Ada.

"Of course, of course," says Ada, nonetheless taken aback by the flimsy nature of her home.

Ivy smiles encouragingly. "Your room is the one at the back."

The room has a window, and is furnished with a low wooden bed, a bookshelf, a chair and a woven bamboo chest. A net hangs over the bed. There is a sagging ceiling of matting suspended on the rafters. Ada instantly imagines a snake curled up where it bulges.

Ivy shows her the spirit stove kept upstairs for making tea or boiling an egg, the water jar and storage boxes down below.

"We have to be so careful about fire," she says. "We have a fireplace, did you notice? All the village houses have a hearth, but it is a frightful hazard. And they fill the place with smoke. I haven't tried this one yet, not having been here in a cold season.

"Now I'm going to meet my women," she says. "You know how important it is to be regular about these things or they get confused."

"May I come?"

"Of course. Of course, you *should*!" Ivy smiles encouragingly again.

"There are only four of them just at present. We've not got to the Bible reading stage yet. I'm just telling them the Good News in my own words. There's a rather nice mango tree where we sit."

Ada finds it is essential to tackle the ladder backwards, even though there is a hand-rail, and in following Ivy too closely she narrowly avoids hooding her with her skirt. Ivy goes into the enclosed storage area under the house. As soon as she has dragged open the door she raps loudly on the house posts with a stick that is leaning against the wall outside.

"Snakes," explains Ivy. "Just like to be sure before rummaging round."

She takes out two folding stools with striped canvas seats and a length of folded cloth.

The mango tree is only a minute's walk from the house. They settle themselves, but no women come. Ada takes the opportunity to watch the activities of the village. The houses are mostly scattered, with trees or areas of garden in between. Chickens peck on the paths. She can hear pigs arguing. A young woman with a baby on her back and a bundle on her head approaches them from an almost imperceptible path between the trees at the edge of the village clearing. Ivy greets her, but Ada can tell she is not one of 'her' women. She gives a friendly reply to Ivy's abrupt question, but shows no sign of stopping. Ivy looks puzzled, but doesn't explain.

Ada is content to sit under the tree, not moving, grateful to be still after the weeks of travelling. Looking up into the tree she sees the heavy forms of green fruits. She is about to ask Ivy when they will be ripe, and who is entitled to pick them, but sees that she is riffling through the Bible on her lap. She feels the heat of the sun just starting to bite on her ankle, so she stands to shift her stool deeper into the shade. There is a sudden clattering in the branches above and it is as if one of the heavy green fruits has taken flight.

"Pigeon," says Ivy. "They're mostly green."

She stands up. "I'm going to have to go and find them. It's such a shame. Of course it doesn't help that nobody has a clock. Perhaps you'd like to make yourself at home and unpack. Ka Pa will make you lunch if you show yourself at the house."

Over the next few days, Ada discovers that there really are some women who come and let Ivy talk to them about the Gospel. She watches while Ivy speaks, trying to pick out words she has come across in her language books. It is a repetitive process, with Ivy saying a carefully prepared sentence, then waiting, watching their faces to see if it sinks in. The women sometimes respond with streams of words that Ada can see are beyond Ivy's comprehension. Ivy thinks through another sentence and then waits to see if that makes an impact. She does not mime or strive to convey the meaning with anything other than the words. Ada wonders why the women are there. No doubt they are curious. But what could Ivy have said at the beginning to catch their attention? Maybe it's not her words but her person that they come for. Her buff-coloured dress and sunhat, her books, her shoes, even her hairy forearms - everything must be dusted with the exotic for them.

Ivy keeps a little notebook where she scribbles the names of the women who gather. She also has a little bottle of iodine in her bag, with a roll of cotton wool. When she spots a scab on one of the women's arms, she offers a dab which, after some bashful giggling, is accepted. The stain is much admired by her companions. Ada knows from training that it does not matter what first draws converts in. If they come close enough, they can be helped towards a grasp of the all-important message. If there should be any problem for which these women could be persuaded to visit the dispensary, that would draw them in at this vital stage of their contact.

After a week of finding her way about, it is decided that Ada should start spending time at the dispensary. It is a way of making sure that for most of the day she is immersed in the language she is striving to learn. Maud Bennett is the only trained nurse and every few months a doctor, also a missionary, comes to discuss difficult cases, maybe taking a stretcher party back to the little hospital near the railway line. Occasionally they get a visit from a part-trained Burmese Sub-Assistant Surgeon sent out on tour to practice his skills on the inhabitants of remoter villages.

Maud wears a crisp white uniform and headdress. She gives Ada a blue scarf to tie round her head. On one wall of the dispensary are shelves with rows and rows of unlabelled tin boxes full of drugs and equipment. Maud's hand moves unerringly to the right one. Ada has to recite to herself – "Aspirin, bit of blue label, gauze pads, high white tin, quinine, battered red tin". She learns to sterilize and handle sterilized equipment. The dispensary is often hotter than outside because of the primus stove they use. She develops a knack for holding small children while Maud probes their mouths and ears and injuries. The mothers, once they see that there are two women in the dispensary, insist on handing the children over. Maud is always busy, but as she tells Ada when they first start to work together, "This dispensary is nothing if not a fountainhead of Jesus' love, an object lesson for our patients of how God gives them healing. So we have to tell them," she says. "I will find you lots of little tasks, rolling bandages and cleaning up after me, but the real task is to tell them."

Ada doesn't like to point out how little she can say as yet. On their first day together, Maud makes the task easier. As she finishes with each patient she gives slow and careful instructions about tablets and dressings and then, just before ushering them out of the chair, puts her hands on their shoulders and tells them firmly in their own language, "Jesus loves you", which they seem to accept as part of the cure. Ada adopts the phrase, offering it as they pass her by the door. At the end of the first day, during which Ada has dropped a sterile hypodermic, broken a bottle and lost several tablets in the cracks of the table, Maud says, almost gleefully, "There now, you *are* doing well. We could develop your contribution as your language improves, but here you are, doing the work of the Gospel!"

Ada ponders this as she trudges up the path homewards. She enjoys Maud's approval and enthusiasm but it seems too simple.

She sees the other missionaries coming and going and often thinks about Lydia and Bill in their outpost in the jungle, waiting until it is not a sign of weakness to return to be closer to the doctor.

Andrew receives a telegram. Frank Mann is to return from furlough. He is bringing with him vital equipment, the telegram says. The news generates a flurry of enthusiasm among the missionaries. Diana and Maud speculate as to the nature of the equipment. Maud is hoping for some rather specialist forceps but does not think Frank would have known of her need. Ian Pavey, on the other hand, can't help mentioning that a better harmonium would make the hymns so much more tuneful, and it's quite possible Frank will have thought of it, being a keen singer. Listening to the pleasure they seem to share even in mentioning his name, Ada senses that it is Frank himself, far more than his luggage, that they will be pleased to see. They're like children, eager for the return of a parent, Ada thinks.

His bullock cart, when it arrives, contains a suitcase of normal size, a tin case half as big, and a large wooden box. Frank Mann is tall, younger than she expected and has the kind of skin that responds to the heat by gaining a sheen like polished wood rather than flushing and looking saturated or cooked. He greets Ada with an enthusiastic handshake, and seems to savour her name as if in recognition that, as one of this close group of companions and colleagues, she is going to be part of his life. *Oh dear,* she thinks. *We're all going to be competing for his attention.*

That evening Diana's cook roasts chickens on a spit and bakes sweet potatoes and they sit at a long table on the veranda, with mosquito coils sending question marks up into the air around them. After a heartfelt grace the mood is cheerful, with Frank regaling them with stories about his journeys, and Andrew updating him with news of local converts. After the meal, while the servants clear the veranda they take their chairs inside. The youngest Sinclair child, Donald, is taken off to bed by his ayah. Andrew hangs a bamboo pole horizontally against one wall and Diana suspends a sheet over it. Frank's wooden box has been opened to reveal a magic lantern. Frank lifts out the black tin lantern with a hat-like cowl on the top, and puts it on a tall plant stand. He opens the brass-trimmed door at the back and strikes a match. A square of light appears on the sheet.

"Here we go," he says, "The Baptism of Our Lord". He fiddles with something at the back of the lantern and a delicately coloured scene appears on the sheet.

"This is not the most recent model," says Frank, "but I felt we would benefit from the reliability of an oil lamp rather than electric cells. The disadvantage is the weight of the slides." He rattles the box of wooden frames.

Jesus stands waist deep in a turquoise Jordan with a cloth draped over one shoulder. A similarly bearded John stands amazed beside him, while the shape of a dove can just be discerned in the white light above Jesus's head.

Almost all the light in the room is gathered into the scene on the sheet. Frank's face hangs in the dark behind the projector, the low angle of the light giving him surprised brows and sculpted cheeks. A moth has somehow circumvented the screens on the windows and, as Ada watches Frank's face, it flutters towards the back of the lantern.

"Oh no!" cries Ada, and flaps her arms. The moth changes direction and clamps itself in a cool furred kiss onto Frank's cheek.

"Miss Henry!" he exclaims, and as he leaves the light the moth abandons him. Ada retreats into the dark, uncertain whether he thinks she touched him.

They view the remainder of the slides - the wedding at Cana, the healing of a blind man, the crippled man being lowered through a roof.

After a while Ian Pavey laughs to himself.

"These images show Our Lord so pale - a pale northerner, the sort that astonishes people here. The reality, that he was of dark, Middle Eastern stock, would make it so much easier to persuade our friends here of his kinship with them."

There is a pause while his colleagues assemble their responses.

Andrew speaks up. "The truth of the matter is, Pavey, we don't know what our Lord Jesus looked like. And it doesn't matter. He comes to us in our hearts, clothed in heavenly light."

Diana's brow puckers. "I don't know why you would worry about appearances, Mr Pavey. We use these devices to warm their hearts and speak where words alone will not touch them. All that matters is that the colours and the light enchant them."

Then Frank says, "Simple as they are, they do not think, and we do not want them to think, that this magic vision is truly magic. It calls to their attention a truth and a history that we have knowledge of, and they have not. They must see it through our eyes."

"We see Jesus here with locks down to his shoulders," says Diana, "and a beard and flowing robes. None of us shares that appearance, yet that does not make *us* less able to come close and hear his call."

Ada and Ivy return to their house, having borrowed an electric torch. "Just to dazzle anything that moves," Frank says as he gives it to them. "Tread firmly and check the path for snakes. You'll get used to it," he adds, patting Ada's shoulder. "As ever, we are in his hands."

Towards the end of November Andrew comes up the track to the house at the crossroads, leading a pony because he is about to make a small tour of nearby villages. But there is something he wants to talk to Ivy and Ada about first. The Hocknells must leave their post up in the Valley. Lydia is getting near her date and they must stay within reach of the doctor, who is based twenty miles to the south at Mogaung, on the railway line, for the birth and the first couple of months. Now that Ivy and Ada are used to working together could they feel called to occupy the Hocknells' station, once Christmas is over, until their return? They could keep up the rhythm of simple services and baptism preparation work and, even better, would be there to host a visit from the Bishop, if his tour should take him so far.

Ivy's women from the village could be encouraged to go a little further for meetings together with Diana's group of women who gather in the compound. It would be a timely little test of their commitment, Andrew suggests, and no bad thing.

Ivy looks at Ada and away again. Ada feels it as a flicker of rejection. Ivy, she has begun to suspect, does not like her. She cannot altogether work out why, though she still feels she is neither very useful to Ivy's work, nor able to step out on her own, because of the primitive state of her grasp of the language.

"Shall we all undertake to bring it before God and talk again on my return?" Andrew says, before turning his pony and riding off.

Ada dwells on the question for the rest of the day. She would much prefer to continue spending most of her time with Maud in the dispensary. At least she can pass the scissors and even handle a hypodermic. She knows that the point of the dispensary is to tell the great story of God's care and healing to all who come. But there is no doubt the medicines and practical care are what attract the people.

Just as she is getting used to the rhythm of days at the dispensary, Andrew takes Ada on a visit to the house of the headman of the village that adjoins the mission. He has decided that she should spend time each day learning the Jinghpaw language with a boy who lives there. He cannot walk and as a result does not have other responsibilities. Ada has seen the boy from a distance shuffling about near the headman's house. Now that she sees him close to she wonders if, indeed, he is a boy, or rather a shrivelled man. He has dull, powdery looking skin but his eyes are bright enough, when he looks up sideways from under the brim of a cap that must have been the gift of a European. His hands seem larger than they should be at the end of his arms which, although stick like, have the strength to haul him around. His lower body is a bundle entangled in cloth, which mysteriously stays in place as he drags himself about.

After a short conversation, Andrew tells Ada that she and Mahgawng Kajee will meet at the church each morning and sit on the veranda there for their conversations. Ada wonders how Mahgawng Kajee will get there. Andrew just says that Bill Hocknell has seen to that. The next day, she decides to do some small jobs at the church, dusting and tidying the mats, and to let Mahgawng arrive in his own good time. She hears children calling and laughing and then sees that Mahgawng is heading towards her on what must be the chassis of an old pushchair, punting himself with a short length of bamboo. The children are prancing about delightedly, kicking aside stones and other obstructions. He reaches the church and shuffles up the three shallow steps to the veranda. As he leaves his vehicle, he turns and snarls a few words at the children with a startling authority so that they abandon any ideas of borrowing the trolley, and disperse again.

Mahgawng turns to Ada and giggles charmingly. They settle down and Ada tries her prepared phrases: "My name is Miss Ada."

He starts asking questions, working away at each one until he has found out that she is not married, that she came across the sea, that she can read and write. He keeps his eyes fixed on her face and reads the flickers of understanding and confusion. When they reach a dead end and she is completely bewildered, he taps her hand with a finger as if to say, we'll start again.

At their second meeting he seems to take his role as teacher more seriously. He begins to tell her what she ought to know.

The Jinghpaw people don't have many things, he tells her. Europeans, Kala, have many things. Ningkong Wa, who made everything in the world, the rocks and the trees and the rivers and the mountains, called all the people in the world and gave them books. Mahgawng enacts this with a hymn-book. He shows the people cradling the book, keeping it carefully. Then he says, "Jinghpaw. Jinghpaw people are always hungry," and with a great greedy snort he pretends to devour the book. Ada laughs as she has not laughed for months. But she demands an explanation. "No one eats books, they don't taste good." So then she gets an elaborate story of the slaughter of a goat, the stripping of its skin, which is cleaned and smoothed and written on carefully and rolled up. Then the Jinghpaw comes, sniffing eagerly, snatches the parchment and takes it away. Then he quite clearly toasts the parchment in front of a fire and eats it with a look of great satisfaction.

Ada can't help thinking practical thoughts about how Mahgawng manages with his disability. She thinks of how often she has shuffled Louise to the privy and wonders if he needs help. The villagers are not often very particular about where they relieve themselves, depending on the pigs to tidy up after them when necessary. In the middle of one conversation, Mahgawng taps her hand as he does when it's time to start a new topic, then spins round on his arms and shuffles down the steps to his trolley. He punts his way to the nearest bush and after a few moments during which she averts her gaze, he returns.

She does not use their conversations as an opportunity for evangelism. Andrew had said, when introducing the plan, "He's bright and, I would think, highly teachable. This will be a way of drawing him in to our work." But Ada has begun to value the odd friendship that is developing. He shows respect and curiosity towards the Kala but doesn't show any sign of wanting to become like them. And she finds herself unwilling to over-simplify the Christian message for someone so sharp and direct.

One day Ada leads a conversation to the nats, the spirits. She has seen a chicken being sacrificed, and the tuft of feathers fixed to a bamboo cross to show that it was an offering. Mahgawng explains that the nats take the spirit of the chicken. The household can eat the meat. Nats don't eat meat.

"Where are nats?"

"Everywhere."

"I can't see them."

"Of course not."

Ada feels a little flush of embarrassment at having patronised him.

"Who rules them?"

"Karai Kasang rules everything, nats, people, everything."

"Are they bad?"

"Some are bad, some are good. But they will all bite you if you forget them."

"Are you afraid of them?"

"Not really." He tells her that a nat bit him when he was born. "When you get ill, a nat has bitten you, but you can make friends again."

On the way back from the church, Ada descends the hill, crosses the channel that is sometimes a little stream, and finds herself toiling up the path through the village behind an old woman who was at the dispensary that morning. She recognises the woman's garments, and when she comes close and tries a greeting, the woman turns and reveals a bright white dressing on her neck. San Lu, Maud had called her.

The woman walks awkwardly but effectively, swinging her pelvis as though to compensate for a drag in the legs. Her bare feet with battered toes seem to grip the ground for slow and steady progress, like tractor tyres. She grins a black grin and stops to draw breath, laying a friendly hand on Ada's forearm. She passes a few remarks. Ada understands nothing but the sociable intention. When they reach the junction of the track and Ada is about to turn aside to her house, San Lu says something and when she hesitates takes her elbow and gestures hospitably towards the village. The hands are distorted and arthritic.

San Lu leads Ada to one of the larger houses in the village - not the chief's house, but the other long one. But instead of directing her up the ladder she indicates a little log stool under a bit of lean-to matting roof. Ada wonders if San Lu is an aged parent, or perhaps a poor relation of the main householder. They can hear a man's voice above them, chuckling in a leisurely way, perhaps teasing someone. She points towards the voice and mimes holding a baby. Is he San Lu's son? The old lady chuckles and denies it forcefully. She reaches under the overhang of the thatch and pulls out a little woven box, intricately patterned with dark and light reeds. There's a toggle to close it. The woman's knobbly fingers unbutton the toggle and flip the lid open. Ada expects to see nuts and leaves for chewing betel, but there's nothing inside. And then she realises that the box is being proffered to her. A gift. As soon as it is in Ada's hands, San Lu sits down and begins to shuffle through a tray of flattened reeds. Ada crouches down to watch the gnarled fingers selecting, interlocking, gripping the pattern in place, as another box begins to take shape.

Just then, an adolescent boy descends from the upper part of the house and approaches San Lu, seemingly barking commands. Immediately she pushes the half-made box into the space under the thatch, gathers her skirt around her and bustles round the back of the house without a further word to Ada.

On a day when Maud says she won't open the dispensary because she needs to restock, Ian Pavey invites Ada to accompany him on a bicycle ride to Ku Yaw, the next village round the hill. They will be following the contour, he assures her, so they will be able to ride for most of the hour it takes to get there. He has an errand with the chief and it will be good for Ada to meet him as his villagers form a large proportion of the patients at the dispensary.

The track is well-used and not too rutted. Ada learned to ride one of the old bicycles at Meredith Hall. This one is heavy and too large for her so she has to stamp on the pedals to get going.

She asks Ian Pavey a question that has been on her mind: "Are some of these people slaves?"

"It's supposed to have been eliminated," he says. "But you can't change things within a generation. You can't change how people think of themselves. All the village chiefs are hereditary. And I guess if you are the child of a slave, being told by the Governor General that it doesn't mean anything anymore isn't going to make a lot of difference. Actually it makes our work easier in a way."

"How do you mean?"

"A gospel given out in the Roman Empire makes more sense, doesn't it? After all, we are asking them to grasp that, until released and forgiven, we are all slaves."

As with the two villages adjoining the mission, it is obvious which is the chief's house. It is taller and better made, with checkerboard patterns woven into its walls. The chief greets them with what seems to be amusement, and places stools for them to join him in front of the house. Ian Pavey has told her that they are trying to arrange for one of the chief's sons to come and live at the mission. The boy would widen his knowledge of the world and it would give the mission a channel of communication with this village. It won't be insignificant, Ian Pavey says, that the mission will bear the cost of feeding him.

They settle on the stools. Other men gather and stand or sit, watching the two visitors, waiting for the performance to begin. The chief looks from one to the other. Mr Pavey introduces Ada, and she understands that he is explaining that the mission is expanding and growing. There will be even more people in the next few months. Ada plans to ask about this afterwards as she had not heard that more newcomers were expected. Ian Pavey talks about the dispensary, using the word in English, and saying how good it is. The chief assents. Then they are talking about the boy. He will be taught to read, says Mr Pavey. He will have three meals a day and some new clothes. Ada tries not to laugh as he uses his nice square hands to mime the books, and the meals, and the boy's delight in them. She watches the chief's impassive face to see if he is responding to persuasion.

At last the chief's face creases. Then he tells them that the boy is already on his way. He has gone to his uncle's village to repay a debt and he will arrive at the mission by the time they return. He imitates Mr Pavey's efforts at mime and the audience laughs. Ian Pavey shakes the chief's hand heartily, enjoying the joke.

On returning to the village at the crossroads, Ada decides to start work with some of the children. She has a little pair of sewing scissors, and paper she has taken from the wastepaper basket in the compound office. Armed with these she goes out and practices her greetings on a group of village children. It is not difficult to attract them. The minute she appears they are distracted from their game and whereas the moment before they were running, now they just stand and stare.

"Hide and seek!" says Ada jovially. "Grandmother's footsteps! The big ship sails on the Ally-Ally-Oh!"

The children return her smiles and approach closer. Ada sits on the bottom step.

"It doesn't matter what I say to you," says Ada, encouraging herself, "But come and play with me". She folds a sheet of paper and quickly cuts out a row of dolls, fanning it out like a magician. The children are pleased, but she is not sure they recognize what is represented.

She separates one little figure and marks a face with the pencil stub from her pocket. She holds it up and the children step back, as if a strange child has joined them. Ada persists, marking a second face and walking the two dolls to meet each other. She tries a conversation. "My name is Ping," "Hello, my name is Jing". She sits the little figures down. The children are mystified, and slightly anxious. They watch the scissors as she carefully cuts out another figure, taller, dressed in robes.

"Jesus," she says, as she holds it out to show the children.

"Jesus love you," says one of the children, who has recently been to the dispensary. Ada is enchanted.

Ada sits the child figures at the feet of the Jesus figure. She frowns as she struggles with the language. "Jesus says come child. Come little child." The children look dubious. The paper Jesus pats the paper children on the head and says again, "Come little child". A gust of wind blows one of the child figures away. The children shriek and draw back to avoid it. Ada stamps to catch it with her foot but it escapes. "After it!" she says in English. But she can see that the children will do anything to avoid touching it. They are keeping their eyes on the two remaining figures, fascinated and suppressing giggles. Ada hears Ivy's heavy tread coming down the path from the hill. She gathers up the pieces of paper and crushes the dolls in her hand. The children scatter as Ivy arrives at the foot of the steps.

"I thought I should start trying to make contact with the children," says Ada, not sure why she should be embarrassed at having taken an initiative.

"Oh, good!" says Ivy in a preoccupied way. "We've got a baby due up in the next village. Now just think how wonderful it would be if we had a little hospital with beds for such occasions."

"Would they go?" asks Ada. "They probably don't think much of it, do they?"

"They do cherish their privacy, it's true. They wouldn't let me in the house just now. What's this? What have you been doing?"

She pounces on the lost paper doll.

"You're not trying dolls, are you?" she says, with disappointment in her voice. "Someone should have said. It really isn't a good idea. You *know* what a fear they have of spirits and manifestations of spirits. They should have taken you through this in training. Adults, children, everybody, they all carry a terrible burden of fear that there are evil spirits lying in wait at every turn. And if you personify them in a figure like this, it just confirms it for them." She shakes her head sadly and tears the little figure into pieces.

"Well, we all live and learn!" she finishes brightly. "There are plenty more children around to make a fresh start with."

Ada goes to her room, downcast by Ivy's assumption that she has "spoiled" one set of children and will need to find some fresh ones. She had so much enjoyed the gap-toothed grins and the excitement in their dark eyes.

Two days later Ada and Ivy are at the compound for a meeting. After prayers and discussions of future strategy, plans for the Bishop's visit and for imminent tours, Andrew asks if there is any other business, looking expectantly at Ivy.

When she says nothing, he says, "There is the matter of sustaining the work at the Valley Station. Can we consider asking Miss Smith and Miss Henry to undertake a tour, or rather to take over temporary responsibility for the Valley Station?"

There is silence.

Then Ivy clears her throat.

"Speaking for myself am not yet sure that I can commit to that amount of responsibility. On a more general point, I feel we should think hard and pray about how best to support each other's work, particularly where there is a lack of local expertise. We should ask ourselves whether perhaps our newest recruit, Miss Henry, is sufficiently supported and trained in local ways. I am thinking for example of the issue of dolls and figures, which was such a problem when they were sent for us to distribute as Christmas gifts. There are in fact probably very few mission fields in which dolls would be appropriate as a teaching aid, and they certainly are not suitable here. In fact, they are positively harmful."

Ivy looks around anxiously, as though there might be some disagreement.

Andrew rolls his pencil, then frowns gently at Ivy.

"And are you saying, Miss Smith, that you are unable to offer suitable support to Miss Henry?"

"No, no! Of course not! I think I can say that we work together well. But I am myself a relative novice in this respect, having been here in the north just for months rather than years."

"Come, come, Ivy," says Diana. "It is surely a year now."

"Not yet," says Ivy firmly. "I arrived on the 27th of November."

Diana concedes graciously. "So it's next week we celebrate your anniversary. But you have in any case a head start on Miss Henry and will have much useful knowledge to share with her."

"Indeed. And I do. And I look to her for the support of a fellow Christian. I am indeed grateful not to be alone in the Crossroads House."

The meeting is clearly not going as Andrew had hoped so he offers some persuasion: "For at least the first part of the tour across to the Valley, the journey outwards, the ladies will have at their disposal the very valuable experience of Mr Mann."

Everybody looks at him, so Frank smiles and says, "On the question of dolls, has there been a problem? Do we need to show some of our friends in the village that there is nothing to fear, and do more to introduce them to the idea of the protection of a loving but invisible Father?"

He's looking at Ada encouragingly, as though he, at least, has faith in her.

"Of course we do!" says Ada. "That is what we are here for is it not? I simply tried to attract the attention of some of the children with paper dolls. I think they reacted as children do, with curiosity and uncertainty. I am not convinced that they saw in them evil spirits or anything to fear. Not really. It was just a new thing to them."

"We do have to be careful of too quickly assuming that their minds are like ours."

"What I mean is that we don't have to take remedial action," says Ada, "Just carry on with the work."

Despite the embarrassment of having her efforts discussed at the meeting, Ada is beginning to enjoy being one of a team. She has not been used to spending time with men. She can't help noticing their strong hands, their bony wrists, the tender places behind their ears and the distinctive ways their hair finishes at the backs of their necks. Ian Pavey's hair, she noticed, is a colour rather more mouse than blond. It finishes on his neck with two softer, longer streaks growing down the tendons. Frank Mann's, on the other hand, finishes with a dark central point in the hollow at the base of his skull. Ian Pavey's hands are solid and square with broad, square nails. Frank Mann's fingers are long and narrow, stemming energetically from bony, brown hands. She's even noticed that the two men smell different. Ian Pavey smells grassy, while Frank Mann is more like fresh carved wood – not the resinous pine her father worked with so often, but something more exotic and spicier.

What would Jesus smell like, she wonders, as sleep kicks aside the guardians of correctness. Dusty, perhaps, with the dust of the roads clinging to his clothes.

A few days after the meeting Ada arrives at the main building in the compound just as Frank is approaching from the track. He climbs the steps to the veranda and throws his sunhat onto a chair. He's frowning and Ada is reluctant to make a demand on him by speaking. She jumps up to fetch tea but he says, "Don't abandon me, Miss Henry". She pauses.

"I have been up to the top village and down as far as the river trying to find somebody able and willing to dig a little grave for us. A still-born baby. Everybody looks serious and helpful and makes suggestions but not one of them will actually do the job – not even at twice the going rate."

"Surely they know it has to be buried,"

"It's the spirits again. They cannot bring themselves to contradict the spirits."

"In a few years' time," he goes on, "when they have come to see a better way, I shall remind them of this. They'll see the chasm they have crossed. Purchasing the favour of their filthy little spirits. Even when they've sacrificed more than they can afford to give, killing all their best animals, they're still full of fear."

Ada hovers, waiting for him to say more.

"Maybe you could find me a cup of tea and I shall go and dig the grave myself."

After her sessions with Mahgawng Kajee most mornings, Ada is still accompanying Maud in the dispensary for the rest of each day. On a day when Maud has to take an injection to a woman in a hut across the river, Ada heads for the Mission House for a break. As she approaches, she hears screaming and raised voices. She hurries past a slow procession of men in white turbans and arrives panting on the veranda. The Sinclairs' middle child, Carol, is screaming, gulping and twisting about, trying to evade her mother's arms. Her younger brother is stepping from foot to foot and shouting incoherently. Diana tries to command Carol's attention and keep her still by grabbing her frock.

"It come out of a bush," shouts Donald. "It got her!"

"What did? Show me. Do stand still!"

Ada can hear panic in Diana's voice and knows why. It could easily have been a snake.

Ada puts her arm around the boy and follows his stare. Something dark is dangling from the girl's elbow – a splinter or a sting.

"Here, it's a bee sting, just on her elbow."

"You should have told me, you foolish child!" Diana darts into the house and fetches tweezers but is trembling still and hands them to Ada. Her eye catches the silent group of turbaned men who have ascended the steps, and stand waiting for her attention.

"Can I help you?" Diana asks, but one of the men gestures towards the children. She's to see to them first.

When the sting is removed and vinegar has been applied, Carol is still sobbing and shuddering but Diana pats her back and tells her to run along, what a fuss about nothing. The tallest of the visitors starts to speak in Jinghpaw. Neither Diana nor Ada understands immediately so the man removes his turban. Something falls out of it, covering his eyes with a crimson fabric, which he quickly reaches up to replace. With a shock Ada sees it is his scalp. The top of his head has been slashed just along the hair-line and Ada realises she has been hearing the word for tiger - *shdraw*. A slash from a tiger's paw.

There's sweat on his cheek and a pale line either side of his nostrils. Ada grabs him by the shoulders and presses him into a chair. She runs to the dispensary to see if Maud has returned and to fetch forceps, antiseptic and stitching thread if she has not.

The man sits steady as a distant mountain, never flinching while his companions squat on logs below the veranda, chatting and chewing betel.

Half way through the procedure, Ada hears footsteps. Between the twenty-seventh and twenty-eighth stitches she looks up and sees that Frank is there, watching. She stretches her neck and returns to the work until the neat line of bulging red beads is complete from one temple to the other. She splashes iodine, mops the man's forehead and lets him go.

Then comes Advent. Mahgawng Kajee knows that the missionaries are preparing for a festival. "Is someone big coming," he asks.

"No, not like the Bishop," says Ada.

"Not someone who can tell us the story? Or bring us good things?"

"There is a story," says Ada. "That's what it is, the beginning of the story."

There's a footstep coming round the corner of the church. It's Frank Mann.

"Excuse me, Miss Henry," he says. "We need you for the meeting that was to have been tomorrow morning. We are doing it now, if you are able to come."

As they leave the church Frank remarks, "Your language is coming on apace. You seem to have a real rapport with Mahgawng."

"Sometimes I wonder how much of it is words," she says. "He makes me understand, and he understands me, but then when I try to think of the words I've learnt, I realise that it was a bit of mime, or just his expression that put the idea across."

"Well, it's good to see you finding your place here," says Frank. A single down-curving crease forms to the side of each grey-green eye when he smiles, adding a touch of mischief to his normally dignified face. Ada walks alongside him to the veranda of the Sinclairs' house where they usually hold their meetings.

Ivy gets up as they climb the steps. "Here. Sit here Ada," she says. Ada thanks her and sits and then wonders if there's a reason why Ivy is now sitting on the double seat alongside Frank. It reminds her of the way bossy Lilian used to manage to sit next to her favourite among the boys at the church camps and she suppresses a grin.

They make plans for Christmas, deciding that it should be celebrated more publicly this year, with a tree and a party and presents, as well as the usual services. The Sinclair children, Patience, Carol and Donald will decorate a tree with paper streamers and twisted sweet wrappers.

On a Wednesday, when Ivy gathers her group of women and Diana is about to be busy schooling her children, Frank and Ada set off in the late morning to conduct a baptism. Ian Pavey has had an errand in the town and will meet them at the riverside village where the baptism is to take place. Frank assures her that it is not a long walk.

"It's an easy walk," declares Diana.

"I don't mind a walk," says Ada, tempted to add "as you well know".

"Except for about twenty yards of it," says Andrew. "It's the High Strung Bridge – a bit of a challenge the first time.

"The High Strung Bridge?"

"That's what we call it. It's written differently on the map. It's one of those suspended things. But it gets quite a lot of use so you can reckon that they maintain it. Hai Taung, it is really."

The bridge, when they get to it, consists of a pair of ropes suspended from a framework of poles on each side of the river. Bamboo rods are bound between the ropes and make a wobbly platform to walk on. A rope on either side makes a handrail. Suspended a foot or so above the ground, it would be nothing. But the bank slopes steeply and the drop is hidden by bushes and trees of unknown height. She can see glimpses of the brown muscle of the river and hear its steady roar.

Frank is watching her taking it in.

"Look," he says reassuringly. "The main posts are really stable, nicely braced and dug right in. The rope is handmade but it's not too old."

"Is this the way everybody crosses?"

"Yes. It's the only way from this direction. There's a wider river to the other side of the village."

"And you've crossed it before?"

"Lots of times."

"Do they get animals across? Horses and mules?"

"No, they have to swim them. Further down, beyond that bend. They'd panic on the bridge and cause all sorts of damage. Whereas you, even if you do panic, you're not going to do it any harm."

The creases form by his eyes.

"I'm not going to panic," says Ada.

Frank steps onto the bridge and the bamboo rods jump to one side.

"You want to get your second foot on there, nice and steady so it balances out," says Frank. "Do you want to cross on your own?" he asks. "It'll move more with both of us."

"No. It'll be all right. We'll get a rhythm. Like breathing."

She reaches up to grasp the rope on either side. It's an uneven twist of some kind of fibre.

She steps onto the rods.

"Feet right in the middle, see where the worn bits are. Keep close behind me."

He steps forward and his weight causes another heave.

"Gently forwards."

She shuffles after him. The whole thing sways so that their arms are going one way and their feet the other.

There's a patch of bright sunlight falling amongst the trees on the bank on the far side of the river. Two dark-clothed women hunch there with baskets of clothes. Ada sees them glance up at the figures on the bridge, then bow their heads to their washing again.

We're just an everyday occurrence, thinks Ada. *We'll soon be there.*

As they step forward, the ropes they're holding get lower making it easier at first. Frank's hands are running loosely along a little way in front of hers. When they get to the centre section the river runs below them like a strip of worn khaki webbing, frayed and distorted where rocks break through the surface. The constant fierce roaring seems to have nothing to do with it. The side ropes sag lower to less than waist height. Ada finds herself leaning forward uncomfortably, her eyes distracted by the drag of the water. Frank stops and Ada bumps into him. The movement of the bridge loses its rhythm.

The ropes are at mid-thigh against Frank's long legs. He stands there like a surfer, riding the movement. She wants to cling to him but tells herself that would finish them both.

"Sorry," he says. He's heaving deep breaths.

"Say when you're ready." She is focusing her eyes on the cloth of his shirt.

"Let's go," he says and takes a tiny step. They set off again and gradually the side ropes lift to a more reassuring height. They are over trees and bushes. A black and white monkey bursts out of the foliage below them and swings up the rope to the top of the anchoring structure. The washerwomen are hidden from view by riverside trees. Frank steps off the last of the bamboo rods and turns to clap a hand on her shoulder. "Well done Ada Henry!" he says. "You are a woman of courage."

"I didn't like the bit in the middle," she says.

"I'm sorry, that was my fault. I had a - something happened to my eyesight for a moment. I really thought I was going to pitch over the side." He rubs his temples. "But I was glad to have you with me. You kept me steady."

Pleased, she dares to look him in the face.

"Your eye!" she exclaims. "Does it always do that? Like a squint."

He frowns and tries focusing at different distances then shakes his head. Ada is mortified to have made an offensive personal remark. But she is sure that his eye had not been pulling to the side like that before.

"We have to get on. Pavey's expecting us at about two."

The well-worn path follows the river and allows them to walk side by side.

Ian Pavey has prospected along the river-bank for a suitable spot and gone round the houses summoning an audience to a clear space of withered grass. When Ian leads Frank there, Frank immediately says, "Well this won't do. They've been sacrificing here." He indicates a pair of crossed bamboos, stuck rather lopsidedly into the dry ground.

"No, no," says Ian. "That was me. Just a suggestion of a church."

He looks put out and spends a little while driving small sticks into the ground and trying to prop the cross up straighter. About thirty men, women and children sit in the sunshine, waving leaf fans, chattering expectantly. Some of the men are lying in the dry grass half asleep, as if they were on their own verandas. Children paddle.

The candidate, Ma Kaw, is wearing a white jacket and a white wrapped skirt. Her face is wrinkled like the surface of the river and she turns her deep-set eyes on each of the missionaries in turn. Frank asks Ada to stand alongside her once they're in the river and to help her haul her skirt up out of the water so she doesn't get knocked over. Ian has a little accordion hung around his neck, which will give them the notes for the hymns. Frank removes his boots and socks. He carries his Bible and prayer book in a tasselled bag hung across his chest. He's taken a bamboo scoop from his knapsack and tucks it under his arm.

They step into the water, Ma Kaw clutching Ada's arm as her feet encounter the rounded pebbles and the tug of the current. Ada watches her face, the dark eyes slightly clouded, her mouth ajar like a hopeful fledgling's. Somehow, this little old woman has grasped at the threads of their tale, caught at wisps of it and woven it into something she wants, something that makes sense to her. In a world of journeying and often mischievous spirits it's good to have a friend. Yesu will be kind she has been assured, always kind.

Ian Pavey strikes a chord and the three missionaries launch into *Breathe on Me Breath of God*. Ma Kaw giggles nervously. The river buckles round their calves.

Frank's voice is clear and loud and he fills the prescribed dialogue with drama. Ma Kaw is given her chance to reject the Devil. Despite a lot of coaching, she giggles and forgets her words. Ada prompts her half in Jinghpaw, half in English. The people on the riverbank are restless when they cannot hear what is going on. Frank raises his voice and announces that he is about to wash all Ma Kaw's bad acts away. The audience cranes. Some of them have heard about the Baptist missions to the south and may be hoping to see this frail old woman submerged in the racing river. Frank whips out his bamboo scoop, fills it with water and sprinkles her brow. Never, announces Frank, will Ma Kaw make gifts to the nat spirits. Never again will she do what the Devil wants. He draws with water on her brow, muttering rapidly. She seems shocked by the contact and shifts her feet as if she is going to turn away. Ada holds her forearm and strokes the back of her hand. She can imagine that a sudden lurch would have them all keeling over and what message would that give to the watching crowd?

Ian Pavey is just about to strike a chord for another hymn but Frank mouths at him over Ma Kaw's head. They wade to the bank and once they are safely standing dripping on the shingle they sing the final hymn.

On the return journey, Ian asks to go on the bridge alone as he has a knapsack, a tool bag and the accordion. He won't be able to hold the rope and needs to be able to predict the movements of the bridge.

"It's all right," he says. "The locals do it all the time with great bundles on their heads."

Frank and Ada wait and watch as he steadily makes his way across. Just as they are about to step onto the path of rods Frank stops and says, "Ada, would you mind going first? I'm not entirely confident of my eyes."

"Of course. If you need a hand ..."

"I'll be all right. I just don't want to stop right in front of you like I did before."

She sets off, keeping her feet to the centre and her knees very slightly bent. She thinks she must look like a tightrope walker. She's hardly holding the side rope at all.

"Not too fast!" says Frank behind her. Swallows are darting below them but Ada keeps her eyes on the band of bamboo rods.

She pauses and the movement of the bridge tells her he's getting closer. When they get to the point where the rope is too low for support he suddenly says, "It's happening again. Can you ..." She stops and reaches her hands behind her on either side.

"Steady now. Give me your hands." She takes his hands and places them firmly on her hips. "Now we're going on again. Just look at the back of my neck, don't look anywhere else. Little steps." She keeps her hands on top of his until the side rope rises to waist height. "All right now?" she asks, but he keeps his hands where they are. Ada can see Ian Pavey at the end of the bridge, stooping over his luggage and tugging at a strap.

After a few more steps, as the trees on the riverbank close off all sight of the water, Frank lets go of her but she can still feel the warmth of his body very close behind. They step onto solid ground and Ian Pavey nods approvingly at Ada.

"She looks quite comfortable and it's only her second go!"

"She's a natural," says Frank. There are beads of sweat across his forehead. Ian wrestles himself into the straps of his knapsack and Frank mouths something at Ada. She thinks it ends with the word "angel". She can still feel the tension in her shoulder blades from walking with her hands behind her, and the pressure where her fingers had closed round the bones of his wrists.

8

December 1927

Ada

Ivy and Ada's house is situated at the fork of two tracks, one that leads to a river crossing and the other that rounds a hill and then follows the river into the wilder country where the jade mines are. The latter is the route to the Hocknells' station. Often the two women hear voices as people pass each other at the junction, sometimes exchanges of greetings, other times more complicated interactions where Ada struggles to identify the emotional content - are they angry, or enthusiastic, or just passing on everyday news?

One morning halfway through December, as Ada is brushing her teeth in the kitchen shelter behind the hut, she hears raised voices. With her hair still in bedraggled overnight plaits, she emerges to see a man gesturing and exclaiming to two others, one of whom summons a number of women from nearby houses. Ada thinks she sees a gesture towards their own house. She climbs up the kitchen ladder, passes through the house and finds Ivy listening at the screened window by the dining table.

"'The Laughing Duwa'," she says. "They're talking about Bill Hocknell. That's what they call him." She looks uneasy, as though they could be overhearing a conspiracy.

"Should we not ask them what it's about?" Ada asks, but is not surprised when Ivy shakes her head. She is beginning to suspect that Ivy is not a natural linguist and that unpredictable conversations are still difficult for her.

"Something's stirred them up," Ivy says. "We should go down to the compound."

There is the sound of running feet down the track and a young boy shouting. The small crowd scatters, shooed away like chickens. Ivy and Ada grab hairpins, sun-hats and shoes and descend their ladder to the track. A pony is approaching through the village with a man in a pith helmet close beside it and a pack mule trailing behind. It is Bill, with Lydia on the pony. They can tell at once that all is not well. Lydia should not be on a pony, even sitting sideways as she is. Bill is holding her in place as she droops in the saddle, with the bridle in his other hand. On the pony's withers in front of her is a bundle of dark cloth. As Ivy and Ada stare, appalled, they see tell-tale bloodstains on her clothes, on Bill's clothes and the saddle-cloth.

"We must get her to bed," Bill says. "Here, help us with this." He stops the pony and takes the dark bundle in both hands. Ada stumbles forward and takes it. The stories of tigers and attackers fleeting through her head give way to the certainty that hidden deep in the bundle is the baby.

At first Ivy walks in step with Bill and the pony, then hurries ahead to prepare a bed in the guest-house and to find someone to make the journey to the town to telegraph for the doctor. "Get Pavey to go," Bill calls after her, "Pavey on a bicycle."

Ada holds the bundle close. She can feel that the head is in the crook of her arm. All Bill's attention is on Lydia and the unevenness of the road. Ada can tell he has given up on the baby, and of course, he must be right. He would have seen that there was no hope. But maybe he is wrong. Ada can feel her own heat returning from the bundle. Could there not be a spark of life? She holds it against her moving ribs trying to press life into it, just as she used to soothe Louise to sleep.

Warned by Ivy, Maud closes the dispensary, leaving a milling crowd of patients that suddenly disperses as the procession of missionaries approaches.

Bill lifts Lydia from the pony and Ada feels a physical shock pass through her at the sight of the glistening blood-stain on which she has been sitting. She follows them into the bedroom of the guest-house. Maud lays Lydia, who is now trembling uncontrollably, on towels on the bed and cuts away her clothes. Diana brings water in basins and jugs. There is a prayer stool against the wall with a Bible on the book-rack. Ada sits on the kneeler and begins to unfold the bundle. Now she sees that the baby is indeed dead. It is mottled greyish purple, like a pallid piece of the purple jade Diana collects. Like something excavated from the earth, the deep creases scored into its face are filled with a kind of whitish crust. Where the crust is not, the skin is shiny and tight looking. It looks entirely devoid of life, like an ancient carving, as though it never had lived. In so far as it looks like a living creature, it is humanoid, not human. Ada pulls aside the cloth and sees it was to have been a boy. The umbilicus is left long, but tied with a scrap of white rag - from Bill's handkerchief probably.

A boy. The baby's sex makes Ada think of all that this child will not do. He will not wear shorts and graze his knees. He will not shout and run about, or grow a moustache or wear shiny shoes.

She reaches for a towel from the stack Diana has brought. She lays it, folded, on her lap and swaddles the baby. Bill, in clean clothes, is standing in the doorway. The women look disapproving and concerned, but do not send him away. He hesitates until Ada approaches him with the swaddled baby. He looks at him and touches his cheek.

"I didn't know what to do," he says. "I didn't know what to do. The coolies scarpered. The baby came so fast. I could have lost both of them there in the jungle." With a passionate spasm he takes the baby from Ada.

"Heavenly Father, please take this child to you, in Jesus' name," he says. He pinches his eyes tight and passes the baby back to Ada who continues to hold him. There is no piece of furniture in the room suitable for a dead baby to rest on. She does not want to remove him to the dispensary store-room, sometimes used as a mortuary. But the dressing table mirror gives her a glimpse of herself pacing with the swaddled infant in her arms, like any nursemaid, and she feels a decision has to be made. Diana looks up and sees her. She looks horrified.

"Take it away!" she mouths. Maud, having bathed and soothed her patient, notices Diana's agitation and looks up.

"Here, let me look." She leads Ada to the dispensary where she unwraps the baby and tut-tuts over the trailing umbilical cord.

"I don't think he had a chance," she says. "He needed another three or four weeks at least."

Doctor Barber comes, dusty from the bicycle ride from Mogaung. He sedates and examines Lydia and says that he expects the bleeding to reduce to a safe level during the night. The main danger now is to Lydia's spirits. Everyone must work together to help restore her to strength. Once the doctor has finished, Bill sits on a white-painted chair beside the bed, his Bible in his hands, emerging only for the evening meal.

Less than a month since the last time, the missionaries troop up the hill from the church to the burial enclosure. The doctor will not allow Lydia to attend. Andrew has chosen hymns suitable for children. Ada is uncomfortable with this. The others did not see the inhuman little body. They are imagining the child he will never be. But for Ada, their dealings with God today are not about children. They are about the tremulous line between here and there.

Thick, syrupy sunlight squeezes from beneath heavy clouds and stains the hillside. Then dusk falls.

In the subsequent days Ada and Ivy find Ka Pa more reluctant than usual to address his normal tasks. He fetches water and lights a fire first thing in the morning, but then seems to melt away. Ivy frowns at Ada. "It'll be opium. He hasn't been bad up till now, but maybe someone has given him a present, or he's had a nice little crop from his garden. It is hard to say whether laziness is part of the character, or brought on by indulgence." She whisks a twig broom round the floor of the kitchen area.

"We have an enemy, Ada, and we see his mark in dirt and idleness." She has only just started calling Ada by her first name. On this occasion Ada feels that Ivy's disapproval is smudging beyond the dirt and idleness to herself.

On the third day after the Hocknells' return, Bill sets off to catch a train up the line to the administrative centre with errands at the bank, but also to register the baby's birth and death. Lydia lies alone in the guest bungalow bedroom, not allowed to get up and apparently not eager for company. Ada hears Andrew promising Bill that he and Diana will pray with her morning and evening and that she will not be alone. Diana, however, spends her days with her groups of women and children, or supervising the servants, and when she is not doing mission work she is educating her own children. Maud is still tending to Lydia as a nurse, but has her long dispensary queues to contend with. Ada sees that she herself is the only one not bustling about. She takes her language books and taps on Lydia's door.

"Would you mind if I sit with you?"

"Please..." says Lydia through dry lips. Please do or please don't?

Ada puts her books on the chair and takes the water jug to the bungalow kitchen to find fresh water. There is an earthenware cooler with a tap. Back in the bedroom, she empties the stale water in the glass into the vase of white chrysanthemums and refills it. Lydia reaches for it at once, awkwardly because she is so low in the bed. Ada moves to bulk up the pillows, but Lydia says, "I'm to stay flat." She resumes her position staring at the ceiling. Amongst the clutter on the bedside table is a thermometer in a glass.

"Have you had your temperature done?" Ada asks. Lydia rolls her head and accepts the thermometer under her tongue. Ada then remembers about checking the mercury is down, shakes it and offers it a second time. When she takes it out, it seems to unplug something for Lydia.

"Did you see my son? Was he really gone? I heard his voice."

"I saw him, but he wasn't alive."

She sits, placing the chair between the bed and the door, and opens her books.

"If it's a test..." says Lydia.

Ada is momentarily puzzled, thinking of her language books and the test that lies ahead of her when she completes a year on the mission.

"If God's testing me, I might not pass. I might be angry and unfaithful. I might be too angry to continue my work here."

"Is that how it is?"

"No. Not yet."

The voice is level and the words as short as they can be. Ada is reminded of her own mother in weary moments and suddenly catches an uncomfortable glimpse of the cavity under the words.

"My mother," she says, "My mother had a baby that disappointed her. My sister. The birth went on so long. I can't really remember, but I think it was three or four days. Much too long, and my sister lacked oxygen."

"Did she live?"

"Yes, she lived; she lives. But it is not as it would have been, not as it was meant to be if the birth had been easier. And my mother, I think she has been angry all these years."

Lydia sighs and closes her eyes.

As she walks through the village to collect milk, Ada notices gatherings of women working together round pots and mats, grinding and mixing and spreading the resulting paste out to dry.

"Something's up," Ivy tells her. "Those collections of women mean beer. They can't do any feast or ceremony without beer. Or even stronger liquor, they make that as well."

Ivy's women do not turn up at the mango tree, but Ivy is steadfast and sits there, preparing a little bit of teaching based on the Sermon on the Mount. Ada sits on the veranda with her language books. She is not sure if it is the village's air of preoccupation or Ivy's comments that make her feel more foreign and out of place in the village today. As the day progresses Ada notices that most houses have baskets full of long bamboos propped up against the walls. Ivy tells her they're full of freshly brewed beer.

By evening Ka Pa has not made an appearance so they cook their own supper of fried sweet potato and omelette. Chickens assemble to peck at the peelings they throw out. There are the customary evening noises - a house crow's call pierces the cooling air. There are squeaks that could be birds or could be monkeys. But across the village clearing, a hammer hits a bamboo stake with erratic strokes.

From the veranda they can see across thatched rooftops to the other side of the shallow valley that holds the village. Ivy clutches at Ada's arm.

"I knew something was up," she says.

There's a structure of posts and a palm leaf roof that was not there before, not substantial enough to be a house but with an elevated floor like a stage. Ada smacks a mosquito, freeing her arm from Ivy's grip. These surroundings, which had started to become familiar, are alien again. There's something wrong with the light. The sounds of the village are wrong.

"Listen to them," says Ivy. "They've been drinking all day."

"Are they building something?" asks Ada. "All that banging in of posts. Do they make beer for that?"

"Well, it's not a house," says Ivy ominously. "That's the place they have ceremonies. I told you, we don't walk there. It's a place of fear for them. There'll be a witchdoctor coming. They put up altars and posts all round with weapons on to keep people away. I haven't seen it, but it's what they do if a *dumsa* comes.

"Tonight, Ada, we will say Evensong together. We need to place ourselves under God's wing."

They eat sitting on low stools on the veranda. The sky fills with vivid streaks where the light clings to the clouds.

Across the valley, firelight bounces off the trees behind a noisy milling crowd of men, women and children. There's a clacking sound the two women have not heard before, and exclamations.

As they are eating, the light in the clouds fades and the dome of the sky turns deep mauve for the night.

Ada and Ivy stand side by side on the veranda and read the order of Evening Prayer by the light of a paraffin lamp. Smoke drifts past them. Ivy chooses Psalm 22, which they read in turn, verse by verse. The eyes of the one who is not reading are drawn to the crowd on the opposite slope.

Ripples of yellow and orange light dance from side to side as the fire is replenished. Tall headdresses of long feathers or reeds move among the shifting people.

"Many oxen are come about me; fat bulls of Basan close me in on every side. They gape upon me with their mouths: as it were a ramping and a roaring lion."

Ivy's voice is firm. She pushes the book towards Ada who picks up the next verse:

"I am poured out like water, and all my bones are out of joint; my heart also in the midst of my body is even like melting wax. My strength is dried up like a potsherd, and my tongue cleaveth to my gums; and thou shalt bring me into the dust of death. For many dogs have come about me ..."

At that moment they hear a terrible squealing and yelping. Could they be killing a pig? It is worse than that. Ada decides it must be one of the dogs, a creature who was expecting human understanding and is bitterly disappointed.

"Heaven help us! A sacrifice!" cries Ivy.

She gabbles on, "But be thou not far from me, O Lord, thou art my succour, haste thee to help me. Deliver my soul from the sword, my darling from the power of the dog. Save me from the lion's mouth; thou hast heard me also from among the horns of the unicorns".

Their voices run together, until Ivy, to Ada's astonishment, falls to her knees weeping. There's a crescendo of shouting from the other side of the clearing and then the dog's howls are cut short. Ada tugs at Ivy's sleeve and hurries to the end of the psalm and onwards:

"Lord now lettest thou thy servant depart in peace..."

"Peace," repeats Ada, "In peace. Sorry. This isn't working, is it?" She starts to back away. She wants walls around her.

Ivy is kneeling in the doorway, slumped and shaking. She reaches for the book, and, without looking at it, works her way through the Creed. She clutches Ada's ankle, digging her fingers in. "Let us *pray*, Ada, let us *pray*." Ada joins her in the Lord's Prayer, pinching her eyes shut as she did when a child. Ivy's voice re-gathers strength with every phrase. They skip the prayers for the King, and hasten to the end. Ada can hear that Ivy is putting particular stress on "dost promise that when *two or three* are gathered together in thy Name thou wilt grant their requests". She rises to her feet and shakes her head.

"Oh Ada, you're letting me down!" She finishes with an ungracious grace.

Don't, thinks Ada. *Don't make me feel what you feel.*

She flees to her room but feels as if the whole house is thrumming with Ivy's distress. Peering between the slats of her blind she can see only darkness now except where the trees beyond the clearing are lit by an orange glow. The fire is crackling and roaring and men's voices are raised above it. From time to time there are loud detonations followed by what sounds like an incantation yelled out above the hubbub. Ada sits on her bed and wraps the mosquito net round herself. She finds she is rocking as she sits, and that it makes the floor creak, so she stops herself. She thinks of Louise in one of her frantic states, and of calming her in the rocking chair, catching her wild arms and stemming the stream of snot. She calms herself and lets her curiosity follow the excited sounds from round the fire.

She creeps out of her room and through the hanging bamboo curtain to the back veranda. The sounds from the clearing seem to be of merriment. There is a smell of cooking meat. She listens hard, over the pulsing hiss of crickets. Is it devil worship, or is it a party? She slaps a mosquito on her neck. Standing still, she must be sending out the appetising scent of warm blood in ever-wider ripples of air. She edges, the wrong way round, down the steep ladder on her heels and crosses the track to a path that leads between the nearest houses. There is no light in the houses, but then there seldom is, beyond a very dull glow from a hearth. She hears a child fretting, and a woman calling out. They aren't all at the clearing, then. There are shrubs and spiky little bamboo fences to keep pigs out of vegetable patches. It is not easy to cross the village in the dark. She does not want to be watched creeping about, but avoiding passing the doorways of the houses makes her route more difficult until she gets to the pathway that circles round the outside of the area of houses and bits of garden.

She steps round a banana plant and freezes. There is a tall figure in front of her - a gleaming rounded brow with a tufted topknot, a stick or a spear over one shoulder and a sword jutting in the usual position alongside his chest. He stands perfectly still, and Ada can see the fierce, unblinking glint of one of his eyes. After a heart-thumping moment she realises that he should have blinked. She reassembles what she is seeing - a stout post, a spear tied to it with heavy rope, a sword slung beside it and, tied at the top, a huge ancient pistol with a polished wooden butt. She dares to creep closer and sees that the firearm is not even complete, little more than a butt and a barrel. Even so, the assemblage of weapons seems menacing, and she stops.

There is a platform between Ada and the fire. Two men are sitting on it, backs towards her, facing the bulk of the crowd. One of them has a tall headdress of reeds that flicks about as he moves. He throws something into the fire, which, after a moment, explodes loudly. Someone rakes the ashes to fetch it back and passes it to the pair on the platform. The one with the headdress peers at it, mumbling. Then the other shouts out to the crowd of men in front of them, as if he is making a translation and voices from the crowd shout back a commentary. Ada realises she has seen young boys playing at this game, throwing little lengths of bamboo into a hot fire so they pop. She tries to read the illuminated faces of the men round the fire. Are they playing a game or is it deadly serious? Are they doing deals with the spirits? Most of the men are seated or squatting in an even row. Her eye is caught by one face that hangs low at a familiar crooked angle. Mahgawng Kajee is there, one of the crowd, listening intently, joining in the responses.

She hears a little sound, a rustle, in the grasses behind her. There's a larger sweeping, thrashing sound from tall trees beyond the clearing. Above the highest of the rising red sparks there are sharp white stars. I'm just a tiny scuttling creature in the undergrowth with all these strange and wild creatures around me. Does God want me here? Where am I called to be? How could I think I was meant to be here, so far from those who love me?

Shortly after dawn Ivy and Ada encounter each other, grey-faced. Ivy looks suspiciously at Ada's outdoor clothes and shoes.

"Come on," she says. "We need to talk to Andrew Sinclair, and I'm sure they won't begrudge us breakfast after the night we have had."

She bustles to get dressed, shaking the house as she does so. Irritated, Ada sits at the top of the ladder, waiting. The path is slimy with dew, causing them both to slip.

Ivy marches onto the Sinclairs' veranda, with little regard for the early hour. A child is already crying and a hand opens a window screen and throws a wet sheet onto the veranda. Andrew emerges with his Bible and notebook in his hand, and has slumped onto a chair before he notices the two women. He jumps up politely but looks put out.

"We'll go," says Ivy, bluntly as though no time has elapsed since the conversation before Andrew's tour. "It's the right time. We should take our place in the Valley, while there is a need."

Ada is taken aback. She does not trust Ivy's decision-making, nor her ability to forge relationships with Jinghpaw, or even to speak to them appropriately. A journey where she herself is the junior partner and an attempt to take up the reins of the Hocknells' work seems unwise.

"It is the right time," Andrew says. "Or almost. I have given the matter some thought and it seems to me that if Frank Mann goes with you he can not only assist you on the journey, but he can also finish an exploration project of Bill's and perhaps accompany the baptismal candidates when he comes back. But he can't leave immediately. We have some business to do which requires his signature. None of us can be sure that we will not be quite suddenly called away on the Lord's business, and Mann must be my deputy if that should happen. We will spend Christmas together and then you can go." He picks up his books again, then adds, "We heard the gongs and so forth last night. Was that a witchdoctor affair? I should think they are all the worse for drink this morning. And I imagine you might be thankful for some coffee after such a noisy night. Go through and ask Ma Gam." He waves them away and they leave him to his prayers.

Sipping coffee from a porcelain cup, Ada feels encouraged by the thought of having Frank Mann accompany them to the outpost. He is more experienced, and also so far as she can tell, steadier and less likely to be put off his stride by unexpected or undesirable events than Ivy. Ivy, too, seems pleased by the outcome and is making lists out loud. She decides that as it would not be helpful to have one person riding while the others walked, they should all walk and lead the pack pony. Ada, being still innocent of any experience with ponies, agrees, feeling that leading one will be a better first project than riding one.

Ada stands by the dispensary, trying to engage in small talk with the early arrivals, watching for Bill Hocknell to emerge from the guest bungalow. She greets him and asks how Lydia is. He stops and thinks before answering.

"She is gaining strength. But she feels the failure of it. I think a woman puts herself in God's hands to have a child, gives herself over to it. And then to lose it. It is a blow. Like seeing the collapse of something you have built, all your work going to waste. Heart-breaking."

The last word is a scratchy whisper.

"Your work," says Ada quickly, trying to prevent the welling of sympathetic tears, "And hers. We are going up to your station, Miss Smith and I. Can I talk to Mrs Hocknell about it? Would she mind that?"

"No, of course not. It would be good for her, occupy her mind."

He goes back to see if Lydia is ready for a visitor, and ushers Ada in. Lydia is still in bed, but sitting up against the pillows. A brush and hand mirror are on the bedside chest and her silky dark hair is arranged in a bun. She is still very pale, with mauve patches under her eyes.

She sighs before beginning to speak, but otherwise seems pleased to see Ada again and indicates a chair.

"Can you pass me a wad of those gauzes," she says as soon as Ada enters the room. "The milk won't stop. I'm getting damp down the front. It makes me think of our cow back in Ireland, howling to be milked. We took it in turns, my sisters and me, getting out before breakfast to milk her. She'd come trotting along, so eager. I thought it was because she loved us but now I'm thinking she just needed her udder eased."

She has a lot more vigour than last time Ada sat with her.

"Tell me, Miss Henry…Ada, why would God bring it all to a stop like that? The beautiful miracle of a child. What a down blow. Did I do wrong?"

"No, of course not. I'm sure you were taking every care."

Ada is dissatisfied with this reply because it makes her think of a list of careful things that Lydia may think she did not do well enough. Lydia turns her head to the window. Ada draws breath to say something and is relieved when Lydia speaks again.

"When I knew the child was growing I would look around at all this beauty. You should indeed visit the Valley Station, such a beautiful spot. All those green leaves, great trees reaching up from the valleys, bright-eyed birds and leaping creatures. And I was part of it, nourishing my child within me. How I rejoiced. But was it a mistake, that God brought that venture to an end? And as much as it was his plan, that much I am punished. I have to accept it and see how it schools me."

"Oh, no!" cries Ada. "It's not punishment. It's just how it is."

She lifts the corner of the sheet where it hangs down and strokes the fabric.

"My mother and I, we make shrouds, robes for people to wear in their coffins. Soft white fabric, swansdown it's called – like a very fine flannel. And in fact they're just like baby clothes with all sorts of pretty white trim and ribbons, for men or women, and often the ones for men are fancier because the women are choosing them. I always think they're like christening robes, and that dying is rather like being born. Opening a door and slipping through it."

Lydia turns her big beautiful eyes on her and smiles.

"It is so. We come from the dark and return to it. We do our utmost to listen through the keyhole do we not!"

Lydia reaches for Ada's hand and holds it for a moment.

On Boxing Day, Ada writes a letter to Edith.

My dear Edith,

This is to bring you greetings for Christmas (though I know it will arrive long after) and to share with you some of the oddities of the festivities in this part of the world – and a sorrow that has stolen the sense of promise that I think all of us here were hoping for.

Not surprisingly, I think of familiar old Christmases at Upham, or even our end of term festivities at Meredith Hall, and feel a twist of homesickness. Just that happy trust that something good is coming and that we can take part in it – even if, on the surface, it's only a good dinner. We never made much of the giving of gifts at home, but being here, I've been stitching little purses from the rather nice woven fabrics you can get and even tried knitting some socks, until I decided they were going to be the sort that slip down and make rock-hard bars under the feet.

Anyway, we decided we should give our converts, and a lot of hopefuls, something of the feeling of the gift of Christmas, so we ordered a box of handkerchiefs (they'll never use them for their proper purpose!), some damp-proof matches in very fine boxes decorated with birds, and a lot of sticks of barley sugar. At one of the advent services, Andrew tried to explain about the Magi bringing gifts. He and Messers Mann and Pavey sang the verses of We Three Kings. I learnt afterwards that at least some of them thought he was explaining our British system of government, with tributes being delivered once a year!

We even had a Christmas tree. The Sinclair girls, Patience and Carol, chose it and, being brought up in India mostly, they weren't thinking of a conventional little fir tree. They chose a beautiful, variegated shrub with leaves that are stained red at the tips and that rattle and flutter in the slightest breeze. Actually, it puts me in mind of the burning bush – I keep listening in case it says something!

At the beginning of Advent, Diana and the children started work on a very small nativity scene, with figures made from twisted pipe-cleaners bound round with wool and bits of ribbon, arranged in a stable made from a broken wooden box. They made a baby, very fat and very pink, to be laid in a nut-shell with a blue donkey and yellow sheep all around. But, in the end, we could not bear to look at it. Our colleagues, Bill and Lydia Hocknell, were travelling back to join us for the feast when Lydia's labour came on. The baby did not survive. Lydia is, I think, making a slow recovery. But the episode seems to have tainted our relationships with the people around us. They look at us distrustfully, I feel, and they have been performing their own ceremonies, noisy and involving a lot of drinking, which have made far more impression (at least in terms of aching heads) than our own.

We did have a Christmas dinner – a lot of chickens met their end. It was a bit awkward, in fact. Diana had announced to their cook that we were going to offer a feast to church-goers on Christmas Day and they were to kill and pluck about fifteen birds especially for the feast. Then later in the day, she saw that they had set up a pole with tufts tied to it like they do when they make sacrifices, and they were setting to with a sword, working their way through a clutch of skinny chickens. Diana screamed at them and she actually made them exchange the dead chickens for new ones. We can be sure that the sacrificed ones did get eaten, as they always do, even if nobody has anything much to eat for weeks afterwards.

I do keep wondering how our work of spreading God's love is understood by those around us. I told you about my little tutor, Mahgawng Kajee. He asked me about Christmas – what was this festival we were preparing for all about? He'd picked up that someone was coming. Was it like the Bishop's visit (which we are also preparing for)?

I said to him, no, it was the coming of God's son to earth, being born as a baby many years ago. You can imagine what it is like trying to do this in the simplest terms. He still seemed puzzled – where has God been, how far away is God? So I pulled out my tatty little Jinghpaw gospel and started to read to him the beginning of John.

Shawng ningpawt e Mungga nga si ... In the beginning was the Word. He leant over, terribly excited. "You have it in a book? You can read this?"

He stared at me. "But you are not a Jaiwa." That's one of their ceremonial storytellers who get very drunk and tell the history of their people.

Am I not? I said. Aren't I a European one? You should have seen the look he gave me. Very dismissive and affronted. I wondered if it was because I am a woman, but I don't think that was what shocked him.

He kept saying, "They wrote it down!" It really seemed to upset him.

I wanted to say, but is it not good that the word of God is here for anyone to read? Actually, I was thinking of the discussions you and I used to have. I went on to read the next verse. I could see that Mahgawng was torn between eagerly deciphering what I was saying and disapproving of me for saying it. And he has not made himself available for our meetings in these last two weeks.

I write at such length now because I am to make a journey to the most remote station of our mission and stay there for some weeks.

I send you good wishes, dear Edith, for the new year that will be well under way by the time you read this and I hope that a path is opening up for you that uses your talents but does not endanger your health.

Your affectionate friend,
Ada

9

January 1928

Ada

Despite Ivy's list-making and enthusiastic preparations, Frank Mann takes charge of the expedition, as Andrew Sinclair intended him to. He decides they do need to return the Hocknells' usual pack pony, Teddy, to the Valley Station, but agrees that they will walk rather than ride. This means choosing between a very long day's walk or breaking the journey in one of the villages a little way off the route. Frank asks the ladies their preference and listens carefully to their answers - both feel they are unused to long treks and will probably fare better stopping part way. Then Frank explains that he feels it will be better to do their utmost to achieve the journey in a single day, there being many discomforts involved in staying in a village hut, insects of many kinds being the worst. And if they camp in the open, the pony would be at risk from tigers. Ivy and Ada meekly give way to his leadership.

Ivy has set her large steel alarm clock for half past four, which is when they estimate the dawn to be. Bars of mist hang over the trees above and below the village. Ada has assembled their luggage on the veranda and sits listening through the chaos of bird-calls for the sound of the pony's hooves. Ivy emerges behind her. Planning for their journey seems to have smoothed the awkwardness in their relationship. "I should have asked you to join me for a prayer," she murmurs, just as Frank's "Good morning" reaches them.

The path away from the crossroads is uphill, as they expected. But it continues uphill for several miles. Frank laughs. "There's so much uphill in this journey you'd think you would arrive at the pearly gates themselves, but what happens is there's an extreme descent in the middle where you lose most of the height in a very few minutes. And then you have to make your way all the way up again."

At first the land falls away so steeply to their left that they have wide views over the mist-curled jungle and retreating hills. Ada's thoughts stray, as they always do when she feels the spaciousness of the sky, to Louise, still in darkness far to the west, her head under her elbow and her breathing steady and noisy. After an hour the light warms and the jungle begins to catch the light of the rising sun, with bright trunks gleaming here and there like rising sparks against the smoky green. They have not eaten, pausing only to gulp from their water bottles. Their clothes are damp from the moisture in the air and it has been too chilly to stop. Frank leads them aside to where a rocky platform makes a fine and sunny breakfast place. He lights a fire, brews tea, and boils eggs, which they hold in their handkerchiefs. Despite his efficiency he cannot find salt, and Ivy is gleeful to be able to produce a small jar of it. They shake the last drops of tea from the enamel mugs, dismantle the fire and reload the pony.

As the day grows hotter so the path becomes shadier, but they are plagued with insects. The path is well trodden but very uneven, with dry ruts, rocks and sandy patches. They pass several individuals. The variations in their clothing indicate they belong to the various hill tribes. A train of mules, jingling with bells, approaches them from a side route. The Chinese muleteers do not acknowledge their presence and the mules push their way between them without altering their pace. The second time this happens the missionaries leap to the side of the path at the first sound of bells.

Ada is dreading the steep descent. Her walking shoes, which had seemed solid enough on a Shropshire hillside, are not as substantial as she could have wished and she knows she will struggle if the drop is an exposed one. Her nightmares always involve vertigo. But when it comes to it, the difficulty is lack of exposure, with dense jungle making the path so dark you have to feel for each successive foothold. Frank has cut them each a stick. He has a square-ended sword as sharp as any Jinghpaw's, but he lets the pony carry it tucked into the pack basket, rather than slinging it alongside his chest as they would. "I don't have it as a weapon," he says. "It's just useful."

He wears a pith helmet and a robust shirt with neatly rolled sleeves. The military appearance of his shirt and shorts is belied by the boots, which are of pockmarked brown leather, scuffed and unpolished. Because he leads the pony he lets the women go in front, and that way conversation is still possible, when they have the breath for it. When they pause to drink, shortly before midday, Ada is taken aback to see that Frank's tan shirt is darkly wet down the centre of the back. But of course that is what happens when men exert themselves in the heat. Her own bodice and blouse are starting to cling to her.

For a while the path is level, weaving through tall, rustling, elephant grass and occasionally becoming moist. There is an equivalent path of blue sky above their heads, fringed by the feathery grasses. The heat is intense, but soon they regain the shade and start climbing again. As she raises her foot to surmount a rocky step, Ada catches a glimpse of the back of her own leg and lets out an involuntary squeal. There is a pattern of leeches scrawled on it. Frank asks if she's got her pocket-knife handy, or should he use his sword. Ivy, panting and red-faced, produces her own little knife from a buttoned-down pocket. "Just scrape, ever so lightly. You don't want to slice yourself. Conditions like these, everything infects. You've seen, at the dispensary." Ada feels absurdly relieved to be rid of the leeches, and ashamed of herself for having made a fuss, particularly when she sees, at their next stop, where Frank removes his boots and socks, that his white and angular feet have been providing nourishment for another half dozen.

They rest for over an hour in a glade where, when Ada lies back on the tarpaulin Frank spreads, the tall trees appear to soar to a bright white point over their heads. Curtains of creeper with aerial roots hang around, and clambering plants, some with scarlet flowers, climb to meet them, making a tapestried room in which to rest. They make no conversation, but take the task of recovering seriously. The pony kicks flies and shakes his head restlessly with a clatter of straps and buckles. Ada rolls over to watch a copper-coloured beetle climbing a stem, choosing a path amongst dry roots, diverting round a cylinder of fractured twig, encountering another beetle about a tenth of its own size. Drowsily, she wonders how they both know where they're going, where they should be going. When the travellers rouse themselves, Frank says, "Take heart ladies, we have less than three hours' walk from here and the Celestial City will come into view."

In the late afternoon they emerge from behind a bamboo clump to see an open slope with a scattering of huts around the edges where the jungle begins again. At the top of a rise is a neat bungalow with white painted walls and a teak shingle roof.

"Our destination," says Frank. "The Valley Station."

"More of a hill top than a valley," grunts Ivy.

"The Valley opens out on the other side of this hill," says Frank. "And that's where the jade mines are. But this little hill is the start of the range of higher mountains that isolate the Valley from this side. There are these villages here where you see, and a few scattered in the jungle on this side. But there are far more on the other side. That's why we need a station up here." They trudge up a winding flight of gradual steps cut in the hillside and reinforced with bamboo poles staked in place. The pony seems to know how to manage them, placing his hooves on the centre of each step and scrambling round the turns almost before Frank can, so that he has to repeatedly change hands on the bridle.

There is a shout and an eager dog bounds around the side of the house followed by a broadly smiling Jinghpaw couple. Frank clasps their arms in greeting and Ada hears him saying something about water. "There'll be baths for everyone within the hour," he tells them while pulling the dog's ears. Ada has not had a bath, of the sort you can sit down in, since she arrived in the country, but she is almost too tired to be excited about it. She subsides onto a canvas deck chair on the veranda. She smells smoke and curry and the resinous scent of sun-baked conifers, and then a whiff of stagnant mud as she eases off her shoes.

Waking the next morning on a proper iron bedstead and stepping onto a floor which, although covered with grass matting, is evidently solid cement underneath, feels like luxury to Ada. The doors all swing correctly, unlike those in the hut, which have to be lifted and dragged. The lavatory hut resembles the one they use at the Crossroads Hut in that it is suspended over a small ravine, but to get to it you step along a solid plank walkway with railings on both sides, and when seated you are protected by firm plank walls rather than flapping matting. When she remarks on how well-made everything is Frank says, "That's Hocknell for you. It is part of his gift to make things sound. And you have to admit that the villagers only need to take one look and see that this is not a man to build his house on sand. It's all part of the message."

The morning sky is white and the further hills are obliterated by mist. Gradually the trees and the billows of more distant jungle emerge. Stretching her stiff limbs, Ada feels curiously refreshed and energised by the previous day's effort. They eat fresh soda bread with scrambled eggs, and drink China tea at a table with a bright white cloth.

Ada and Ivy use the guest room, which has two iron beds in it. There is a double bed in the Hocknells' room which Frank uses and Ada sees that, in a third room, there is a cradle made of dark teak planks, curved, interlocked and polished to a shine.

Ada looks about at all the heavy items - furniture, the zinc bath, the cement flooring - and wonders how they could have been brought up the path they have followed.

"I'm sure it would have been possible, with enough coolies and determination," says Frank, "But there is another way, a cart track. It goes down to the railway well north of our compound, just where the railway crosses the river. We are thinking of bringing the Bishop that way, if he does indeed come, but we missionaries - we are light on our feet and are usually all the better for a bit of a trek. Wouldn't you agree?"

A queue of people has formed by the time they have finished breakfast. Although there is no dedicated dispensary building here as yet, people wait patiently at one end of the veranda where the roof extends a little and makes a block of shade. None of the three of them has more than basic nursing skill, but they can do disinfecting, stitching and dispensing aspirin. "We can look after them as we would one of our own number," says Ivy. "We can do no more." Ada tries to organise the queue, bringing small children and anyone with running blood to the front. Up here, the women's turbans don't stand up from the head, so they resemble the men's. Since everybody wears a wrapped cloth as a skirt, Ada has to look carefully to work out the difference. The ground where the people wait is spotted with betel juice, sometimes startlingly similar to blood.

"If only they would look after themselves," says Ada, after cleaning and stitching a jagged cut. "Did I understand him to say that he hurt himself on his own house? That sounds careless."

"That is what he said," says Ivy. "Something to do with a child - the child damaged it or stuck something through the wall. They always have it so dark inside, it's a wonder they don't all come to us with burns, the way they have the fireplaces smouldering there in the dark."

Frank is repeatedly sought out by a number of local men, apparently chiefs to judge by the separate retinues of respectful men accompanying them. He sits with the chiefs on the side veranda and discussions take place, but afterwards he seems bemused. "They come here looking for Hocknell and it's not easy to know where he'd got with them. They seem expectant, as though negotiations had broken off in the midst."

"It all makes opportunities for us to tell our story," says Ivy. "It's good for them just to see that there are more of us, all here with a serious purpose. In the end there is only one thing for them to understand."

"That's putting it very simply," says Frank. "I just feel I could be a bit more tactical if I knew what they were looking for. It seems Hocknell has become a bit like a parent for some of them."

The days take on a rhythm. The two women make themselves available in the mornings to dispense medicines and clean up wounds. Frank goes on excursions with the local men who seem to be accustomed to having Bill Hocknell at their disposal to mediate disputes, of which there is a never-ending supply. There is a holiday feeling, too, as they are only filling a gap in a temporary way. There is no point taking major new initiatives that would have to be interrupted. In the afternoons they tend to sit on the veranda reading and writing, studying language or making repairs to clothes and equipment.

Familiarity develops between the three of them, but three is an awkward number. At first they keep having discussions about minor matters. Who will lead their morning prayers, who will make tea or discuss the meals with the cook? On the second morning, when Ivy has laid the table for breakfast, instead of sitting in the nearest chair, she hovers and shows first Frank, and then Ada, where to sit like a hostess on a particularly formal occasion. Ada privately thinks it is ridiculous that they have to adopt favourite chairs at the table and on the veranda but recognizes that it is probably something to do with putting two women in a house with one man. She does find she notices how close or how far she is from Frank, as though he has a force field, and she supposes Ivy does, too.

The night before they leave they arrange with the caretaker couple to each take a final hot shower - a bucket suspended above a drain in the corner of the bathroom is one of the luxuries Bill Hocknell has introduced. Ivy takes the first turn and Ada and Frank sit on the veranda listening to the chorus of birds and animals that comes with the dusk.

"We'll remember this," he says. "When we're old, it will come back to us, the sounds and scents and colours of our years here. Ada, will you marry me?"

Her next breath hits her rib-cage from inside. The words entered her ears but seem to have formed a jumble in her brain.

He is holding out his hand to her. There's a clank and a splattering of water from the bathroom. She lays her fingers on top of his and he instantly grabs them.

"I hoped you would," he says, smiling broadly.

She wants to laugh, but equally, she wants to go away and paint careful pictures in her head of being married to Frank.

"You really want to?" she says.

"I do." He locks her gaze onto his. "We have such a purpose in our lives here, so much that we share, so much more to share."

They hear Ivy's slippers slapping on the teak floor of the hallway and he drops her hand, grins at her and moves ever so slightly away.

"I've had my eye on you," he says softly.

Ivy is in the doorway rubbing the ends of her hair with a towel. She raises her eyebrows.

"He's not teasing you about those sticking plasters that went missing, is he?"

"What sticking plasters?" asks Frank.

"You know, the tin of sticking plasters that disappeared after the children's class on Wednesday."

Ada steps past her to go and have her shower, letting her make what she will of her beaming face.

On the long walk home, Ada receives every leaf, every pleasingly striped pebble, every line made by the horizon, as a gift, entirely confident that God loves her.

When they get back to the compound, she and Ivy shrug off their kit bags under the Crossroads Hut and follow Frank down to the compound to make an initial report and drink tea.

As Ada climbs the steps to the veranda, Diana waves a letter at her.

"A letter from home! You're the lucky one this time."

In the bustle of greetings and exchanges of news, Ada simply tucks the letter away for the moment, dismissing the trace of unease that it is her father's handwriting on the envelope.

Later, sitting on her bed, by the light of her little hurricane lamp, she pulls the stiff sheet from the envelope and it is as if all the time she has ever known was shaped around this moment. Geological, unalterable. Just a day ago, she experienced what she had thought was an astonishing revelation of the redirection of her life, feeling herself at the tip of a growing shoot of green promise. Now the ground slides from under her.

By the time Ada returns to the compound next morning, Frank has set off with Ian on a visit and it is not until he returns and seeks her out that Ada hands him the letter to read.

She tells him she cannot marry him. She feels that her guilt makes her unfit to marry. She backs into the shady enclosure that serves as the kitchen for the

Crossroads Hut. He takes hold of her upper arms, as if to brace her up. She shakes her head.

"I am not someone you can depend on. Not now."

He gives her a little shake.

"You will be strong now. We will be strong together. I will hold you steady if you'll let me."

Another shudder goes through her but he keeps on.

"We will stick to our plans and then, when we are married, we will take a furlough together. You will see your father again."

"I can't. He will know I am to blame for leaving them all."

"Come now, you are feeling guilty because of the shock. You know it is not your fault."

Her deep, heaving breaths draw in the scent of him and when he sits down on the ladder, she sits with him, resting on his knee, enclosed in his arms.

Later that day he insists that she accompany him down to the town. They are to meet the train and collect a box of printed materials, but it will also give Ada the opportunity to send a telegram in reply to her father's letter. When they enquire at the station they learn that the train is running several hours late. Ada approaches the door of the telegraph office but then baulks. She expects Frank to herd her in, to demand some words to press into the soft paper of the pad of forms but he does not. He touches her elbow. It's too hard just now, he says.

Frank takes her to a house where they sell curry scooped from a huge iron vat into banana leaves. There are a few chairs and tables outside but after exchanging words with the man with the ladle, Frank leads Ada to a doorway at the back and into a dark room with two or three low beds.

"We used to stay here sometimes before the forestry company sold us the house in the compound. You can rest a bit. I can see you haven't slept."

He shakes out a bedcover and takes what looks like a crisp enough white pillow to inspect it at the chink of light from the shuttered window at the back.

"They keep it clean and fresh because of some deal with the dhobi family next door. Lie down dear girl."

She obeys him, lying on her side. She hears him pegging the door shut and soon after she feels the lightly built bed straining a little and the heat of him lowering himself alongside her. His right arm comes over her and fits round her right breast. It does not seem wrong to her that they are close, that her breathing moves his arm. She turns and presses her face into his neck. There, in the darkness, she accepts that this is the place for the wounded, that submitting to his stroking hand is the comfort she needs. Even when his hand begins to push inside her clothing she reaches an arm round his back and clings to him so she will not have to move away or open her eyes or do anything that would separate them.

"You need to know I love you," he whispers, pressing against her. "I am the one who will care for you, whatever happens. Whatever happens."

It is dusk by the time their bullock cart rolls into the compound. Ada's news has become known and she has to face her colleagues' sympathetic looks and offers of prayers. She longs for the privacy of her room but once there she lies, wakeful, pressing her forehead against the weave of the wall, hearing the sounds of others' normal lives going on uninterrupted. She tries to take comfort from the thought of Frank's extravagant promises but since he cannot do the one thing she needs, which is to take her back to the time before the catastrophe, she feels a puddle of resentment accumulating each time he offers more soothing words.

Each subsequent morning Ada wakes to the usual racket of birds and knows at once that there is a reason why she should not have slept. Of course. Nothing is as it was. She has to realise it all over again. As she will with every waking from now on. On the third morning she is unwilling to lie in bed absorbing painful facts until they form a weight of guilt or a flood of self-pity, so she gets up, although it is still very early. She gathers into a little knapsack what she will need for her meeting with Mahgawng Kajee later and takes the path down towards the compound. As she rounds the corner of the Sinclairs' veranda she sees Diana carrying a basket to the vegetable garden. Abruptly, Ada turns aside onto a steeply stepped path that takes her down to the river-bank. She stands by a little bay where seasonal waters have scraped the bank clean of vegetation. Silt-coated shingle slips beneath her feet, but she steps to the edge and peers into the cloudy water. The body of the river is opaque, apparently motionless until a floating branch or cluster of bubbles reveals the pull of it. Her dark reflection, the dome of her hat brim and the pillar of her body, looms like an effigy.

Now, for the first time, helplessly, she dwells on the sense of loss that filled her mother's life for as long as she herself can remember. She has always been impatient at her mother's perpetual mourning for the child that Louise should have been. But now, that loss compounds her own loss and she is overwhelmed. She feels it like a hollow ache and bends, clutching her knees with her hands. Tears well up and as she blinks she sees rings of ripples where they fall. The ripples repeat and expand until they become one with the sheet of morning light on the surface of the river.

"I've found you!" calls Frank's voice from behind her. "Where are you heading so early and all on your own?"

She straightens, staring across the bright water, unwilling to let him see her face.

"That's lovely," he says. "Can you go just a bit nearer the bridge?"

A glance shows her that he is unbuckling his camera from its leather case. She walks upstream a little way to where a simple bridge of planks resting on low wooden piers is rooted in the bank.

"There!" he calls. "Turn to face me! Lovely! I can send that to Mother."

The engagement has become official, as Frank has announced it to the others. Andrew Sinclair starts suggesting when they might conveniently marry. All his suggestions seem to Ada to be shockingly soon. She supposes she should write to her father about it, but feels quite unable to open a conversation with him.

Frank is kind and constantly refers to her grief but somehow seems untouched by it; it feels to Ada as though it is mainly an inconvenience. She wants to tell him, "You cannot meet my mother and my sister because they are dead." In case he has not understood. Every time they are close together, she wants to say it again because it is that sort of intimate fact, a deep and hidden matter, that you can only say to someone very close. Dead and gone.

Then she comes to the lower end of the compound one morning, expecting to plan the Jinghpaw Bible study with Frank, and sees Ian Pavey dashing off on a bicycle. Maud emerges from the Bike Shed, as they call the men's quarters, to tell her that Frank has collapsed and been helped back to bed. He has a very high fever but it is almost certainly just a case of malaria. Maud suggests that Ada should sit with him and bathe his head.

She does so and from time to time he opens his eyes and smiles at her – she's fairly certain it is a smile and not a grimace. Eventually he sleeps, Maud returns and sends Ada away to rest.

After another day mostly spent dozing, he asks to speak to Andrew and reminds him that they wish to be married as soon as possible. Dr Barber, summoned when the fever first set in, arrives on the third day and confirms that it is malaria - to be expected and that it will recur. "Probably at the most inconvenient times," says the doctor. "There is something I haven't quite got to the bottom of, but if you're not experiencing any other symptoms than those you have told me about, it's just a case of trudging on."

Two weeks later, they are married.

The morning after the wedding they have a train to catch. Ada wakes in good time, she believes, but finds that Frank was up before her. He bangs her case shut and hurries her out to the bullock cart. It is easy not to talk as the cart jolts downhill towards the village by the railway track. Both know that if you do talk there is a danger of biting your tongue or having your teeth clatter together. Ada can see that Frank's jaw is shaking in any case and his brow is once again beaded with sweat. When they roll to a halt she wonders for a moment if he has the strength to move. She clambers down and thanks the driver who is taking down the luggage. Frank stirs himself and picks up the biggest case. They cross the rails, making for a patch of shade against a wall.

They sit on the cases and after a few moments two figures detach themselves from a group under a tree and come to join them.

"Father James!" says Frank, attempting heartiness. Father James's companion is a nun with a crisp white veil flaring behind her. They all shake hands; Father James, who has once or twice visited the mission, greets Ada as "Miss Henry" and neither Ada nor Frank corrects him.

"Malaria's got you in its grip," says Father James. "We all go through it. Sister Francis here is becoming something of a specialist in dealing with it. So are you going to the hills for a furlough? Ah, here we go."

There is a tremor along the rails and a stirring among the waiting people and Ada realizes that a distant screeching, which she had interpreted as a flock of panicked birds, comes from the approaching train. It creeps to a halt alongside them, breathing stinking heat. Father James finds them two benches in the last carriage, helps Frank to get the two large cases on board and passes the smaller items through the open window, before sitting heavily beside Sister Francis. He divides the pages of a tattered Rangoon Daily News to provide them each with a fan. Frank droops against the window frame. Ada imagines herself taking his hand or offering wifely comfort. She is afraid of this illness that is washing through him, but more afraid, she realizes, of betraying his expectations.

The train moves at little more than a walking pace. Ada stops fanning with her paper and stands up. There is nowhere to go, and moving down the train involves stepping over the legs of other passengers. But she makes her way to the open platform at the back of the carriage. There are two men lolling on the floor, she guesses under the influence of opium. She watches the rails glinting behind them. The train slows even further, and looking along its curve Ada sees that the engine is about to advance onto a rickety wooden viaduct. The river. She frowns and tries to remember how it fits on the map. This must be the place from which they were going to bring the Bishop up to the Valley Station. There is a small thatched hut, which possibly represents the halt. She watches the ground creeping past, then clambers over one of the semi-conscious men and down onto the step. She feels the eyes of passengers who are leaning from the windows, and so, with an attempt at insouciance, steps down, staggers, and turns to wave to the slowly parting train. She is wearing a long-sleeved cotton dress, stockings and her walking shoes, a hat and white mesh gloves. Under her left glove is her wedding ring, hard and heavy. She has with her a canvas bag, which contains an aluminium water bottle, two handkerchiefs, a notebook and pencils, her passport and some boiled sweets. Also her father's letter, which she will never look at again.

If she is right, there should be a track, even a road usable by motor vehicles, heading westwards up into the mountains. She does not suppose that a train would be stopped just because a woman got off in an apparently orderly manner, but she stands in the shadow of the hut just in case, watching for the front of the train emerging from the riverside trees onto the central span of the viaduct. It takes so long she fears it has stopped, but eventually it appears, tentatively edging out across the water. It finally pulls out of sight, dragging away its many sounds and leaving just a hint of its sooty stench.

Jungle sounds close in around her, hootings in hollow throats and half-formed vocalisations. She realises she must have a plan of sorts, to do something so definite as stepping off the train. A small and hopeless voice inside is saying, *I want to go home.* She knows that is impossible. Home is a charred stump. She doesn't want to return to the "home" of yesterday, the hut shared with bitter Ivy. But clear in her mind is the white bungalow on the hill, where the floors don't shake and aromatic air passes through the rooms. Bill will be there taking care of Lydia, who is still sad but knows there is a path out of sadness. Frank cannot help her because he needs her to be a wife, the right sort of wife, not one chosen hastily in error, under the influence of passion. She will find a path to the Valley Station, following the rise of the land upwards, but never crossing the ridge to the left. She walks a little way along the railway track to the left, looking for a road, and after five minutes decides she had better check the other direction. Sure enough, shortly beyond the point where she stepped from the train, there is a gap between clumps of bamboo, and a dusty road winding away in the direction she wants to go. There are thatched roofs showing through the trees on the low hill to her left. If it is a sizeable village, perhaps she can find a bullock cart to take her some of the way.

She recalls Frank's voice describing the hills and valleys, and mentioning the road by which the Bishop, were he to come so far north, would be brought to the Valley Station. She assures herself she knows how to make her way there.

She has a nagging awareness that she has done wrong, parting from Frank without explanation or farewell. But she is filled with a strange and cunning urge to escape from what feels like an impossible situation. He will be angry. How can she expect to be forgiven?

She ascends the first part of the track, passing the villages on either side, but never approaching them closely. When she comes to a fork in the track she decides that the left turn leads only and immediately to a village of about ten houses. She can see the tattered thatch of the roofs. The other fork looks wider and more rutted by use, and so she assumes it is the principle route up to the Valley. While fleeing from Frank, she wishes she could consult him. He'd know these paths. She is quite quickly confronted by choices of ever-smaller paths all winding through denser, darker jungle on more and more precipitous slopes. At first she is pleased to be shaded from the sun. But after a while, after she has heard some mysterious rustlings and shrieks in the undergrowth, she begins to feel uncertain.

The sky darkens. She comes out onto a rocky slope where the trees and undergrowth open out, and sees that thick clouds are covering more than half the sky. She can see ranges of jungle clad mountains stretching ahead. There's no longer any human habitation in sight. With a pang of anxiety she recognizes that she is starting to feel quite hungry and thirsty. There are a few mouthfuls of water remaining in her bottle. She decides to save them, but takes a rest for the time it takes to suck two boiled sweets from the small stock she has in her bag. The tree tops are twitching, everything about her is restless and rustling. She overcomes her fear of snakes and sits on a rock. Then as she gazes across the uneven slope, trying to see where the path goes, she realizes she is not alone. A column of moving heads is visible above the bushes and rocks up the hill from her. Above the heads is a great bundle on a stretcher, an awkward, heavy burden. They are twisting and turning and moving with difficulty as they descend. She thinks of retreating into the jungle in case they see her, but at that moment there is a flash of lightning. The trees thrash more than ever and there are the first spatterings of rain, and then a deluge. It is the worst, most violent thunderstorm she has ever experienced. She curls up on her rock and feels the thunderclaps shaking both her and the rock. Her ears are ringing. She tries to hide her eyes from the lightning. It is as if her eyelids are transparent and the flashes are almost continuous. The sky is cracked all round, like the shell of an egg, and the terrible light comes through. She thinks she should pray, but fears that to raise her voice, even her inner voice, would be to expose herself further to the terrible fury all around her.

After a time she begins to understand why this part of the hillside is clear of trees. Little torrents gather and start to pour downwards. They accumulate grit and flakes of shale until the entire hillside around her is a shifting mass, building up behind rocks and then bursting away downhill. She begins to fear that the rock she is clinging to will go the same way, but there is nothing more solid to brace herself against. Through the tumult she hears shouts and remembers that there are others on this mountain enduring what she is enduring. Then there is the most terrible blow against the rock she is on and an agonizing pain in her leg. She cannot move. A great and grinding weight lies against her left leg. A boulder has come down the slope and lodged against her rock, with her leg trapped in between.

The night creeps past. The storm lessens. She is deeply chilled. She has no hope, no thoughts at all about what could happen next. Sometime after the storm subsides, she is startled by a shout almost in her ear. She opens her eyes to see a man's head against the grey sky. He is shouting and waving to others she cannot see, and soon she is encircled by about five mud-caked men talking in a language she does not recognize. She tries to move but cannot and the attempt starts her trembling. But, as she peers at them, she realizes that the men are not looking at her or trying to help her. They are studying the rock that traps her and shouting excitably. Three more appear. Eventually one of them fetches a bamboo pole, all tangled up with rope, that is lying nearby. They start to lever the rock. Every movement hurts her, and after a while one of them jams stones on either side of her leg, between the two boulders. As she watches them helplessly, she sees that the boulder that had come crashing down the hill has split right across. It seems to be this that interests them. They peer in between the two parts in the poor light. Eventually, first the smaller part and then the larger part are removed and the men all squat round the wreckage shouting at each other. One of them starts hitting the two parts of the boulder with a little pick, seemingly trying to smash it further into fragments. They keep trying different tools from their packs, a hammer, some kind of a wide-bladed pickaxe, a bigger hammer. Ada realises they must be miners, jade miners, bitterly disappointed by the revelation that their great rock is just plain and solid rock. No nodules of jade, no promise of a fortune, nothing worth carrying down to the railway line.

It is only when they have despaired of the rock that they turn their attention to Ada.

It is impossible to tell from the look of her swollen lower leg what damage might have been done to it, but quite clearly she cannot walk. Once it is full daylight and they are able to tear themselves away from their worthless boulder, the miners assemble some more of the bamboo poles which had formed the framework with which they had carried it. Bound together in a square, the poles are offered to her as a carrying chair. It is both painful and undignified. The poles dig into her armpits and behind her knees, but what other choice does she have? The men are remarkably skilful at getting along the rough and winding track, and compared with their rock, she is a light enough burden for them.

10

June 1928

Esme

At Moorside House Esme Mann moves through the empty rooms, empty of people but full of things. She wonders if she has too many things. As she and Joe and the boys moved from one place to another, she had attached these things to their life, pulling along bits of their story that, once they were settled in one place and the objects all piled up together, began to seem irrelevant. She touches a sinuously carved giraffe, a pair of brass vases, an inlaid table-top of multi-coloured soapstone that had remained forgotten, wrapped in a Hindi newspaper at the bottom of a trunk, and when it was rediscovered it looked too garish for this sombre room. This has been her house ever since she married though, for most of the next forty years they only returned to it occasionally. There had been an interlude round the time her younger son was born when she stayed on her own with the children, recovering and building up her strength. Gregory learned to walk on the rugged oak boards of the sitting room floor, concentrating hard and planting each foot several times before shifting his weight. Frank, on the other hand, had set off like a little dancer across the tiles of the bungalow in Darjeeling, arms in the air where his ayah had released them.

It is mid-afternoon but seems duller than it should be. She goes out of the back door and across the little yard to the cottage. They always called it the cottage though it barely deserves the name. There's a room downstairs with a small iron range and a staircase that is as steep as a ladder to the bedroom where an adult can barely stand at the highest point. Cecil and Rosemary Tinknell had come in middle age when their son, Thomas, had left them to work as a farm boy, so that the cottage was just sufficient at the times when Esme and the family were there, and they had had, after all, the whole place to themselves for most of the next forty years.

Rosemary cleaned and cooked and fed the fires, and Cecil had filled the orchard and the little meadow that they called the Lea with beehives. Now that they are gone, with all that Thomas could squeeze into his little van, the windowsills are still stacked high with jars of honey. The westering sun is catching them so that the light in the room seems solid, even impenetrable, like being inside a gold bar. This is what she has come for, a jar of honey. She has it on her porridge and stirs a little into her tea, loving the waft of flowers that creeps into the back of her nose. When Frank went to his prep school he insisted on taking a jar. The second term he demanded a supply of two jars and she learned that one jar was for rewarding himself with a teaspoonful each day when he got back to the dorm and the other was for rewarding his friends and enemies with a sticky spoonful "when they were very good". At the time she had laughed and taken this as a sign of coping, but now she wonders how it felt to be one of the boys never rewarded.

Esme knows there is a way through a narrow storeroom to the house, though the door on the other side is at the back of a cupboard and never opened. She tries the door on this side and is greeted by the sweet smell of beeswax and cedar-wood. The space is stacked up with sections of hives, frames of wax, smokers and gauntlets. Amongst it all is a tall pale figure with a gaunt, dark, face. She reaches a hand to confirm what she knows, that it is Cecil's overalls and hat hanging from a beam and, as she does so tumbles, to a booming accompaniment, over a large zinc barrel that is lying on its side on the floor. She hisses at the pain in one elbow and feels the swinging of the frame that is designed to spin inside the barrel-shaped honey extractor, as if she's lying on the panting belly of a rather large beast. Furious with herself, she clambers up and returns the way she came.

The next morning she telephones for a car to come and take her to see her optician. Here she is, stranded at the edge of a small village, with a car sitting uselessly in the outbuilding. She's never liked driving in steep-sided Devon lanes, having learned in a part of Kenya where one seldom met opposing traffic and, if one did, could usually run onto the strip at the side, which hardly differed from the road. She has always let Cecil do the driving. Now she will have to learn the times of the buses and time her trips accordingly. Then with a chill she realises that, with her vision getting dimmer as she now admits it has been, she probably will not want to go very far. If she falls over a large object in her own premises, how will she cope with the steps, kerbs and parked vehicles of the town?

The optician confirms her suspicions that this dimness is not going to retreat and her doctor writes for an appointment with a specialist.

She has a week of grimly trying to brace herself for these truths. Then a telegram arrives. She has hated opening the envelope of a telegram ever since the announcement of her younger son's death in the last days of the War, but this one is good news, written in round black letters by Mr Cann at the Post Office. "Awful bout of malaria ever since marriage. Coming home. Docking Liverpool twenty first July. Frank."

She rejoices, chiding herself for feeling abandoned. That word "awful" gives her a little throb of anxiety but the word "malaria" is almost consoling. She hasn't known a white person who died of malaria unless they were already ill with something else. She can help him recover; he can sit in the garden, or now the weather is getting cooler he'll want to sit by a window and read and join her round a fire in the evenings. Except now he has a wife. She visualises triangular arrangements of chairs. They will get to know one another.

It is less than a year since she last saw Frank. She remembers the solemn meal the two of them had with an extra course of soup and all the best silver the night before his dawn start. She had kept her eyes open while they said grace together gazing at his bowed head and shining dark hair, just as she had when he was a child. When she thinks of this she feels another little bubble of concern. Why would they send him home again so soon if he was not seriously ill? But it is probably because of his marriage. They will know that he needs to introduce his bride to his family (that is, to her) and, although they always take good care of the funds so painstakingly raised in missionary boxes at the back of every church, they are not inhumane with their staff.

She thinks about the wife, Ada, and hopes he has been wise in his choice. They have not known each other long, just a few months, but she thinks he has the confidence to make a serious decision. She is young, he told her that, but "strong in spirit". She will have passed through the selection process at one of the missionary colleges, which is probably a good sign. Frank did send a photograph showing a shortish young woman in pale clothes standing next to a low bridge of logs slung over a gleaming river. Esme had pored over the little scrap of card but the picture was taken in bright sunlight with sharp shadows and the upper half of the young woman's face is deeply shaded by the brim of her hat. She's wearing a knapsack, which gives her a sturdy, practical appearance, Esme supposes. Not unlike herself when young.

August 1945
Esme

Frank came home and lies, just up the lane, in the churchyard. And home, for Esme, has darkened, lost its shine, changed from a promise to the limit of possibility.

It was her influence, she believes, that led Frank to became a missionary. She had travelled so widely with her father and then her husband in the colonial service. She was thoroughly accustomed to making herself at home surrounded by the babble of foreign voices and the curious flourishes of other people's customs, while always carrying a small shining picture of "home" in her head.

A number of trunks and cases followed Frank's return, filling the house with clothes that were never to be worn, equipment for photography, for expeditions, for the keeping of records, for the cultivation of the mind. And of course, there's Ivy, who at least is useful, and continues to be useful for reasons best known to herself.

Esme needs Ivy. Not only is she completely blind but her legs have swollen and stiffened so that she is becoming less and less able to manage the stairs. Some days she spends downstairs but more and more often, she stays in her room. To her joy, Ivy accepted the little evacuees, solemn Dennis, striving so hard to be correct and useful, and the wordless little girl who wafts into the room and around it, never afraid to touch, to lean, to spring away and settle back again. She listens attentively, Esme knows, and, while most children would pick things up and fiddle, Annie never leaves anything out of place, as though she shares Esme's heightened sense of the space between things. It is for Annie that Esme speaks her stream of memories.

Esme has made her way downstairs in search of a piece of cake when she hears a noisy engine, a motorbike, that falls silent just outside the front door. And soon enough there's a rapping at the knocker. She knows Ivy and Annie have taken the bus into town so she makes her way to the door.

"Mrs Mann, you probably don't remember me – I visited with Frank many years ago." It's the bashful missionary who stayed a night at the end of Frank's last furlough. "I've changed a bit since then," he says. There's a pause while he takes in the fact that she can't see him at all. He's probably passing a hand over a bald head, she thinks. Frank would not have been bald. None of the men in her family ever got bald.

"Ian Pavey," he says. "I visited just the once.

"I've got a few of Frank's things. Not much as we had a bit of a trek to get out of Burma during the invasion in

'42, but I held onto a bundle of letters and so forth, and some cufflinks and a bit of jade he probably bought for you. Rather special, that. It's the multi-coloured variety.

"I'll leave these with you," he says, placing them in her hands and holding them to ensure she has grasped them all. With her hands in his, his voice suddenly assumes a priestly tone.

"It was such a sadness, the death of such a fine man, and just as he was about to become a father and when poor Ada needed him so much. So sad his daughter could not know him, so hard to accept it was God's will."

She pulls her hands away from his.

"I'm grateful to you Mr Pavey," she says. She fingers the jade. Multi-coloured? It's just hard and cold and, as far as she can tell, shapeless.

January 1948

This girl who has materialised where Ivy should be – she's either naturally clumsy or she's angry. Esme can hear her moving about, light and quite small, but, in the way she sweeps things aside or plumps them down, there's anger.

Where did she pop up from? Why doesn't she say?

But once she starts, she doesn't stop.

"I believe you are my grandmother," she says. Esme's heart trips. But she has already thought of this. Ever since Ian Pavey left her by her front door, just before the end of the war, with the bundle of papers and the jade paperweight, she has done her best to estimate the age of every unknown young woman she meets; there have not been many.

"You wrote a letter," says the girl. "You'd heard about me. I'm the child of your son."

Esme stays silent.

"My real name was Frances. Frances Louise Mann. I didn't know anything about it, but we found my birth certificate when...recently."

She did that – she named her daughter after Frank. She admitted the connection. And now here the child is, in front of her, and she cannot see her.

"So you have another family. The ones who brought you up."

"My parents, the ones who adopted me, have died."

"How old are you? You must be 18. They got married in April '28 and Frank died later that summer."

"Nineteen. I'm nineteen. What did you say? They were married? I didn't know they were married."

"Well, of course, child. What did you think?"

Nancy flaps the counterpane and says nothing. Then she mumbles, "Is it all right? That I'm your granddaughter? It doesn't make you angry – or sad?"

"Of course it makes me sad, you silly girl. I shall never see your face."

The girl stops fiddling about with the covers. Esme feels her hand grasped by the wrist.

"Feel it then."

The edge of the bed sinks as she sits down and Esme feels breath on her palm. Her fingers meet a jawbone that seems to be shifting nervously, grinding the teeth – with impatience or anxiety. She lays one palm on the cheek and raises the other hand to the other cheek.

"Calm down, child. You know I will find you beautiful."

Her thumbs stroke the cheekbones, pass over the fluttering eyelids and smooth the brows. Then the girl takes her fingers to the hairline.

"Here, I'm like him here, my forehead. Like the photo downstairs. Can you feel it?

Esme holds her breath and passes all her attention to her fingertips.

The girl exclaims, "I couldn't believe it until I saw that picture. Do you believe it?"

"Of course I do. Of course."

A few days later Esme says: "I knew who you were as soon as you came. When Ivy ran away."

"Why? Why did she do that? She wouldn't say anything; just a jumble of things about how it was when she arrived here."

Esme laughs.

"She probably thought I didn't know! I don't know what your mother was like and I never will. But I knew with certainty that Ivy was not the woman Frank would have married. And anyway he told me. In that nightmare time of his illness. 'She stares at me,' he said,

'Those dreadful blue eyes, staring. Tell her to shut her eyes.' Almost the only thing he told me in the letter announcing he was getting married was that his fiancée had 'eyes like pale glass'. Well, that wasn't Ivy. After he died I asked the girl who came and did for us back then, what colour are her eyes. Blue. Most definitely blue. Weren't they? You saw them."

"I saw them," agrees Nancy.

11

February 1948

Ivy

Ivy inserts a hair-grip into the corner of the envelope. The paper tears easily to the half-way point but she pulls the hairgrip out again. It's not addressed to her. She had truly forgotten that she had put this letter, addressed to Frank, in the dark pocket of artificial silk in the lining of her suitcase. It was a time of such turmoil, a time when she was telling herself again and again that she had to play her part, since Ada was not there to play hers. The letter - she can see the fat wad of small pages in Ada's handwriting - is on brownish airmail paper with the red trim on the envelope, one of those they used to get in a dark little shop in Kamaing. It looks suddenly familiar now. She remembers how the first sight of this letter on the Moorside doormat had made her gasp. It was easy enough to tuck it out of Esme's feeble sight. And it no longer mattered once Frank was dead so she had pushed it out of her memory.

She takes brisk walks along the Bournemouth sea-front and up to the cliff if it is not too windy. Margaret keeps suggesting shops she might visit – hat shops, book shops, tea shops. She accepts the implicit suggestion that they do not particularly want to spend all day in the house together, but nor does she want to hang around the shops. In fact, she is almost as likely to encounter Margaret in the shopping streets as she is in the house, scuttling with short steps as she tends to do, and with one or more brown paper packages tied with the haberdasher's distinctive ribbon, or a cake box dangling from her finger.

Since her night in the woodshed Ivy has felt that there are still pockets of sluggish cold lurking in her veins and she fears them. So she braces herself and wraps up and tries to walk at a pace that makes her blood sing through her limbs.

She found the letter in her suitcase when she arrived and unpacked at Richard and Margaret's house. She has been carrying it around ever since, slipping it from one pocket to another. She doesn't know what it says - what it said so long ago. But she knows, now, after that icy night, that it has power over her.

Sitting in the not very adequate shelter of the arcade, watching the grey sea heaving itself up the beach, Ivy imagines Ada sitting in the well-worn Sunflower Hotel that the Mission used in Rangoon, with its arched windows looking out onto the noisy street. She sniffs the paper and thinks she can still just catch what she always thought of as the scent of foreignness – drains, curries, wood, dust.

While she has been sitting there, the tide has crept up the beach and is now toying with the line of shrivelled weed and scraps that it left in the morning. She stuffs the half-opened letter back into her bag. Pulling her gloves back on and tightening her scarf, she heads back into the town.

She walks up the path to the Overcliff, ignoring the griping of her calf muscles, thinking she might look for a tea-shop. She's not happy in Richard and Margaret's house. Richard says how pleased he is that she has come to visit at last, but he is seldom at home. A dentist, he shares a surgery a few streets away. Margaret makes much of her, ostentatiously making all sorts of arrangements and adjustments. She has changed the picture in the guest room, taking the blurry infant leaning against its adoring mother's silken knee to the landing and putting instead something green and jungly with sharp shafts of light slicing through it. She has rearranged the chairs in the dining room, claiming that the chair she herself takes is too awkward for a guest as one has to sit with one's back jammed against the piano.

When he married, Richard, whose work could have been established anywhere, brought his new wife to a good-sized house in a healthy seaside town, with a garden backing onto heathland, expecting that she would soon be walking a pram along the paths and waiting outside the nearby school. That was not to be. It seems that Ivy, the spinster sister, equally childless, heightens Margaret's sense of lack, expressed in her care of little things. Even when she shuts herself away in the guest room, Ivy feels she may have to answer a tap at the door at any minute as Margaret brings a clean towel or a little bunch of flowers in a vase.

Ivy follows the incline rather than streets that she knows, hoping that she might come across a cafe. Her hopes are raised when she sees ahead a Georgian style shop-front with a large copper kettle hanging over the door. But when she approaches she sees that the painted sign above it says "S Warren, Antiques and Curios". Ivy doesn't expect to take much comfort from treats such as tea or cake, and she pauses without disappointment to peer through the panes. Low sunlight is glancing across below grey clouds and it strikes an object beyond the thick glass – a transparent globe on a stand. A crystal ball, thinks Ivy. You can buy such pagan paraphernalia in a shop in Bournemouth? She has been meek and polite for five days. She would quite like to have a more abrasive conversation. She pushes open the door which, predictably, rings a little bell above her head. The shop is long, narrow and cluttered. She makes her way to the back where a man is sitting at a counter, almost hidden behind a cabinet full of medals and costume jewellery. With an eye-glass gripped to one eye he is peering at the back of a large steel watch by the light of an angle-poise lamp.

"That object in the window," says Ivy. He looks at her unenthusiastically. "The glass sphere, I mean".

"The lace-maker's flash", he says at once. "For getting a better light. To save their eyes." Then he gets up. "I'll show you." He lets his eyeglass dangle from the buttonhole where it is attached.

He's tall and angular and as he squeezes past her he rocks a small fake marble pillar with one of his large feet and kicks a wooden dog on wheels with the other. He brings the glass ball from the window and Ivy sees that it has a wooden stand and is actually more like a very round bottle with a little neck at the top.

He goes through to the very back of the shop where, behind a Chinese folding screen decorated with a flight of cranes, he evidently has a sink with a tap. After some splashing he comes back with the globe full of water, and wipes it dry. "It should ideally be snow water. Purer."

He goes back to his counter and sets up the globe next to the angle-poise lamp so that a band of intense light falls on the watch. He shakes back his sandy-coloured forelock, sets the eye-glass back into his socket and peers at the watch. He takes up a tiny screwdriver and seems to be counting something. There's a rumbling sound from behind the screen.

"Would you mind turning the kettle off?" he says, contorting himself to keep the watch in the light. "Now, would you mind? I don't want to be making steam in here."

She makes her way behind the screen where, below a high window, there is a sink and a cluttered table with a bottle of milk and the kettle. She can't see a switch on the kettle so she follows the cable, grips it and pulls the plug from the socket.

She flies backwards into the screen, which bears her like a stretcher and lays her down in the shop amongst a clatter of falling objects.

"My gosh," says the man. "Are you all right?"

She lies there while the shop settles into stillness. Her arm is stinging and she tugs at her coat sleeve helplessly.

"Was that the kettle? Did the kettle get you? You've done for the lights, look. I should never have asked you to touch it. It should have been me. It's been out to get me, I know. It started to smell the other day. And it was fizzing; just a funny little fizzing inside the plug from time to time. It was meant for me, I know."

"I dare say I deserved it," says Ivy. "One way or another."

"Not for me, you didn't. Can I help you?" He reaches a hand down. "Listen, is everything working? Heart ticking away okay?"

"I think it must be." She laughs a little gustily. "Just my arm. It feels burnt and a bit odd."

He helps her up and helps her undo the buckle of her coat so she can pull her sleeve off. He leads her to the front of the shop, holding the part of the coat she's not wearing and they study the arm, definitely reddened and tender looking.

"Now Miss ... You must let me take you for some tea. Hot sweet tea after that. I should introduce myself. I'm Stephen Warren."

"Smith. Ivy Smith."

They walk four doors along the street to a little cafe with steamed up windows, which smells strongly of steak and kidney but promptly serves a pot of tea under an embroidered cosy. Ivy still feels a little shaky and ready to be indulged and accepts a slice of cold bread pudding. Stephen Warren eats hungrily and absent-mindedly. He glances quickly at her and then out of the window.

Ivy finds an urge to treat his anxiety.

"It wasn't so bad, what your kettle did. I've never experienced that before, a shock. But I seem to be all right. Tell me, what brought you into this business?"

"My father had the shop. He was more of a specialist in pictures and fine furniture. And picture frames, the carved and moulded ones. The street was a bit better then with more fashion and so on. The street went downhill and I'm afraid I let the shop slip. I'm always beguiled by the curiosities. When I look through an auction catalogue it's the mixed lots that get me excited. My Pa wouldn't have looked twice."

"So the lace-maker's thing, the flash did you say, how much would that be?"

"It's only a middling good one, woodwork slightly scratched, but the glass is nice. But you, Miss Smith, must take it. It's the least I can do. I'll wrap it up for you. Just as soon as we get back."

He looks at her sternly and directly. But she is not resisting. When did she last receive a gift? When, in fact, was she last part of a joint plan, even if it is only to return four doors along the street?

She returns through the dusk to Richard and Margaret's house with a brown paper package under her arm. She uses the key Richard has lent her and, creeps quietly up the stairs. She had been toying with the thought of getting something for Margaret, something that sits as awkwardly in Margaret's carefully coordinated house as she does herself. She is not sure she wants to make a gift of the lace-maker's flash. She doubts that Margaret would like it, but that had not been her original intention.

After the evening meal and half an hour by the fire in which Margaret asks Richard about his patients and Richard asks Margaret about her shopping, and then they both ask Ivy where she walked, Ivy retreats to her room taking a cup of tea and a box of matches from the kitchen. She fills the glass flask in the bathroom, rests it on its stand and lights one of the pair of candles in the porcelain candlesticks that Margaret no doubt intends to be purely decorative. Ivy slips on her dressing-gown over her clothes and then places her hands in the pool of light. Her right hand is still reddened and she peers with interest to see that the hairs on the back of her hand seem to be standing up stiffly. She tries to imagine what lace-makers have to do, peering at fine threads and twining them around each other. She makes her fingers do a little dance in and out of the light. Stephen Warren had told her that sometimes ten or a dozen lace-makers clustered round a single candle, competing for the best quality light. Then she pulls Ada's letter out of her pocket, uncreases it and lays it in the light. On the envelope, Diana's firm italic handwriting has scratched out the address at the mission and superimposed the Middlecombe address.

Manager's House
Harris's Sugar
Kamaing

27ᵗʰ May 1928

Dear Frank,

This is a very difficult letter to write.

I owe you an explanation. Perhaps by now you will share my view that it was wrong of me to marry you – you deserved better.

I may have seemed to you like something I was not, someone with a true calling to work at your side.

Struck by a blow that hit me somewhere deep inside, where perhaps you couldn't see it, I proved flawed. How could I have let you bind yourself to me? I gave in to the comfort of your kindness. A part of me felt that you had come to know me deeply, but it was never true knowledge, was it? What of myself was I hiding? I feel I deceived you and that by stepping off the train so thoughtlessly I revealed something of my true self.

I do ask your forgiveness.

I have been punished, if pain is sufficient punishment.

I was drawn to suffering; drawn to Lydia's intimacy with death and loss. I believe I felt the need to travel closer and closer to whatever and wherever awaits us beyond this life. And so I made a desperate journey up that mountain, following what I remembered of your description of the route towards the Valley Station as a storm closed in. I endangered myself and could so easily have died, pinned between boulders in a landslip as the storm crashed around me for most of a long night. I have never known nature so angry.

But I was thinking entirely selfishly and not thinking of your weakness and suffering. I knew you were not well that morning when I parted from you, and I am sure you expected more kindness and responsibility from a wife.

I know that I have wronged you. But I beg that you might think of releasing me, and yourself, from a marriage that was born of circumstances and not from true knowledge of each other.

Whether forgiven or not, I hope that I may remain

Your friend,
Ada

She didn't love him. That is Ivy's first thought. *I could have loved him better. She doesn't even pretend she loved him.*

Her second thought is, *she has indeed been punished. God hurled a rock from the splintering sky and punished her. Would God do that, to make things tidy?*

Then she begins to fit herself into the picture.

She had heard nothing about Ada having sent a letter to the mission in the belief that Frank would have returned there. Maybe it came some time after she herself had been dispatched to Maymyo, ready to accompany Frank on the long journey down to Rangoon and the ship home. She had heard something of Ada's strange journey from Maud who had heard from Dr Barber of the state she was in when stretchered in to Harris's Sugar Factory by a band of jade miners.

Those miners, how surprised they must have been to find a woman, a white woman, on the mountain in the midst of a thunderstorm. They must have abandoned their dream of riches, but they saved her. They disentangled her from the jumble of rocks and saved her life. Was it really God? Did God send the miners, build the desire that took them to that remote place, that made them lash together a cradle to bear a great weight down the mountain? They would have been disappointed in their search for jade, but they didn't see the full wonder of what they had done: inside that crumpled, drenched woman was a child.

Restlessly she blows out the candle, reaches to the light switch and stands under the dull, even illumination of the bulb.

Why had Diana forbidden Ada to return? Ivy knows. There are very few moments when Ivy has made a difference to anybody. If she had not helped Frank on the journey home, someone else would have done. Caroline Mason from the mission office in Rangoon would have been only too pleased. If any of the Jinghpaw she met did turn to Jesus, she does not believe it was her stumbling teaching that made them do so. But that morning, the morning after Ada married Frank, she, Ivy, had set a chain of events in motion that had turned the course of someone's life.

12

February 1929

Ada

Each dark morning in the days that followed her baby's birth, Ada lay on the hard bed where, a few weeks earlier, she had lived through the drama of the birth. She felt trapped in the time when it was too early to make the floorboards creak, to run the taps or to force the day to begin.

She had to find a new beginning, to climb out of the valley she was in.

Spreading her hands on her own softened belly, she remembered Lydia, on that dull Upper Burma morning, drooping in the chair that would carry her home to the bungalow on the hill, gazing into her empty lap. At the last minute, Maud, normally so precise and timely with her well-trained hands, had pulled forward just as the four porters raised the chair and began to move. She reached over the arm of the chair to put something white in Lydia's lap.

"You should have it," she said. "I made it for you, and you should have it. For hope."

Ada, standing a little further along the path ready to clasp Lydia's hand, saw her shake out the tiny garment and lay it on her knee – a baby's nightdress with twining green vines around the cuffs and across the bodice. Maud must have known, she always knew, what she was doing. *This will hurt for a minute*, she would say, as she brought the needle close. *But it will bring you relief.*

So, had Lydia accepted her lesson - the sting of it and the mystery of it? Ada had less confidence that she herself was someone who would be able to pass God's tests. In her weeks in the narrow, white house in Ely, Ada had stopped praying. In the emptiness left behind, especially in those grey dawns, she had found herself talking to Louise – gabbling, muttering, even wanting to shout, as if to an unresponsive, retreating back view: Louise shuffling away with their mother beside her. Sometimes, her face pressed into the pillow, Ada wanted to call to her mother but dreaded that she might turn, might show her bitter face.

Ada heard the milkman's handcart rattle against a kerb in the street below and allowed herself to kick off the blankets and stand. Her nightdress was damp at the front.

She listened to the wheels below and remembered Mahgawng Kajee bumping along on his trolley and looking up at her as she waited on the church steps. Why, she had asked him crossly (on Frank's behalf), will nobody dig a grave for a baby? He had shaken his head as if to get water out of his ears. Was it a bad question? Had she offended him? He shut his eyes, recalling the details of a process which he then went on to describe, with gestures and emphatic words: how the baby must be placed in a jar made of bamboo, with leaves, lots of leaves, and the bamboo must be bound round with cord and carried a long, long way. An old man must carry it. He must take it to – Ada had not been able to make sense of the next few words but it was clear it was a tree, some kind of tree. Did he say it was a mother tree? A tree that makes milk.

Her baby, wrapped not in leaves but in the soft blue blanket she had bought for her, had gone far away to another mother. To her real mother. While she, Ada, stood woodenly in a shadowy room and leaked milk.

Jennifer had said she could think of leaving after eight weeks.

The life had gone out of her relationship with Jennifer. Jennifer was solicitous, she nurtured her with carefully balanced meals, but they had nothing to look forward to together. The absence of a baby hovered darkly between them so that Ada felt guilt on two accounts. One morning Jennifer opened a letter and quickly suppressed a smile.

"The next one," she said. "Due in September."

Ada felt a flash of panic.

That night she slept fitfully and arrived with a sense of familiarity at the time before dawn when sleep would desert her. She was breathless, striving. It was as though she had come into the dark room directly from a mountainside, a path winding upwards, with an urgent need to make progress, to catch up.

"Northwards," she muttered. "He said they go northwards."

She sat up, pulling herself back into the room. She stared at the faint grey lines around the edges of the curtains.

"Beautiful death," she said, steadying herself. "A place for beautiful death. I shall go to Scotland."

So she had arrived in Portobello with a fiery sunset – copper light bouncing off the folds of the hills, and streaming like flame on the steam from the factories.

She had to surge past her own doubts; she had nowhere else to go.

She had pushed her way into the front hall at the Pavilion, past painters' trestles and dust-sheets, and startled Bernard Callandar who was standing there, his face illuminated, staring up at a skylight.

"I want to work here," she said. "I did nursing in Burma."

He recognised her but appeared to have forgotten about a promise, kindly made in the bustle of Birkenhead Dock, many months ago.

"I can be useful now," Ada said, remembering how you have to tilt your head to talk to such a tall man, "But I will be rather more useful if I can be trained."

"Follow me," he said, and led the way across a patch of windy garden to a low stone house. He opened and pushed his way through the front door, reached back to rattle the knocker and ushered Ada in.

A woman appeared, tall and stately, with hair more ginger than auburn.

"Alison, my sister," said Bernard. "And this is Miss Ada Henry. She has come to work with us."

He then whisked out of the door and back to the main building, leaving the two women to decide what happened next.

A year or so later, Ada asked Alison, "Was I so very bedraggled and pathetic that you felt you had to take me in and treat me with such kindness?"

"Bedraggled? You were like a wild beast in flight. I thought you were about to run away," she said. "You were driving yourself; you'd have dragged yourself onwards, anywhere, up the nearest mountain, however hard it got. I thought I should make sure you stopped and sat down for a bit. Ate something."

It was one of the first things Ada learnt about Alison, that she loved to cook, but her moment of satisfaction came not when the sizzling dish was placed upon the table but when the person being fed chased the last traces round the plate. Alison would always finish last because she forgot her own plate in her eagerness to watch a guest being nourished by her hand.

Ada stayed in a small spare room in the cottage for the next few months. Alison's husband, Daniel Russell, was a joiner, with the development of the Pavilion as one of his many jobs. He was friendly but not talkative; Ada liked to breathe in if he passed close by her, to capture the familiar scents of pine shavings and linseed. At the first meal they sat down to together he nodded at the pie and piles of potatoes and sprouts on the table and said, "Thank the Lord there's someone else to take on the task of eating all this."

When, the morning after her arrival, Bernard clarified that Ada's hospital training so far had consisted of approximately four afternoons, he agreed that she should apply to train as a nurse at the General in Leith. Until her training started she could make herself useful cleaning the rooms of the Pavilion as they became usable, stocking the storerooms and making up beds.

Ada had not realized until after she began that the training would involve at least three hard years. The Matron had looked doubtfully at her clumsy ankle but accepted Ada's assurances that she could walk for miles and was really very strong.

In fact, Matron seemed keen to test this claim as often as possible, stretching Ada's shifts, sending her on all the most distant errands, down to the basement, along the barely lit corridors full of pipework, and up again at the other side of the hospital to collect a slip of paper or deliver a specimen.

She shared a dormitory in the nurses' accommodation with three much younger women who treated her as a mystery to be probed at every opportunity. Why had she been abroad? Why do her training so far from home? How had she hurt her leg? Had she had a boyfriend? Was she running away from someone?

Meanwhile, a couple of miles away, honey-coloured paint, copper pipes and electric wiring spread through the corridors and rooms of the sprawling quadrangle of buildings that was the Pavilion.

Gradually, the patients' rooms began to be occupied. Besides Alison, who was fully qualified, there were two other nurses ready to start work.

Bernard led the venture with a kindly earnestness but he sometimes troubled those who worked with him. From her very first encounters with him on the *SS Bhamo*, returning from Rangoon, Ada had been aware of a subdued charisma emanating from Bernard: people noticed him, listened to him, wanted to be heard by him. The little community that was gathering round him to live and work at the Pavilion seemed warmed by the glow of his energetic pursuit of a vision. But Ada could see there was a deeply embedded combination of admiration and frustration in the way Alison, the one who knew him best, responded to her brother.

"I'm the practical one," she said. "He's the dreamer."

Ada soon discovered what everybody else took for granted, that Bernard practised a routine of meditation every day. It seemed to mean that he was often not available, and his little office filled up with scraps of paper and notes left there by people who had looked for him and not found him. Nonetheless, when there was need of an impassioned speech to drive the builders on a bit faster or to gather together a board of governors, he was always able to find the words.

While Ada was training, he encouraged her to keep one of the nurses' rooms at the Pavilion for when she was off-duty so that she would be thoroughly familiar with the place by the time she started working there full time. Alison, remembering hasty meals in the nurses' home, baked treats for her to take back with her.

As the months went by, Ada noticed that Bernard seemed to be paying more attention to her than he did to the other nurses at the Pavilion. It was as though she, unlike those with experience, could be more perfectly adapted to the kind of nursing they would specialise in at the Pavilion. On summer evenings, he took her for walks along the seafront and quizzed her about her motivations for working with the dying. One balmy evening when she had been in Scotland for just over a year, they sat on a low wall, he cross-legged, she with her legs dangling just above the pebbles below. He asked questions about what she was being taught at the hospital.

"Is each death a failure, a disappointment even?"

The question was odd, quite foreign to the routines that were being instilled in her at the General.

Suddenly she laughed. His dipping head and earnest questions reminded her of Mahgawng Kajee and her own failure to pass on a proper Christian understanding of what it meant to die.

Bernard's voice recalled her.

"Can you see that we must make a death the culmination of a meticulous process of care? A process that always remembers that dying is connected to living," said Bernard, "Isn't it? Part of here and now, what we are doing all the time. Don't make it just the end of something."

"It's as much about the people around us, isn't it? The waiting before and the grieving after."

"You're right," he said, jumping up. "We're making space for the grievers. That's what the room with the windows onto the lavender garden will be."

But Ada was still far off in north Burma.

"Shall I tell you a story?" she said, unsure if he was going to hurry away. He sat down again so she went on.

"Out in Burma I visited a house of mourning. The village headman's wife had died. The mission leader took me with him; he said it was 'to plough and sow in the fertile soil of grief'."

"And did you reap a harvest?" Bernard asked.

"We were invited into the dark of the house and offered stools. My colleague had his little gospel translation and was all ready to offer that kind of comfort. But the headman was so eager to talk, even to gabble, so that Andrew didn't get a chance to give a Christian interpretation. He just had to mutter agreement – *Rai sa*

- 'And so it was.' It was the same word we used for 'Amen'. He wasn't very comfortable. He held his handkerchief bunched in front of his nose as though there was a stink. It all smelt as usual so far as I could tell – smoke, forest floor, mustiness of unwashed clothing and you could tell there were pigs underneath the floor."

Bernard chuckled. "Sounds a bit like where I went in the Highlands to try out general practice."

Ada cast her mind back to that morning when she had become aware, perhaps for the first time, that although Andrew Sinclair was her superior and guiding her in her work, she was not entirely willing to trust what he had to teach her. What had she learned, though? Maybe Bernard would understand. She spoke slowly, remembering:

"There was grief, real grief: wailing voices calling out from time to time, 'Why do you leave us?' Women were going to and fro from the room opposite the guest area. After a bit I realised there was the shape of a figure on a raised bed. A girl, a little one who was still too young to wear a turban, carried a dish of steaming rice past them all and set it down beside the bed.

"After we left I was wondering if that could have been the body there on the bed. I asked Andrew and he said he was sure the place would have smelled even worse if it was as she'd died several days ago.

"But I asked my little language teacher, Mahgawng Kajee: The women were saying to the thing on the bed,

'Why did you leave us?' and then they took in a plate of rice, so do they think she's still alive?' And he said, 'No. Of course not.' 'Does she need to eat?' I asked. 'No. Of course not.' He laughed at me. So then I asked him, 'If they don't think she's still there, why do they do it?' And he said, 'She's not there. *They are.*' And that did make perfect sense when he said it."

Bernard seemed to like this: "Ah yes. All those bonds and connections, they still exist, just as much as they always did. Except that you could say they were never anything but smoke."

"Smoke? Not real?"

"Well, we can let them go, we have to let them go. And when we do, our compassion spreads beyond our little circle of kin and companions."

Ada reflected that so many of her close relationships had dissipated like the columns of smoke from the industrial area she could see across the firth. Had it made her more compassionate? There was just her bond with her father – everything that was familiar about it now twisted into an ugly, ragged cord that yanked at her painfully from time to time. She involuntarily screwed up her face, but fortunately Bernard wasn't watching.

He chuckled again. "Beyond humans even. I am at this moment summoning the courage to say to Alison that I am disinclined to eat other animals anymore."

They watched a long-legged wading bird at the water's edge, its bill pointing first one way and then the other as it peered down between its own toes, between the glistening pebbles where, presumably, it hoped to spot a meal.

"We could feel compassion for that bird there," said Ada, "Or we could feel it for the creatures that live between the pebbles. How are you supposed to disentangle where to put your feelings? Shouldn't we care most for what is closest to us? What brushes up against us?"

"That's what meditation practice is for, to let go of your own point of view," said Bernard.

Ada frowned, doubting.

On another occasion when she had a free weekend at the Pavilion, she asked him, "Why *do* you meditate? What difference does it make?"

"It's all right," he said dismissively. "I'm no missionary. You don't have to pray with me to work with me."

Ada felt offended, thinking she must have intruded and did not press him further. But then later in the afternoon, when she'd helped him check through a list of medications, he took up the conversation again.

"I was like you. I went to the East to test my vocation – but as a doctor, not a missionary. I'd trained to please others as much as for my own satisfaction. It was a family thing. Both parents. Alison. My uncle Stanley. But very early on it occurred to me that we cannot truly heal people – all are dying. All we can do is make people suffer less. So then I tried to understand suffering.

People are so reluctant to talk about it. So I travelled. I found suffering sure enough, more than I'd ever seen before – lepers and beggars, all before one's eyes. Maybe they didn't suffer without complaint, I'm sure they did complain, but, out there, those around them have the habit of accepting that suffering is inevitable. And while I was in India, near Chittagong, I found a teacher who introduced me to Buddhism. You asked me why I meditate. I do it to face reality. And then I can help our dear dying guests to face it, too."

"But what words do you use? What do you reflect upon?"

"Oh, it's beyond words. It's so very simple. I pay attention to the flow of my breath. In and out, one breath after another."

That sounded suddenly familiar to Ada. He must have read an understanding in her face because quite suddenly he flashed her a warm and confident smile.

"Are you eating at Alison's tonight?"

"Yes. Then afterwards I'll get the bus back."

It didn't surprise Ada to find Bernard at Alison's table that evening – nor to see the struggle Alison was having with Bernard's refusal to eat roast chicken.

"Turning down God's good gifts!" Alison muttered to Ada in the kitchen, as they carried through the warmed plates and vegetable dishes.

Daniel was washing his hands at the sink. "You should know your own brother by now," he said to Alison. "He's quite sure he knows what's what today but he'll change his mind in a week or two. Or he will if he wants to keep eating at our table."

Ada thought the last sentence would have been perfectly audible to Bernard, and worried that there would be a falling out between the brothers-in-law. Maybe Alison felt the same, as she piled double helpings of vegetables onto Bernard's plate and smothered them with gravy that was deliciously infused with chicken.

When he walked her to the bus stop, Ada remarked, "At the Mission, the Buddhists were always a problem for us – all the *pongyis*, you know, monks and young boys. They were so sure of themselves. They couldn't be converted."

"I'm not so sure of myself. And I'm not a Buddhist. But what makes me uneasy is not the clarity the practice brings to me but the question of what other people *need*. There seems to be an impossible amount of foggy feeling in most people's lives."

Ada gave a dry laugh that disappointed her by its cynicism. *I sound like my mother*, she thought.

That night she lay on her narrow bed in the nurse's home, eyes closed but wide awake, and tried hard to remember her mother in the days before Louise. Was there a time when she had a different laugh? Did they sit together in a garden – was it Aunt Marion's garden? – under a tree that dropped little apples, apples you mustn't eat and tried not to sit on because they were so hard? But they gathered them up and made an A for Ada, A for apple. Gripped by the memory of having been the focus of her mother's loving attention, Ada rolled onto her side and tried to burrow deeper into that afternoon under the tree – the woman in a dress with stripes, yellow stripes, the child beside her... . How she longed to meet that woman now that she herself was no longer a dissatisfied, critical child.

When her next holiday came round, she took a trip to Norfolk to see her father. She thought about writing first but dreaded an angry reply. Better to turn up and surprise him.

When she knocked on the door, he peered through a window but, instead of coming to open the door, he stayed there, staring. Eventually he opened the window a little and said, "I don't know you. Go away and leave me be."

"Father!"

"I'm not your father. Leave me be."

She had a moment of shock when she thought he might be right. He didn't look like her father. His hair formed a wild halo round the top of his head. But the voice, light, with little breath behind it, was utterly familiar. Was he still punishing her for having a baby, or for not keeping the baby? Or had he truly forgotten her?

She realised it was still too soon for her, and possibly too late for him; she could not stay and demand that he recognise that they share a painful past, that she had a story to add to his own, that they could both remember the woman in the yellow-striped dress. She turned and hurried back to the station. Heading back to Edinburgh straight away meant spending a night at a station hotel in York but that was better than staying within reach of people who knew her, when her father didn't.

When the three years and three months at Leith General were over, Ada moved full-time into her room at the Pavilion, a room that projected into a bushy bit of garden from one of the corners of the main quadrangle. She began to take her full share of shifts, bustling through days or, at night, sitting in the glow of a lamp beside a patient drifting further and further away.

She loved the work. Unlike the work of a missionary, which had filled her with doubt and hesitancy, or the work at the General, which had seemed to involve endless routine repetitions of tasks in order to demonstrate obedience, caring for patients at the Pavilion made her feel useful and connected - something like the bank of a river, easing the flow of water round a corner.

Patients died. There was always that anticipation. Ada thought of Jennifer Parry, alongside her young women guests, waiting for births that were only a little more predictable than these endings. There was the same careful observation of bodily changes, the same willing flow of attention from one person to the other – and the same expectation that pain was inevitable. The patients at the Pavilion were often sole members of depleted families, with no one to care for them at home. But sometimes there were relatives. After a death, Ada thought, Bernard could, if he wanted to, estimate the Pavilion's success as a place for beautiful death by the reaction of the relatives.

Cecily was one of the lonely ones. She sat in a pool of pain. Ada could see that if she opened her mouth, or even her eyes, the pain pushed deeper. She rocked, very gently, letting it ripple out from her. She had to wait. It would evaporate as it had before. Ada watched, alert for the brief times when drugs released her but before they carried her off into silent torpor, or sleep, if such a heavy, congealed unconsciousness could be called that. In such interludes, Ada listened to scraps of Cecily's memories. In service. Living and working in the Manse, where cleanliness was very close to godliness. As the weeks went on, her memories crept backwards in time until she was sharing mischief with her sisters – putting a dead sparrow in the teacher's desk drawer, stitching up the sleeves of their brother's shirt. Recounting this episode gave rise to a laugh, a gruff chortle that did not last long - it let the pain back in.

"Oh not again," said Ada in frustration.

She sought out Bernard to see if he could bring forward Cecily's next dose. As the main building got busier, he had taken to using the Folly, a stone summerhouse in the garden, to retreat to. She pushed through the bushes and peeped through the window, hesitant to disturb him. He wasn't there.

In the portico there was a pile of furniture that Bernard had removed when establishing the Folly as an empty cube for meditation. Curious, she pulled at the legs of an upturned sofa and revealed the curved back of a bamboo rocking chair. She hauled at it and stood panting. She tugged again and the chair freed itself and lurched into her arms as she staggered backwards. Her face was momentarily pressed against the woven back. A panting breath of damp rattan took her straight back to her bed in the hut at the crossroads; the bed where she lay with her forehead pressed to the flimsy wall, weeping silent streams of tears. Her arms started to tremble and she lowered the chair.

Bernard came upon her kneeling on the garden path weeping into the seat of the chair.

She recovered herself and together they carried the chair through the archway and back into the main building. Ada bumped gently backwards through the door of Cecily's room bringing the chair with her. Cecily was sleeping and Ada hoped she would wake in sunlight to see the rocking chair in which she would voyage through the pain that came in like the tide.

Ada was aware that Bernard was spending more and more time with her. Was it merely kindness? She knew he was kind. Had he not sought out people to be kind to? The Pavilion was dedicated to a robust tenderness that she knew flowed straight from him. That day when he found her weeping on the path from the Folly, she had seen him press his lips together in a line that said, "I knew this was how it was."

She had needed his kindness, still needed it. He had asked very little about her past but she accepted that he had seen her at her weakest. Gradually, as he spent more time with her, she began to suspect that he was prescribing himself as medicine for her. But it troubled her that she might be developing a dependency. She had started to notice the detail of him - how he placed his long limbs, awkward but always somehow elegant. Like an ash tree in a winter gale.

"We've got Professor Rook coming in today," Dr Marriot told Ada at the start of a shift. Ada could tell that she should have heard of Professor Rook, and Dr Marriot could tell that she hadn't, because he explained.

"He's trained more doctors than most people encounter in a lifetime. He saw Bernard through medical school. Apparently, he was ferociously critical, never satisfied with anyone. Told Bernard he was too clumsy for surgery and too pessimistic for medicine. And he should focus on his career, not go gadding about the world."

"And now he's dying."

"Afraid so. There's no cause for optimism there. I'll see you next week – I'm off for my own bit of gadding."

Ada was working on the other wing but she heard raised voices at several points during the day.

Later she saw Bernard, unusually flustered, leaning against a corridor wall as if flung there. She was about to say something light-hearted and then realised he was beyond that.

"He loves it!" he complained, gesturing towards Professor Rook's door. "He's just indulging in hating the fact that he's dying. What did he expect? Immortality? And the wife. She's doing whatever she can to encourage his rage. What is there for us to do? For God's sake don't let them infect the other rooms. Can we move Mr Traske around the corner?"

But as chance would have it, the Pavilion was busier than it had ever been and there were no empty patient rooms.

It was a long day and Bernard approached Ada at the end of it. The Professor had become sicker but no quieter. "I'm going to have to make a demand on you," Bernard said.

His face was pale, almost luminous. She followed him to a bench in the little garden. He collapsed onto it, spreading his arms across the back of it so that she was left standing, waiting for his demand.

"You could get out of your room, scrub it down and go over to Alison's for a bit couldn't you?"

"Have you asked her? Would she mind?"

"She's on shift tonight. I haven't seen her since – what day is it? I didn't stop all night. Get me a locum! We *have* to find another room. We need to move bloody Mr Traske."

"It's not his fault! Listen, the first thing is, you need some sleep. You're not safe, doctoring in this state. It can't all happen tonight."

Bernard's room was stark, a large almost empty box with white walls, a moulded ceiling and a dark-stained wooden floor. Opposite the door stood a huge carved oak bed that looked as though it belonged in a castle. To one side of the door there was a pair of step-ladders brought in to use as a bookshelf.

Ada hesitated in the doorway. Bernard had turned as if to push past her to go back to work.

"To bed," she said, nudging him. "Lie down."

He sat on the bed and tipped over sideways. She unlaced his shoes and pulled them off. He drew his knees up and got his legs under the blankets before she could have any thoughts of helping him with his trousers.

"I can't sleep," he said. "I don't know what to do. It's not enough to face reality. It's not enough to help people rise above suffering. They don't want to. They want to keep it by them. Clinging on. Bloody Rook. Shouting and screaming as if he can turn round and go the other way if he makes enough fuss."

She went to the door, which was still ajar.

"Ada! Don't go!"

She pushed the door shut, flicked the light switch up and felt her way to the bed.

"I only know one way to do this," she said. She kicked off her shoes and lay down beside him. "Roll over. Now breathe. You breathe and I'll breathe."

At some point in the night she tugged the top blanket over herself and they both turned round. Ada was aware of a great sense of peace. She had not breathed peacefully alongside someone since Louise. With Frank their closeness had never been peaceful – more an agitated yearning for peace.

In the morning Bernard was himself again. He had slipped out of bed before she woke and when she opened her eyes, he was sitting cross-legged on the floor, eyelids dropped, brows lifted. She watched his motionless face and remembered the warmth of him. His skin seemed to have a translucent layer, in which the freckles floated, beneath which the solidity of him began.

She sat up and his eyes snapped open. "I think you can count that as a night shift," he said.

"But I slept so well!" In fact she felt a little embarrassed, conscious of having taken advantage of him.

A few days later he came up behind her as she stood scrubbing instruments before sterilising them.

"I watched you sleeping," he murmured.

So the night of gentle breathing had created an intimacy between them.

Before the end of a week, Professor Rook died, much sooner than expected. Moira, his wife, was offered time at his side, a cup of tea, a place to sit and weep but she merely gathered her things, tied her headscarf and hurried away. Ada saw her leaving by the door to the street, looking from side to side for a convenient bus.

A favourite with the Pavilion staff was Brother Cedric. He arrived in the cab of a small battered lorry and a sack of potatoes was unloaded alongside him. He and the two men with him wore faded blue tunics with big pockets on the front and trousers underneath. The rope tied around their waists made it clear that they were from an order of monks. Brother Alan, the driver, explained it was a brotherhood established at the end of the previous century by one Thomas Carder; their daily routine was divided between gardening and "sitting beneath the Cross".

Cedric was the most patient of patients, weak and sometimes racked by coughing, but able to enjoy some food and, it seemed, the company of nurses whenever he could persuade them to sit with him. They joked about making sure they had quiet shoes so they could sneak past his door and get their work done.

Bernard, too, was persuaded to spend time with him and was often sitting there beside him when the day nurses left for the night.

One morning Brother Cedric reached for Ada's hand. "What do you think about dying? What happens?

Where do we go? Can you give me hope of a shining heaven?"

"Isn't that your job?" she asked.

"But you tell me, what do you hope for, for us, as you watch by our sides?"

She carried the question with her and the next time she stood beside him with the blood pressure gauge she gave him the answer that had been running through her mind.

"It feels like watching someone obeying a rather difficult instruction. It fills me with respect. As if they ... you ... are trudging along the difficult last mile or so because you have to. But then, the ones who fight and struggle, I respect that, too."

"We are going where we're going," said Cedric. "But we can take a backward glance, can't we?"

"People have to worry about those they leave behind. They must do."

Ada had watched Bernard's uneasiness with the fighters like Professor Rook. But she herself wanted to be comfortable with them. What was anything worth if you didn't fight to hold on to it?

Talking to Cedric made Ada think again of her mother. All her life, that terrible fiery end was ahead of her. The only way past it was to slip through that invisible crack that opened just for her. Was that the only way she could be properly herself – to die the death that lay before her?

This troubled Ada because alongside her mother had been Louise, helplessly swept away in the current of her mother's despair.

Some days later, Ada was rolling Cedric's skinny body, changing the sheet under him. As she finished, he settled back on the pillows. His dry lips were clinging together as he pulled them apart to whisper an answer to his own question.

"... find the rest of ourselves, the whole of ourselves."

Ada strained to hear: "A bubble on water, it bursts. What sweetness."

Unsurprisingly, he died serenely in his sleep, and really did seem to have a smile on his face.

The lorry came back with a coffin – rather big for Cedric's shrivelled body, Ada thought – and carried him back to the community in the Borders so he could be buried with his Brothers. Bernard went with him and stayed away for several days.

Later that week Bernard summoned the staff to a meeting.

"This war we're about to have - the General Board has sent me my instructions. We entirely lose our independence. We've got to take the patients that are sent to us. Just normal convalescents. Two to a room if necessary. And then we're to be ready for wartime contingencies as they occur. Which includes finishing off the shelter of course."

It didn't suit Bernard. He seemed to lose his sense of purpose. He began to spend time away from the Pavilion, visiting the monks of Cedric's community. Ada felt it was his way of putting his hands over his ears, denying that the war was happening. War was declared during one of his absences. As part of the general sinking of hearts, Alison and Ada grumbled together but Ada was struck by Alison's lack of energy and uncharacteristic absence of interest in food. Eventually she admitted to being unwell – tired and off her food. "It's 'The Change,'" she murmured to Ada. "Just got to grin and bear it."

A week later, Ada watched her in her kitchen pulling herself upright after putting a pan in a low cupboard.

"Are you sure it's 'The Change'? You're ... do you think you could be ...?"

"Pregnant?" said Alison, shrilly. "Just fat. Surely just fat!" She began to giggle. "It's never, ever happened in all these years! Now?"

"Have we got a midwife's horn somewhere," asked Ada. "I only ever used a borrowed one – didn't think I'd have much call for one here."

"I have a nice wooden one somewhere," said Alison. "It's on the top of the bookshelf there."

Daniel was startled to find the two of them on the living room floor, Ada transfixed by what she could hear through the polished wooden instrument pressed to Alison's belly.

A few days later, Bernard returned. He spent a day in his office, catching up, he said, and late that afternoon invited Ada, rather abruptly, she thought, for a walk. Beach-side strolls were no longer possible so they headed for Rosefield Park and sat on a wall with a flat sun-warmed coping. Bernard stood again, arched his back and then shuddered his arms and shoulders.

"Too much bending over the accounts?" said Ada.

"Definitely too much desk work."

He stretched again. "Can I lean on you? Swing round and give me your back."

She turned her back and almost toppled as his bony shoulder-blades made contact. But once they settled, it was comfortable, to be receiving both the September sunshine and the radiating warmth of another body.

"That's my grumble. What's the matter with you? You're not rejoicing at Alison's happy news?"

It was good to be out of his line of sight even though she already knew he was a friend she could safely talk to.

"When you first met me, remember, on the ship – you know I was expecting a baby then? I had a baby. A girl."

"I guessed there was something like that. When you turned up here, in such a state. What happened to her? Did she die?"

"Oh, she's well and happy, I dare say. I hope so. I had to give her away. Oh, God, I hope she's safe – now, with the war. But the awful thing is, now I no longer know why it was so obvious to me at the time that I had to give her away."

She felt him tip his head back to look at the sky so that the vibration of his next words was transmitted through his skull to hers. "I've got a feeling you might have done it for strong and generous reasons."

She held her breath, like an animal suddenly aware of being watched.

"You think so?" she said, dubiously. "I had a burden of guilt. I simply did not deserve..."

"Everybody says that, all the ones who come to us still carrying a horrible little parcel of guilt."

"You can't just dismiss it. I can't dismiss it or I couldn't then. I had deceived myself and others. A pregnancy, if you think about it, it's like a vocation. A special conversation going on, demanding your attention, demanding your submission to it. But promising a future. And I was no longer ready for that. I had been hunting for a future, pretending I was called away from my family. And in the end, I was empty. Not like Maud, or Lydia, my colleagues. I didn't have a gift of faith to give away. I was all questions and no answers. So then, when I realised I was pregnant with Frank's child, I didn't feel I could be relied upon."

She could feel tiny movements of Bernard's shoulder-blades and wondered if they meant anything. Was he fidgeting impatiently? Wishing she would stop talking?

"So why is it," he said, "that you are so very good, so very reliable, at being with the dying?"

"Reliable? It's not so difficult. I'm just being a nurse. We have duties. I fulfil them. I don't see what's so special about that."

A small tufty dog ran up and cocked a leg against the wall. The dust resisted the liquid for a moment and it stayed like a pool of gold while the dog bustled off.

Then he said, "Do you ever think you might marry again?"

And she thought, but didn't say, *Well, perhaps I might.* Instead she said, "The war. What's going to happen? Do you think you'll be called away?"

Alison struggled through the pregnancy. She stopped work almost immediately. Her long body arced and her slender ankles swelled and finally she was sent to a maternity home to lie down for the last six weeks. The child was a girl, a disappointment for Daniel for about ten minutes, until he became besotted with her. He only had two weeks to get to know his daughter before he was called up for military service.

With Alison preoccupied with baby Bridie and the staff greatly reduced, those who remained often gathered to eat their meals in the Pavilion kitchen, once the patients' trays had been taken round. While they avoided, when they could, conversation about the progress of the war, the sense of great disturbing movements going on beyond their walls gave a feeling of being the remnant crew of a ship making a voyage of unknown length. Bernard would sometimes grumble that the place had become like a hotel, which provoked Alison to berate him for getting professionally slack.

"You should employ a matron," she said. "Everybody needs to be kept up to the mark. This place doesn't smell right, do you notice that?"

"Perhaps a bar or two of carbolic would please you more than a matron," was Bernard's response.

Alison recovered her strength almost immediately and didn't ask for help with the baby. The other nurses queued up for cuddles with her. Ada hung back until she recognised that Alison somehow knew better than to push the baby towards her.

As it turned out, any additional demands made by the war were within the capacity of other local hospitals, but the Pavilion staff had to become accustomed to the expectation that nobody would die in their care. They looked at each other and laughed about it.

Dr Marriot had been sent, almost as soon as the war started, to France. Once Dr Carrick was seconded to a military hospital, Bernard was the only remaining doctor at the Pavilion.

On an autumn morning Bernard took a telephone call in his office. Ada was sleeping after a night shift but when she emerged at lunchtime Bernard took her by the elbow and steered her to the office.

"Sit down," he said. "This is something you won't want to hear. They called from St James's hospital in King's Lynn."

"My father," she said.

"Your father. He has been depressed, refusing food for some time. And when they were practicing an evacuation procedure he escaped. He was missing for most of the day but then was seen stepping into the river – is it a big, fast river? They have recovered his body. I am sorry, Ada, to bring you this news. They said he was terribly perturbed by the war, by the sounds of planes and bombs. But above all, he was refusing any help, any food."

"It's an estuary," muttered Ada, "Tearing out to sea."

After more telephone calls, Ada learned that her father would be refused a Christian funeral because he died by his own hand. She had to make a grim trip to Norfolk to hear the hospital chaplain intoning a brief prayer at the edge of the borough cemetery in the area used for suicides. Susan Sands joined her but was so angry that the man who provided respectful endings for so many was treated with such disdain that she could barely speak. For Ada there was some relief that it was at least an ending.

After her return to Scotland it turned out that Alison's warning about sloppy standards was prescient. In the winter of 1942 a gastric infection took hold, swept from one end of the Pavilion to the other and then back again, so that the nursing staff spent hours scrubbing and sterilising. Extra nurses were brought in, and in addition a band of rather young cleaners who were obliged to listen to a lecture on germ theory before Bernard released them into the corridors with their buckets and mops.

As that winter's snow diminished to a few crusty patches, Ada took a hasty walk in the garden before dusk, looking to see if the bulbs planted in the earth that had had to be disturbed when the sunken garden was converted to a bomb shelter, were showing. Work had become drudgery, the war seemed interminable and she was desperate for a sign of spring. Alison no longer had time for friendly cups of tea – or was it that she herself was a little afraid of the powerful magnetism baby Bridie exerted? Even Bernard was no longer the bubbling pot of ideas and enthusiasms that he had been, and barely mustered the energy required for running his hospital.

She peered at the dark earth, still frozen into coarse crumbs. There, shouldering the earth aside, were two green stems, one tall and one short. The tall one was just beginning to show a swelling where the bud would be. She drew a deep breath. *It can't be stopped, this promise. There will be spring, and then there will be another spring. And eventually one spring will be my last but the hope it brings comes fresh again and again.*

She turned for the door to the main building, then changed her mind and headed for the gate to Alison's garden. She rattled the doorknocker, heard Alison's voice singing out, "Come in!"

"It's only me," she said, opening the living room door. "How are you both?"

Alison was reassembling her blouse, with Bridie on her lap. "She's had hers and now it's time for mine. I'll put the kettle on."

With the baby in her arms she hesitated, looked from the cradle to Ada then passed the baby over. "Say a nice hello to your Auntie Ada," she said as she went out to the kitchen.

Bridie's dark eyes fixed Ada in a stare; a curious hand reached erratically towards her face.

The last baby I held like this, she thought, was Louise, and I was only six. Of course she had held babies in Burma so that Maud could stick needles into them. But this was different. Bridie's gaze, dense, intense, seemed to be absorbing knowledge of her, accepting her as different from all the looming presences around her.

The door from the hall opened, Bernard appeared in the room and banged the door behind him. The baby jumped and her face crumpled.

"You didn't have to do that," she said. "We were ... being quiet together."

"Ah," he said. "You've got her."

Alison heard the child fretting and came back into the room to take her.

"You could bring the tray," she said to Bernard. "Get another cup down."

When Alison took Bridie upstairs to be changed, Bernard asked Ada, "What's happened? You've barely looked at my niece up till now. I know you had your reasons. But today you couldn't stop staring at her."

Ada felt herself blushing.

"She was telling me something ... something that matters. It's as if ... she's like the snowdrops I saw earlier, swelling and pushing and making promises. But calling for a response."

Bernard pulled his head back quizzically.

"So what does she say to you with her mysterious cloudy eyes?"

"Something like, 'I'll be me if you'll be you – whoever you are'."

"And that fills you with hope?"

"It does."

"There you are, full of painful feeling – loss and sadness. And guilt. And you turn it into hope. And all the while this war is rumbling on, turning half the world into enemies ..."

He sighed and his eyelids slid slowly closed. This gave Ada no warning of the next thing he was to say.

"Ada, I think we should get married."

"Do you? Can you say why?"

"Something to do with snowdrops. We both need a new project. We need hope."

Ada couldn't help smiling. She thought he was right, if unromantically impersonal.

He wasn't looking at her. But she was fairly certain that this was not an intellectual exercise for him.

He frowned in a pained way: "So do you agree?"

"I do."

"Can you say why?"

"Because here we are bumping along beside each other, getting closer and closer, and it could get really awkward if we don't. And I care for you, and if I don't marry you, who will? And it will be good for you."

She was almost certain about that last sentence.

So in April Bernard and Ada got married in the boxy church, with its domed and pillared porch, where Ada had been attending services. Alison was delighted but incredulous right up to the day itself.

Over the subsequent weeks, Ada watched Bernard rather clumsily making the switch from kind and trusty colleague to husband. He seemed to enjoy their physical closeness in a startled sort of way, but it began to seem to Ada as if there was a price to pay, a sacrifice he was making. In bed, she was charmed to discover that he could be quite light-hearted. He had a one-sided grin that she had not seen on any other occasion. But when he reached orgasm he would sob, his ribs heaving, and afterwards he turned away and retreated inwards as if he was stricken by grief.

When they realised she was pregnant, he was fascinated, as if she was a pattern in the clouds, or a particularly special vegetable. As her pregnancy progressed she herself marvelled that her body should do this again. She loved to see Bernard's interest in the miracle and smiled when he placed the chilly disc of his stethoscope and listened, every evening, to the hurrying heartbeat. The child was born into the arms of his aunt, amid the flickering shadows of a power cut. Afterwards Ada's eyes overflowed with streams of joy and sorrow and she was glad of the gentle darkness.

Bernard delighted in the baby's first few months, not even minding night-time crying. But, to Ada's astonishment, when Rufus began to meet his eye, to smile beguilingly, to expect things from him, he began to withdraw. At first she couldn't believe what she was seeing, though she couldn't help enjoying that it was always her arms the child fell asleep in. But after a time it dawned on her that this baby, not himself, was the remedy Bernard had arranged for her. Whereas what she had planned for him was something he appeared, after all, to be proof against – being gently tapped into place like a well-made joint of woodwork by the daily knocks of loving interaction.

The war ended and they were back on track again with patients travelling gently through their last days. Daniel Russell returned, more or less in good health. Alison spread a table with good things and invited Ada, Bernard and baby Rufus to join them, but part way through the meal, Daniel retreated to the kitchen from where they could hear him gasping and sobbing. He sat on the floor, his stockinged feet, which were the only part of him visible from the other room, twisting and clenching. Bernard and Ada crept away, leaving Alison to join him on the floor and Bridie to solemnly watch from the doorway.

Ada marvelled daily at her child and the fact that he looked for her, leant on her, loved her. He opened vistas of the life that never happened, where another child snuggled close, held her hand and, proudly, in the course of time, could have walked away.

When they first married, Ada and Bernard shared a flat created around what had been Bernard's bedroom, the "music room", where the great carved bed stood under a ceiling with a frieze of plaster trumpets and viols. By the time Rufus was a year old, Bernard had retreated to what had been Ada's room.

Ada was aware that soon enough Rufus would discover that most children do not live in a hospital where people come to die; most of them live with both their parents, have fathers who hold their hands, reprimand them, ask them questions. Bernard was friendly enough, still loving, but ever more remote. He had begun to take more and more frequent trips to visit Brother Cedric's community. They lived, so far as Ada could tell, in separate huts beside a walled garden at the bottom of a wooded valley and mostly ate what they could grow. His long, pale fingers sometimes had dirt under the nails when he returned. He now had little time to discuss the management of the Pavilion.

Ada had begun to think it was time to take Rufus away. She tried to imagine another life. She was qualified, she could work almost anywhere. But she was a mother. Not many hospitals would be as accepting of a nurse with a child as the Pavilion. She hesitated.

But on a day in the third summer after the ending of the war, on opening the door to the music room she saw a letter on the floor, half hidden by the door curtain. Edith's handwriting. Edith had seldom written. When she opened it, the letter was puzzling. Frank's mother, Edith said, was ill and needed someone to help her. Possibly Ada may feel able to go. She gave an address in Devon, which carried echoes of Frank's voice making plans for their trip "home". Having assisted Dr Grover until his retirement, and stood in as his replacement for a while, Edith was still at Meredith Hall, at the centre of a web of connections to the Scripture Pathway Missionary Society and all who were associated with it, including, apparently, the aged mothers of former missionaries. Should I let myself be summoned, Ada wondered. Called to a duty that has been very long neglected.

She didn't immediately tell Bernard about the letter. Then, while she was still waiting for the moment to do so, he summoned all the Pavilion staff and the chair of the Board to a meeting. He was putting it up for sale, he told them. They would take no more new patients. "I have done what I can of this work," he said. "Others must take it on."

He was met by astonishment. Would it even remain a hospital?

"It will sell quite easily as holiday accommodation or a comfortable rest home," Bernard assured them. Ada saw the white line around Alison's lips and expected an outburst, expected that Alison would stay behind after the others had filed out in order to berate her brother. But she did not. She strode away, speechless.

In the doorway, Ada turned and countered Bernard's announcement.

"We're leaving, Rufus and I. We're going south. To Devon."

"Oh, good," he said, then heard himself and added, with a puzzled frown, "That'll probably work out, won't it? If it's what you want?"

She let his question hang, then ran down the corridor behind Alison, and tried to put an arm round her shoulders.

Alison was too angry for that. "Did he consult with you about this? Did you let him make this mad decision?"

"Goodness, no. He doesn't consult, does he."

"What is he doing? To abandon his dream just as it's getting right again after the War."

"I think he'll go to live with the Brothers over near Hathaway, where he's been visiting. The place has a powerful pull on him. I've been trying to understand. It's because it liberates compassion like no other discipline he has known. That's what he says."

"Is he leaving you? This I cannot believe. His dream, his child, his wife ... He must be ill. Liberating compassion indeed!"

"He has kept his distance for some time. I think – you must know this - he is someone not really suited to family ties."

Alison had started to cry, clenching her fists, picking up and pressing down her feet. But Ada needed to run and fetch Rufus from the kitchen before the cook would need to hurry the suppers along.

And now, less than two weeks later, the train starts to carry them past the flurries of blossom and foxgloves that grow beside the line. Rufus is wriggling excitedly and pointing to everything he can see.

"Look, Mumma, a cat! Who knocked that shed down, Mumma, that broken shed?" And, as the train takes the first big bend, "Is that our train I can see, making all that smoke?"

13

March 1948

Nancy

On a day that had begun with a promise of spring but has now become threatening, with grey clouds and a snatching wind, Nancy and Annie are returning from a walk to get eggs. There's a notice flapping on a board propped up outside the village hall, an ancient building with arched windows and doors. Men are stacking furniture or large wooden boxes under the part of the roof, supported by wrinkled oak posts, that extends beyond the front wall. Nancy walks closer so she can read that there is a gathering of the Beekeepers' Association. She sees that the boxes are various versions of the hives that stand crookedly in the meadow behind Moorside house.

"Can I come to the meeting?"

The two men and a woman who are standing outside the door look at each other.

"We need young blood," says the woman. "Do you have any bees on the go now?"

"There are some in the field behind the house."

"What, some hives? Have you been feeding them?"

"You have to feed them? No, I haven't."

"There's not much chance they'll have made it through the winter then."

"But we saw bees, didn't we, Annie, that sunny day, the day before yesterday, they were going in and out."

She had sat on a boulder that protruded from the bank while Dennis and Annie stooped over the little marshy patch under the elder trees looking for tadpoles.

"You wanted some pets," she had said to Dennis, nodding at the rickety hive and the bees coming and going over the sill. "It looks as though we've got some."

Now she asks, "Don't they feed themselves, fetching pollen or whatever?"

"Not much of that about just now, is there? But if there's life in your hives, seems to me you need to come in here and find out how to look after them."

She goes home with an extra jar in her basket. She shows it to Dennis when he gets home.

"What do you think that is?"

He holds the unlabelled jar up to the light. It is quite a vivid green and a little cloudy.

"That," he says confidently, "is honey from the wartime. We've got lots in the back of the larder, down on the floor. Auntie Ivy was giving it to Mrs Mann because it doesn't taste any different. It's just from the bee ration sugar. And we don't mind it being green, me and Annie."

Annie licks her lips.

A month later Nancy attends another meeting, this time getting a lift down the road in the back of Mr French's pick-up with a bundle under her arm of hat, overalls and gauntlets, all taken from the cottage. The spring is advancing and Nancy knows she needs to open the hive and see what state it is in. She watches closely as the host beekeeper, Ken Brown, lifts out the frames one at a time. She is the baby of the group and he makes sure she sees the queen and understands the significance of the waxen structures. She found a dusty green book on the mantle-shelf of the cottage and, reading round the tunnels made by book-worms, she has gained some idea of how a colony survives and reproduces. When it's time to reassemble the hive Ken Brown nods at her.

"Are you man enough, maidy, to get that super back on top?"

He keeps puffing smoke at them but the bees are becoming impatient and panicky, swirling back and forth above the frames.

"Don't keep them waiting. Do it as gentle as you can."

She bends to lift the box and immediately feels the buzzing life inside. There is a bee tangled in her veil and she arches her neck to keep it off her face. Now she has to line up the heavy box with the one below. There are bees everywhere and she doesn't think she can put it down without crushing some.

"Just don't kill my queen," says Ken Brown. "Don't matter about the rest."

She staggers forward and sets the super in place with just a little bump and at the precise moment she does so feels a piercing pain on the back of her wrist. She rips the gauntlet off and they all laugh at her.

"That won't be the last!" says Sandra Mallett. "What do you think? Are you going to pack it in now if that's the price of honey?"

Ken is gathering up his equipment. "You'll want to nip that sting out," he says. "Michael, here, you know what you're doing."

A young man not dressed up in protective clothing has come into the orchard. He takes Nancy's wrist and pinches her skin to squeeze the sting out.

She sucks air through her teeth as the pain burns across the back of her hand.

"Just the one? You've got off lightly! Tea's in the kitchen," he addresses everybody.

They troop back to the house.

"So who's going to help this young lady check her hives this week?"

"I've got my own to do," says Sandra. "Eight colonies."

"I'll be on the tractor all week," says one of the men, and "I'm minding my back just at present," says another.

"All right, I'll do it," says Ken, shaking his head.

That evening when Nancy goes up for Esme's supper tray she sits down in the chair by the window.

"Will it be all right," she says, "If I start to do the bees for you? I've been learning how to do it, going to the club. We've got the hives and everything."

Esme's face looks very calm and she doesn't say anything. Then Nancy sees that a tear is running down beside her nose and she is rummaging under her pillow for a handkerchief.

"I thought ... I'm sorry."

"You could make me very happy," says Esme. "We've always had bees here. Even when we were far away the bees were out amongst the gorse and the heather and the wild roses, working as hard as they could for us. And the boys, they loved everything with honey. We never had to stint them. It's how they knew they'd been naughty – no honey for tea. You keep at it, my dear.

"There's a book somewhere about. I read it when I first came here, even before the boys were born. It tells you how the bee colony works and what's happening through the seasons. And it says the queen of the hive is like the mother of a happy family, or the other way round. I liked that – the mother at the centre."

Still clutching the handkerchief, she smoothes the counterpane over her knees.

Nancy takes the tray from the side table. "Do you want the radio for a bit?"

"Not now. You go on down. I'm sure you've got plenty to do. Lord only knows what it's like downstairs now."

Ken Brown had promised to help Nancy check her hive but, as it turns out, it is Michael who skids to a halt on a bicycle, bangs on the back door and starts to step into his white overalls.

When they've finished their inspection he leaves his instructions, like a doctor.

"So you keep feeding them, make up a syrup at least once a week, until there are more flowers around. And then you need to inspect again in a couple of weeks' time. We need to see what's happening with your queen. I'll come again if you like."

"Oh would you? I don't feel very confident yet."

"I could try to mark your queen if you like – put a little blob of white on her. But you've got to learn to spot her for yourself. And the other thing is, you've got the makings of four or five hives there. You need at least another colony. You could catch a swarm, maybe, or I'll get Dad to split a colony off for you."

The weather is improving and once Dennis has set off for school in the mornings and the breakfast dishes are tidied away, Nancy gets into the habit of slipping out to the little meadow, which her grandmother has told her is called the Lea, to watch the bees at work. Annie follows her. As the bees lift from the sill of the hive they quickly disappear against the dark woodland. Sharp-eyed Annie spots returners when they are no more than glistening dots, and points at them with a wavering finger till they find their way home.

Looking after the bees makes Nancy feel that, if she can just bring a harvest of honey at the end of the season, she could win her grandmother's confidence. The rest of the time she feels she is less than satisfactory as a housekeeper and carer. Her grandmother asks pointed questions about what she is planning to cook, which polish she is using for which furniture and whether she is quite sure the pantry shelves are free of weevils and silverfish, so that she has to tell herself that this is a woman who, for much of her life, was accustomed to a house full of native servants. But then, from time to time, she tells her to for goodness sake to leave the housework and keep her company for just a few minutes.

So then she helps the old lady into the big armchair and sits on the edge of the bed and listens to her deep voice.

"I forget what they looked like," she says. "When they were young. I had those photographs downstairs, all tidy and looking at the camera. Not what they were really like, of course. I can better remember the smell of them. Running in from outdoors, with the scent of grass and moss and bark and a bit of mud. Or when they were tiny, all that Johnson's baby powder and what not. Like some kind of special privilege, being a mother and having that silky head against your cheek."

When she goes downstairs Nancy checks again the photograph fixed just to one side of the sitting room chimneybreast. Two boys aged about six and four, with rounded cheeks and their chins dropped a little as they obediently gaze at the camera. Both are solemn but the older one has a more direct stare than the younger. His hair shows the trace of a damp brush, but with that familiar square hairline. It's what she sees when she's washed her own hair.

When Nancy goes up with the following day's tray of lunch, her grandmother says to her, "You know this coming Sunday is Mothering Sunday?"

Nancy has not been paying close attention to the calendar so she is taken by surprise.

"Every moment feels like forever, doesn't it?" says Esme "Wherever we are in the story we feel this is it, this is the moment that matters. Or we carelessly look forward to the next stage and forget that we have to give this in exchange, this precious moment, to be whisked away forever.

"Sit down, why don't you? You can help me with the condiments."

Nancy's own plate of egg salad is sitting on the kitchen table exposed to flies but she sits.

"I thought being a mother was everything. But they grew up, my boys. Each term's school reports dragged them away further and further into manhood. I got better and better at letting them go, enjoying the space, the chance to set the pattern of my own days again, not having to make arrangements with Nanny or Ayah or anybody else.

"Then it gets so that you have to recognise them as men. They walk into the room and there is someone rather unpredictable, maybe not even particularly friendly half the time. Effectively a stranger."

She sits forward almost as though she's confessing a secret.

"I began to realise it with Frank when he would insist on keeping up a friendship with such an unlikely boy from school. His father and I both hoped he would give up on it but he kept going over to Taunton for weekends in the summer. They seemed so oddly matched at first. Quite candidly, we began to fear there could be something unhealthy about it. But some years later Frank told me - this boy had a terrible guilt. He had, he believed, caused the death of a little sister, a fall from a window, I think. And Frank, at sixteen, once this terrible secret had been confided, felt that he was the only one able to understand and forgive; he had an obligation. Only he could protect the boy from the other boys and above all from himself. And that was why every conversation I had with him about why he owed it to us, his family, to stay with us, to meet our guests, would end with him insisting. Because somehow the other responsibility was greater.

"It was the same for Gregory. When his call-up papers had come and he came back from the first training camp before going off to France, he was completely content, I thought, that others now had his loyalty. It's obvious really. But it startles you as a mother.

"I knew all along that I wanted them out in the world; of course I did. Oddly, I thought Greg would be the missionary and Frank the soldier. Well, they both did their bit of soldiering, but that was all Greg did, all he had the chance of. It was Frank who had the opportunity to carry on and take the message into dark places. Dark and, as it turned out, dangerous in their own way. I didn't expect that. He'd survived the war. He was my gift to God and so well able to look after himself. Not clumsy like Gregory, nor argumentative. Where Greg would have been a stubborn stalwart, resisting the ingrained ways and terrible habits of people brought up believing in witchcraft and evil spirits, Frank was more subtle. He'd get people to agree with him before they understood what he was saying. They'd want to follow his example, repeat what he said, sing the hymns he sang with that lovely voice, and before they knew it, they'd be leading a life as good as his.

"I wanted them to do something worthy, my fine boys. Was I prepared to sacrifice them? I suppose I was, in a horrible way."

She sits back against the cushions again as though she's completed a piece of work.

When Easter approaches and Nancy brings a palm cross from church to tuck into her grandmother's Bible, she is taken aback to be asked, "Are you a proper Christian? Were you brought up going to church?"

There's always an awkwardness in their conversations because neither of them knows how to address the other. Nancy never dares to claim the relationship with her grandmother in case she uses the wrong word. She knows there's a lot of snobbery in the distinction between Nan and Grandmama and all the possibilities in between. She suspects that the old lady, who no doubt approved of the name she knows was on her birth certificate, doesn't like her replacement name and thinks of her as Frances but refuses to say it out loud. It makes their interactions seem brusque. Now Nancy is additionally a little defensive.

"We went to church. Sometimes my mother liked to go to the cathedral for the music. We went quite regularly really."

Nancy knows this sounds non-committal and sure enough, her grandmother huffs through her nose as though she has confirmed a suspicion.

"Not tempted to go to the mission field, then? You've not inherited that particular calling?"

"No ..."

"Don't worry, I don't expect it of you. It's not for everybody, I'm well aware of that. About a year before Frank died he met up with a colleague before travelling back out to Burma and they both came here for a few days before going up to Liverpool for the boat. Ian something. A nice enough young man, but insipid, I thought. How does *he* get them to choose Christianity, I asked myself, because it seemed to me he'd hardly decided himself. But Frank liked him and told me he was reliable and a sound enough Bible scholar. We got into such a discussion after dinner one night. All about whether the Gospel gives us one message or several. Whether it is up to us to search our way through to an interpretation or whether we take the vital blocks of it one by one and build it into the house we need. Something like that. This Ian was too vague to be effective, I thought, too much inclined to let them weave their own ideas into it, too little inclined to sort what was essentially heathen from what was sound.

"And then, as it turned out, God took Frank and left Ian to carry on with his work. Why would he do that?

"And so I gave my sons away, two sacrifices, one for the nation and one for God's good work. What have I gained in return? They weren't mine to give, were they? Off they went, as children do, growing apart. Beautiful. Even quite good. I trust they are rewarded. But I cannot expect a reward, not for what they have done."

Somehow, she has been taking mouthfuls of egg salad all the time she was talking. When she falls silent Nancy gazes at the empty plate, wondering what she is expected to say.

Day by day, Nancy watches Annie, marvelling at how you could tell what is passing through her mind even while she says nothing. Her face softens and firms up, opens and closes, flickers like the wind. Her eyes lift regularly, as if to check that she is understood.

She has had a sad and confusing little life, thinks Nancy, but seems grateful for every look, smile or plateful of food.

Nancy's relationship with her parents was affectionate but did not involve much touching. Mummy would kiss her cheekbone, the left one, Dadda her forehead, but only ever at moments of formal departure or arrival. Mummy used to pat her hand in praise or comfort, or perhaps gently straighten some item of clothing.

Annie creeps up at every opportunity, snuggling against her if she sits on a sofa, leaning on the arm of her chair. Nancy is often surprised to find a small hand in hers if she happens not to be using it.

She wonders if the child is anxious. By denying herself speech, Annie has made herself unable to complain. But, oddly, it seems to bring her closer to other people, even strangers.

When Dennis is there she becomes his shadow. This is only a problem when Dennis has a friend to play with. Nancy has heard him trying to get rid of her: "You really need to change that jumper, Annie. Look, it's got egg on it." Or once, in desperation, "Annie, you should be doing some jobs now – go and sweep the stairs this minute". By the time Annie has wandered back into the house to find the hand brush and heavy metal dustpan, the boys have disappeared into some shrubbery. Nancy, preparing a meal in the kitchen, summons Annie and gives her the peeler and a bowl of carrots.

Nancy thinks of the situations when she herself has failed to find the words she wanted and wishes she could have remained silent instead. But she knows that a child of almost six should, normally, be speaking and she wonders what should be done about it. She has a vague understanding from something Dennis said that the infant teacher at the school had last year suggested that they wait before sending her. That cannot go on indefinitely. The summer term is about to finish and there should surely be a plan for September.

Nancy goes to see Mr Tranter, the headteacher of the village school, and persuades him that it is time for Annie to start. She will be shy. She won't talk. But she is capable of learning and it is time she started. She hears the assertiveness in her own voice and recognises it comes from Mummy. To her surprise, Mr Tranter consents at once. Annie should join the infants for a few days before the summer holiday and be ready to start properly in September.

Soon after this, when Dennis has just returned from school and is upstairs changing his jumper, Nancy answers the door. Annie is behind her as usual, peering round the newel post. As soon as the heavy door is pulled open, Nancy hears Annie scuttling up the stairs and then, from the landing, a suppressed version of Dennis's high protesting voice. It seems that the children know who this is.

"Sylvia Morris," says the solid-looking woman on the doorstep, sticking out her hand. "WVS. It's about the children."

Nancy frowns. "What about them?"

"Obviously they should've gone back months ago but there was a hitch. Now they've got this scheme for sending the orphaned ones out to Australia. But they're not doing it from here. You have to get them back to London. So if I just leave the forms here, we'll get their journey all fixed up from Exeter to London, and then they get joined on to a convoy, if we can call it that. And they start lovely new lives in the sunshine!"

She peers into the dark of the hall.

"You are managing all right, aren't you? I haven't seen Mrs Mann for a bit. And the old lady? I understand she's really not very well now."

Who's been gossiping, Nancy wonders? The doctor came two weeks ago. Or could it have been the headteacher?

"We're managing just fine. I'm here. I look after everything. I'm used to looking after people. And I'm doing the bees for her," says Nancy, as if adding a few hundred more living creatures to her responsibilities makes it better.

It puts Sylvia Morris off her stride. "The bees. Of course, there've always been bees here." She nods at the lichen-covered board shaped like a bee skep that hangs by the gate. "Well, I'll leave those papers with you and call back in a few days."

She turns back.

"It'll be a wonderful life for them, you know. A young country, full of opportunities. And it's not as if they have anyone to stay for."

There were two sets of forms for completion and two copies of the "Instructions for Guardians". Nancy tucks the papers behind the big turkey plate on the kitchen dresser.

The following Saturday Nancy encounters Carol Ormes, a motherly woman from the bee club, at the baker's van.

"Is the little girl deaf and dumb, then?" she asks.

Annie is only a few feet away, hanging off the top bar of a gate and pedalling with her feet to find the bottom one.

"Why do you ask?"

"Mrs Morris was saying." She's nodding wisely. "They might not take them in Australia if they're defective. They'll take the boy for sure. He's quite a bright spark, isn't he? I heard him read the lesson at the carol service. It is an amazing opportunity for someone like him. A young country."

"Well, they don't have to go, do they," says Nancy lamely, taking her large white loaf in one hand and Annie's bony little fingers in the other.

Nancy has no idea how these things work. She feels as though she, the child who was never properly adopted, is going to have to do battle with the same authorities for whom she herself never properly existed.

When the children are brushing their teeth in the bathroom she stares hard at Australia on the globe on the bookshelf in their room. It's a nasty slatey colour, almost too dark to let her read the names of the cities. Of which there are few. Sunshine and oranges, Mrs Morris had said. And opportunities for Dennis.

"He'll be all right anywhere," she says to herself and jumps as she finds Annie has crept close and is smiling grotesquely up at her to show her shining teeth.

They sit in a row on the sofa, Annie with her knees drawn up and leaning her bony back against Nancy, waiting for Dennis to open the book he has chosen.

"What do you remember of your life in London?" Nancy asks.

"Just the park, really," says Dennis, a bit cautiously. "And going to the shops. The greengrocer, with rhubarb and apples, and her dropping onions. I can remember picking up onions and potatoes when she dropped them. My mum I mean. She sometimes dropped them, I think." He frowns.

"Our house. There was a bushy bit of garden at the front where I could stand and look in at the window. It was the living room. I had a fire engine with very good wheels that I wanted to keep on the windowsill. But I wasn't supposed to. It had to go in the box with the toys."

She can see his mind wandering round the familiar room and suddenly, clearly, knows it is going to hurt.

"Tell me about the park," she says quickly.

"It had good bushes. You could hide. That's what I liked. And there was a roundabout you could spin. Do you remember the roundabout, Annie? It made a noise, like a howl, when you got it going."

"I remember one of those," says Nancy. "I played on one of those. But what I really liked was the swing. That made your hair fly. If you spun the roundabout to make your hair fly it made you dreadfully dizzy."

"*My* hair didn't fly," says Dennis and his statement of the obvious saves them. She wants to hug him, but that might bring the tears they have so narrowly avoided.

"Read to us," says Nancy and Dennis pulls their book from behind a cushion. They listen to a chapter of *Brendan Chase*, read very correctly but without any suggestion of emotion, just as Nancy has heard him reading the newspaper to Mrs Mann. Annie sits very still, watching Dennis's jaw moving, but letting one warm hand relax and mould itself round Nancy's forearm.

When they have trailed off upstairs to bed, Nancy flops until she's horizontal, pulling a cushion over her head. She puts her shod feet on the arm of the sofa. She longs to hear Mummy's voice objecting.

The next morning when Nancy knocks on her grandmother's door there is no answer. She finds her twisted on the bed, her face distorted and mouth working.

The doctor listens through his stethoscope for long minutes, pressing the old lady's shoulder against the pillow with one hand to keep her still while he frowns and holds his own breath. Eventually he says that there is something wrong with the activity of her heart and she's "casting clots towards the brain". It will happen again, and next time will be worse, and then there will be a final time. There's nothing to be done. He's very brisk. Does he know she's her granddaughter and not just a hired companion?

He says, "You're going to need some help. You'll be nursing full time until she goes. Are those children still here?"

Nancy sighs. "I've done it before," she says.

But the doctor's words set off a trembling inside her. Once again she's waiting for an ending. Everything will change. And if she is cast adrift, what will happen to the children?

She has come across an old wooden writing case on one of the bookshelves and inside it is a stack of pages of headed writing paper, yellowed at the edges but still crisp. That evening she takes a few sheets, puts the date and starts a letter to the only person she can think of who is likely to help her.

14

March 1948

Ivy

Ivy has spent time sitting in Stephen's shop while he
attends auctions. He has replaced the electric kettle
and trained her in the use of the receipt book. She has
never done this kind of work and worries about how
to describe some of the goods in the shop so he pulls
out a sheaf of paper supposedly listing that month's
stock. There are so many crossings out and additions
that she thinks she will do better making up her own
descriptions in her even, loopy handwriting. There are
not many customers. Stephen has a side-line in mending
clocks and watches, but only if they are of what he calls
everyday value. There's a locked cabinet where she is to
put the watches for repair. The key lives in a separately
locked drawer, along with any takings.

Across the shop from the counter a grandfather
clock ticks gently. Above the dial there's a mournful,
staring moon face peeping out from behind a globe.
She had thought the tick would be annoying after an
hour or so, but she finds it neutrally companionable
in the otherwise silent building. The case is of figured
mahogany and she imagines she can see more shadowy

faces beneath the gleaming surface that conscientious maids have no doubt polished every week of its previous existence.

On the end of the short counter sits a glass-sided cabinet full of small, precious items – jewellery mostly. A ruby ring, or perhaps it's garnet, with the setting formed into tiny leaves that grow out of twining stems, and another, probably a man's ring, with a flattish green stone set deeply into a heavy gold band. How strange it would be to have a place for such things in one's life – flashy, foolishly expensive, unwearable on most occasions.

There's a cupboard full of polishes, chamois leathers and waxes in the storeroom and most items have been buffed up to gleam and entice. But she starts to play a game, seeking out the signs of use and wear. A stain almost lost in the inlay of an occasional table. Little scratches where a key has been clumsily searching for the lock of a writing box. The very slight flare round the axle of the handsome wooden duck on painted yellow wheels that stands on a low shelf just above the bald shoulder of the velvet dog that had gazed into her face when the bolt of electricity laid her down beside it.

Stephen returns from his expeditions with cardboard boxes and wooden crates full of items for the shop. He brings them in to the back room, one at a time, and they go through them. He gives her a clipboard and she records the details as he tells them to her. The final column is "condition", and she lists the marks of use or misfortune that make the items imperfect. She leaves blank the column for "Value". Stephen goes through afterwards and estimates a value, which she comes to realise he will ignore when it comes to a sale.

They are still there by the back window, going through a stack of plates, when Ivy says, "I must go. I'm late for dinner."

"All right," says Stephen, taking the clipboard from her. Then, "You don't have to live there, you know. If you're working for me you could live in the flat upstairs. It's been empty for a while but it's not too bad."

"I'd better hurry now," says Ivy, bustling into her coat.

The next time she arrives at the shop, Stephen flips the sign on the door to Closed and leads her through to the back of the storeroom. A cream-painted door stands open, revealing a staircase.

"Go on," he says. "Have a look."

At the top of the stairs there's a long room that goes through from back to front of the building, with a wide, slightly bowed window over the street. A tiled hearth is half hidden behind stacks of books and maps. To one side there's a kitchen with a slit of a window from which you can look down and see the copper kettle on its bracket above the shop door, then a dark little bathroom lit only by a mossy skylight, and at the back a long narrow bedroom with a plump armchair by the window that overlooks the cobbled yard at the back.

Her voice won't come out. "What's the rent?"

"I'll pay you your hours and as long as you're working for me, you can stay here."

She gazes out of the window. He steps round in front of her, tilting his head and frowning.

"That sounds a bit like slavery, doesn't it? It's not that you have to work for me of course, that's up to you. It's better all-round if someone's here keeping an eye and keeping it warm and I just thought ..."

"It's a very kind thought," says Ivy. "When ..."

"Today! As soon as you like."

Margaret does not seem impressed that Ivy is choosing to live "in a junk shop", but she looks out some old sheets and pillows and insists that Richard gets the car out to help her move.

Sometimes, when the shop is closed, Ivy chooses to sit at the back window, reading one of the books that she has now distributed two or three deep along all the shelves in the sitting room. She looks up to see gulls perching on the neighbouring roofs and washing blowing in the yard next door. At other times she sits at the front and watches people toiling up the street with their various burdens.

She's reading a rust-coloured book about travels in Alaska when there's a rap on the stairs door.

"Hullo!" calls Stephen. She goes down and finds him with a tall wooden box in his arms.

"This is for you," he says. His mouth is a little pursed as though he is suppressing laughter. Fleetingly she is reminded of her brother, Alan, doing one of his teases.

"You'll like it," he assures her. "You're the only person I know who would have a use for it."

She takes the box and puts it on the workshop table. There's a lot of corrugated cardboard packed with crumpled newspaper, more cardboard rolled into a cylinder stuffed with shavings and inside is a tall brown earthenware pot with a lid. It doesn't look sufficiently special to need so much careful packing. She reaches to lift it out and snatches her hand back.

"It's all right," he says. "Just a bit cold."

"I thought for a moment it was hot," she says. She opens the pot and sees that it is packed full of snow.

"Snow! Where did you get snow?"

"At Harding Hall where they were doing the auction. They have an ice-house. My friend works there as a chef when they need one. He also gave me this."

He shakes a rustling brown paper package out of a canvas bag, unrolls it and reveals the stiff, stretched body of a hare with cloudy blue-brown eyes.

"Oh!" says Ivy. "Poor thing!"

"I was thinking," says Stephen, "of doing a proper job of cooking it the way he told me. But I'll need that." He nods at the jar of snow.

"Snow?"

"Not the snow, that is your present. The jar."

He starts reciting a recipe. "Tomorrow. It'll be ready tomorrow."

He's single-minded, thinks Ivy, and feels reassured because of it. He pursues things with a strange determination that cannot be diverted by the usual things like embarrassment; eccentric projects that he sees the value of for the time being. Such as befriending her.

By the next evening, the hare has been skinned and quartered, marinated in the jar overnight and has filled the flat with its rich, meaty scent as the jar stood in a pan of simmering water. The snow, tipped into an antique tureen at the start of the process, has lost its luminosity, slumped and become water, filling the flash plus a bottle for spare, and the flash now stands in the middle of the round table with a five-branched brass candelabra beside it.

Ivy finds herself hosting a candlelit dinner for two, a meal eaten off unmatching but very beautiful plates with heavy silver cutlery. The remainder of the bottle of wine with which the hare was cooked glitters in a pair of crystal glasses.

A car passes in the wet street below. They sit down and raise their glasses silently. It's a moment of conspiracy. Suddenly Ivy stops worrying that she must make conversation. Stephen eats enthusiastically, greedily even. Ivy hears, very far away, her mother's voice criticising such manners. Returning to the present, she wants to laugh. She lifts her glass again. She has very seldom had wine, apart from sips of communion wine. "Let's drink to the hare," she says. "Poor old hare."

Then she leans forward and says, "You don't have to be nice to me, you know."

His brow crumples. She has confused him. He shifts to the edge of his chair. The movement causes his forelock to fall forward again making his expression suddenly blank. But he stands up abruptly and says, "I'll make us a nice cup of tea." So she knows he is thinking about the kettle and what it did to her.

The next day is Sunday. The shop stays closed. She doesn't know what Stephen does on Sundays, but he won't come to the shop. She sits at the front window with Ada's letter in her hand. She might read it again.

Later that afternoon she goes downstairs and into the dimness of the shop. The telephone is on a shelf behind the counter.

Dennis answers, as she had trained him to, "Middlecombe 334. Who's speaking?"

"Dennis? It's ..."

"Auntie Ivy? It's you, isn't it?" He makes it sound as though she may be playing tricks on him.

"It is me. Dennis, are you all right?" Suddenly, before he speaks, she knows he is not. She knows his face is stiffening, she suspects tears may be gathering in his lashes.

"Um," he says. "Um. Mrs Mann has ..."

"What's happened, Dennis? Who's there with you?"

"Nancy is here. We're all right," he says firmly, "Except that Mrs Mann is going to die. The doctor says."

"I'm coming back," says Ivy. "She'll need some help. I'm coming back."

"That's right," says Dennis and hangs up.

15

May 1948

Ada

Ada has one case for the pair of them and Rufus is carrying a bulging beach bag that is a little too heavy for him so that he swings it from side to side and it causes him to stumble each time it passes in front of his knees. Walking behind him in his neatly buckled raincoat, under the echoing station canopy, Ada sees him as she seldom does, as an independent person, facing the world, forming the first sketchy framework of his adult self. She's startled into taking a gasp of the acrid air. "Rufus, wait! Don't bustle! I can't keep up!" He turns and waits and lifts his big green eyes. Her own eyes fill with tears so that she has to laugh and pretend to be short of breath. Then they walk more slowly side by side, and a stream of travellers parts to overtake them.

A woman in a light grey coat has stopped in front of them and is rummaging in her handbag. Something about the stance with legs firmly planted and the involvement of her whole upper body in the little action of feeling for a ticket in a handbag makes Ada look again. And then she sees the suitcase on the platform beside her and knows it as part of the furniture in the place that was her home for nearly a year.

"Ivy!"

The woman turns and freezes. Her stiff hair still frames her face as if she's facing a gale. She has an envelope in her hand, which she shoves back into her bag. But in the instant before she does so, Ada is sure, with a twist in her chest, that she recognises her own handwriting.

"Ada!" There's none of the heartiness Ada remembers. "Is this ...?" Ivy looks questioningly at Rufus.

"My son, yes. Rufus, say how do you do to Miss Smith."

Rufus unwinds the rope handle of the bag he's carrying and pokes forward a crumpled hand. Ivy tucks her bag under her arm and takes the hand.

"How very nice to meet you," she says, distractedly.

Rufus contracts his brows.

"I knew your mother many years ago. We had some adventures together. Now where are you heading?"

"I'm going to look up Frank's mother. I heard she is not well, may need some help," she says.

"How remarkable!" Ivy fixes Ada with what feels like a calculating stare. "Well, I expect you'll need to stay for a while, since she's ill. Do you know how to get there?"

"Well, no. Not yet."

"It's best to take a car. It's a bit of a distance but if you go by bus you'd have to change and there'd be a wait and you wouldn't get there until after this one's bedtime."

"I don't want to trouble her, of course. I know she's elderly and she probably won't want a child visiting."

"You'll get a surprise there, then," says Ivy softly. "You know I travelled home with Frank. I took care of him at the end. And then I stayed on. Poor Esme is blind, had just become so when we arrived, so I stayed to care for her. She's been less and less able to manage stairs and get about."

Ada's reawakened guilt gets in the way of wondering why, in that case, Ivy has been able to leave and who has been filling the gap.

"I'm just heading back to Bournemouth," says Ivy, "But maybe we'll meet again while you're in this part of the country."

Before long, Ada starts wishing they had attempted the complicated bus journey. Forty minutes after they set off, Rufus moans and leans back limply. Ada calls to the driver to stop and drags the child across her lap just in time to get his head out of the door before the spasm of vomiting. They have to stop twice more before they get to Middlecombe. The driver tries giving him one of an old pair of galoshes to hold in case he doesn't have time to open the door but he gags at the smell of the rubber and Ada tucks it away under the seat.

"Dreadful weak stomach," grumbles the driver.

"He's hardly ever been in a car," says Ada. "We had no need, living in Edinburgh".

She feels quite queasy herself. After the first stop the driver does slow down and takes the bends particularly steadily but when they have stopped three times it seems as though he just wants to get the journey over and the car scurries between the mossy walls and arching branches like a beetle in undergrowth.

Ada, too, wants the journey to end but she is bracing herself. She will have to explain herself to Frank's mother.

"This is Middlecombe. Where do you want?" says the driver, slowing down. There's a fork in the road, with a grassy triangle in the crux and a row of cottages on the right.

Just before the junction there's a cluster of adults and children, all shouting and pointing at something in a young rowan tree in the hedge. The car stops because a small girl is walking backwards into the road, peering and pointing with both forefingers at a brown blob, shaped a little like a horse's head, that seems to be moulded round the branches of the tree at about eye level.

"Annie!" someone shouts.

Ada winds down her window.

A boy carrying a large basket runs round behind the little girl and nudges her onto the verge again. "We're catching this swarm, Annie, so you've got to be sensible. We're going to put it in one of the hives. We just needed another colony. You watch. Nancy's going to get it."

A young woman is pulling on baggy white overalls and a wide-brimmed hat with a veil.

As well as the girl with the overalls and the children there are three adults who are all giving advice. A much older man is shaking out a sheet and one of the women is checking the cuffs on Nancy's suit and knotting the tape that holds the veil in place. A motorcycle and sidecar appears from the direction of the village and skids to a halt.

It is no longer possible for the car to move forwards so Ada and Rufus get out. The driver seems to take this as an indication that the journey has ended. Before Ada realises what he is doing, he takes the cases from the boot and dumps them on the verge. She had paid him when they agreed the price because he insisted he needed to fill up with petrol, so there is nothing to stop him reversing across the road and driving off the way they had come.

The young man with the motorcycle jumps off, pulling off his goggles.

"Just what you want!" he calls out to the girl in the veil. "We'll have them in no time. And shortly before dusk like this, they should settle lovely. You don't need to worry about all that gear. They're sweet as can be when they're swarming."

He spreads the sheet at the foot of the tree, takes the basket from the boy and holds it up to the girl in overalls, now striving for a foothold in the roots of the hedge.

"Look, maidy, you hold this. Up as close as you can get it."

With bare hands and forearms he reaches up and starts scooping handfuls of bees down into the basket. Although some of them get separated from the clump and start flying, most of them seem to have a sort of stickiness and a tendency to cling together, like cake mixture falling from a spoon, Ada thinks.

The young man keeps scooping and brushing the bees off the branches with increasing satisfaction, as though he's just tidying up the last scraps of something spilt. The bees in the basket show no inclination to fly away.

"Why don't they escape?" asks the eager boy, daring to step closer.

"They don't want to," says Nancy. "The queen is down in the middle of the basket there."

"Did you spot her?" the young man asks.

"No, but I think I can tell by the way they're all settling. "

"You're getting the hang of this," he says. "See how they're fanning at the edge here, like they do outside the hive. We'll just give them a little while for the stragglers to work out what's what, then we'll put the sheet round and take them up to Moorside to your meadow. Did you get a hive ready like I said?"

"We did. We did!" says the boy. "There were all the pieces in the cottage. We were just waiting for this!"

Annie is standing close to the boy who is clearly her brother and seems to share his emotions. She does a little skip.

Ada watches the young woman, Nancy. Her face is nothing but shadows under the brim of her hat.

Ada turns abruptly to a woman in a headscarf standing watching the final stages of the capture.

"Can you tell me, is it far to Moorside House?"

"Just a short step. You can follow the young people there."

She nods at Nancy and the young man, evidently called Michael, as they bundle the sheet round the basket, turn and stride away.

Rufus has been clinging to Ada's arm and staring with huge eyes at the bustle around them. The crowd is now melting away, the two children following Nancy and Michael with the bundle of bees and the rest going in the direction of the terrace of cottages a little further up the road.

The motorcycle remains where it had skidded to a halt, alongside Ada's pile of luggage.

Ada heaves Rufus's beach bag onto one shoulder and grabs a case in each hand.

"Come on, chick, we're getting left behind."

There's a squeaking from behind them and the woman with the headscarf is pushing a huge wooden barrow towards them. She lets forth a great yell:

"Dennis! Come and help the lady!"

The boy comes running back.

"What should I do?"

"Aren't these your guests up at Moorside?"

Dennis looks blank.

"Are you coming to our house? To see Mrs Mann?"

"Yes, to see Mrs Mann." Ada puts the bags in the barrow and before she can pre-empt it, the boy seizes the handles and sets off surprisingly fast.

"Young man can bring that back in the morning, can't he," says the head-scarfed woman.

"Thank you Mrs Carrow," says Dennis, stopping to look back.

He sees Rufus, limp, dragging on Ada's hand, and says, "Put him on top. I can manage."

Ada adds Rufus to the pile of luggage but grasps the handles of the barrow herself. It wobbles as she gets it moving. Annie holds the side of the barrow. Ada cannot tell if she's trying to help or be helped. For safety, she heaves her up beside Rufus who pulls away a little and stares at her curiously. Once the barrow is tilted, it trundles readily enough and the procession follows the bundle of bees slowly along the road into the village. There's a pub with a mounting block outside and opposite it a stretch of green shaded with horse chestnut trees. Behind it is the churchyard wall and the tall tower of the church.

The beekeepers turn down a side road. The barrow tugs at Ada's arms on the slope and then Dennis stops in front of it and indicates a gate in a mossy wall in front of the house that extends down a lane from the corner, a house that is built somewhat higher and longer than the other houses on the road, and has a stretch of orchard to keep it apart.

"Do the gate, Annie," says Dennis. She threads her hand between the slats and flips the hook, then pushes open the front door, which is not locked. Dennis gets his shoulders under the handles of the barrow and lets the luggage and the two children slide gently onto the slabs of the hall floor.

"What's going on?" The young woman has come through the back way. Her hair is awry because she has tugged off the hat and veil. She's staring at the newcomers and now first Dennis, and then Annie, line up beside her. Rufus pulls a bit of Ada's skirt around himself.

"I wonder if I can help you with the invalid," says Ada. "I'm a nurse."

Nancy frowns at the top of Rufus's head, which is the only visible part of him.

"I am, or I was, Mrs Mann's daughter-in-law. I owe her something. I want to help if I can."

Without saying anything, Nancy pounds up the stairs and along the landing.

Ada turns to Annie and asks, "Do you think we could find a glass of milk for Rufus here? He's terribly thirsty."

Dennis takes over. "He's too little for a glass. He can have a cup."

He leads the way into the kitchen and tweaks a beaded cover off a milk jug.

She goes to the foot of the stairs and listens. Rufus follows with the cup at his lips.

A robust grey-haired woman is preceding Nancy along the landing, speaking with a strong Devon accent.

"So long as you got your swarm, that's the main thing. She's been very quiet, nothing to worry about. I must get along and make some tea now. But don't be afraid to ask if you need a hand, either with her or with the children. Oh, you've got company."

Left face to face with Ada, Nancy looks her up and down. "You say you're a nurse? Have you come to stay?" Ada can see her considering and rejecting a number of questions. "Since there are two of you, you'll have to stay in the cottage," says Nancy. "It's not been used for a while. I'll find some sheets."

By systematic questioning, Dennis establishes that Ada is "a friend of the family" and that she has been sent to help by the missionary society. They stay in the cottage for two nights but it is soon plain that it is an inconvenient arrangement. Once Rufus has gone to bed, Ada has to stay there and cannot help with Esme. On the third evening, Ada is sitting on Annie's bed reading a bedtime story to Rufus and Annie when Dennis suddenly reveals that there is a spare room, left empty since Ivy's departure. Why don't they use that?

Nancy looks sheepish when Dennis suggests it. "I wasn't sure if she was coming back ... but you could use it for now, of course."

16

June 1948

Esme

She hesitates to sleep. If she lets herself sink into unconsciousness, will she wake? She remains in bed all the time now. Only silence in the house tells her that it is night. Now that she no longer moves around the house, no longer moves around the room, she has ceased to feel the space between herself and the objects she may once have bumped into. She feels her attention gliding from one element of her surroundings to another, mapping out a space that includes her own heartbeat (now that she cannot trust it, she keeps an ear attuned to it); she feels her knee against the bedclothes, hears a bird creating an intermittent tinnitus in the holly bush a few feet away beyond the window, is aware that the window is open to a cool, caressing breath, recognises that the hay harvest is progressing a few fields away. Amongst these mental objects, she encounters the hope that soon someone will come, and by doing so, assure her that some, at least, of these sensations are shared. And wafting through them all is memory, disguising, obscuring, diverting and, she knows, confusing her.

This new woman that comes in the night and sits without fidgeting, listening to me breathing. Her own breath moves steadily, quietly. I know she's not asleep.

Sometimes it's the granddaughter that sits here while I sleep, or fail to sleep. Not often. Is she afraid? I suppose someone must be ready to get up for those children. Are they still here? I'm sure I hear their voices still. Unless I'm remembering.

She, the girl Frances, is all I leave behind – all Frank left. Will she, I wonder, bear children? Children with their thick hair square round their brows. Children to lick teaspoons of honey from the Moorside hives.

17

June 1948

Ada

Ada sits in the tapestry chair in Esme's room, listening to the dawn chorus. The birds begin to sketch a landscape emerging from darkness - a hesitant cheep making a mark here, a more prolonged whistle sketching a line a little further away, some more short little scratches and then a whole tangle of fluent lines. To me, Ada thinks, it seems like a celebration of the relief the morning brings, the joy of being alongside all that there is, as it reappears; but I don't think they can be doing it for fun. Each must be testing its place in the world, risking its own voice, reassured by the sound of others.

Ada stands, pulls the curtain open a little, then leans over the still figure on the bed studying a fold of the just visible white sheet for movement. She is still breathing.

There's a creak of boards along the landing. Nancy has woken and is coming to change places. They move quietly, but Esme stirs. She has come through the night, then.

Nancy's eagerness to be useful reminds Ada of a trainee they had at the Pavilion. She is an earnest but unconfident sick nurse, running through the repertoire of things you can do more often than she needs to.

"Water?" Nancy reaches for the cup.

"Uh-eh," murmurs Esme. Two syllables. But she turns aside from the little porcelain invalid cup of water.

Two syllables again. Nancy guesses.

"Honey? Wait just a little and I'll bring some."

Ada rolls the patient and tugs to straighten the sheet beneath her. She opens the curtains fully to a sky that is suddenly piercingly golden beyond the hill. She wonders if anything of this glory breaks through Esme's blindness. Nancy has left the room but returns noisily, purposefully, with a jar of honey and a spoon.

Ada is about to say something but is transfixed by the sight of the determined young woman, hovering over the bed with the gleaming jar and a silver spoon, like a painting, a moment from a legend, a story in which the bond between the two figures is suddenly revealed.

When Nancy holds the teaspoon to Esme's lips there's no reaction at first. She is about to take the spoon away and then it is apparent that Esme's nostrils are flaring. She is sniffing it, drawing in the flower scents, the waxy warmth of it.

Then the dry lips part and Esme's mouth opens with the tongue protruding a little as if to receive a communion wafer. Nancy lowers the spoon and Esme gulps suddenly. Startled, Nancy pulls back the spoon. But they can see that the active half of Esme's face is relaxing. Is that a smile?

"Is it good?" Nancy asks.

But as they watch the pale face in the golden light they see the cheeks sucked in, the jaw jerking, the colour darkening and realise that Esme is failing to breathe. Nancy turns to Ada and yelps, "Help me!"

Ada lifts Esme up from the pillows for a moment, but lays her back down. They both know then that she is not going to draw another breath.

Ada fingers her neck and wrist, then takes Nancy's hand.

"That's it," she says. "She's gone."

"It was me." Nancy is panicking. "I choked her."

"Don't blame yourself" says Ada. "If it wasn't to be today, it would have been tomorrow."

"It was my fault. She asked for honey and I gave it to her. A spoonful. She couldn't take it. You know how it catches you sometimes."

Nancy perches on the edge of a stool, whispering agitatedly, as if Esme could be disturbed. Ada steps closer, leans against her, takes courage and holds the twisting head against her own body, breathing steadily, rocking slightly.

When the undertaker comes he asks them many questions including whether Esme is to be buried in a shroud or in her own clothes. This question clearly throws Nancy into a panic. She feels she ought to know. She doesn't even know which clothes her grandmother liked or could get into at the end.

"I don't know. I don't know. There's her dressing gown, but it is rather worn and not even quite clean. I don't know what she'd want." She has to take something to the undertaker's this very afternoon and starts rummaging in drawers and banging cupboard doors.

Ada tries to calm her. She offers to accompany her. They can take clothes, they can look at the shrouds, and then come to a decision. But if they both go, they need someone to mind the children. Ken Brown's wife has asked several times if there is any way she can help, so Nancy could just run down to the farm and make the arrangement before they catch the afternoon bus.

When they wait on the green for the bus, Ada is conscious that it's almost the first time they have been alone together, the first time Nancy has accepted her help for herself rather than on behalf of others. They sit beside each other on the bus. Nancy stares out of the window. Ada tries not to stare at Nancy's hands clutching the handle of her handbag.

The undertaker offers them a leather-bound album with photographs of shrouds to flick through. At the first glance Nancy suppresses an exclamation and Ada swiftly suggests they might be left for a few moments to choose.

Nancy promptly turns her back on the book. "They're awful! We buried Mummy in her best suit. That's much more dignified."

"It's difficult if she hasn't worn clothes for a long time. You don't know that anything fits. So it could be better just to have one of these fancy nightdresses."

Nancy frowns, then abruptly changes her mind. "All right then. Let's make it good and fancy. And expensive." She giggles. "Look, all these little rosettes. And what do you call that frill around the neck? And some real silk."

The details of their order are painstakingly written down and they make their way back to the bus.

"We're back!" Nancy calls.

Mrs Brown comes through from the kitchen. "I've got the big kettle on for you. I thought you'd be needing tea. And I made a bit of toast and sardines for young Rufus."

"For Rufus? But where are the others?"

"Well Mrs Morris came for them. She said it was a bit earlier than she'd said to you, but she needed to catch up with the others and be ready for a very early start tomorrow so she's taken them to Exeter tonight to stay in the church rooms. She helped them finish getting their things together and they left."

At the sight of Nancy's face, Mrs Brown starts to sound less confident.

"She said it would probably be easier, in the long run, not to make a fuss about saying goodbye. They've not known you so long and you've got the funeral and everything ..."

"They're not going! They're not going anywhere! I'm going to adopt them. They have to be with me."

She runs out of the open front door. The road is empty. She turns, leans her head on the door, thumps it, kicks it.

Rufus comes through from the kitchen and stares at this thrashing, moaning grown-up.

They are all staring. Nancy flees through the house and out of the back door.

"So that's what she was thinking." Ada subsides onto a chair. "She said something about adoption. I asked her why she was talking to the lawyer when he came yesterday. I thought she was thinking about the past."

"She's kicked the bees!" Rufus has followed Nancy at a safe distance and now comes running in. "They're all over the place!"

The gate to the Lea is open and Ada follows the trail through the grass to the clearing round the hives. The top part of one of the hives is on its side on the grass with bees seething over and above it. Nancy is standing doubled over like someone with a stitch, muttering and weeping.

"Go back in, Rufus, you'll get stung. Come here, child." Rufus and Nancy both stare, checking that it's Nancy she's addressing.

Nancy swats at Ada's extended arm. "Child! That's it. I need to be older. Two years. They've got to give me time."

There are at least two bees crawling up Nancy's sleeve and more in her hair, but she is not flinching.

Ada is thinking fast. "Listen. *I* can do it. We'll get them back and I'll adopt them. If that's what you want, what they want. We'll live on something. I can get a nursing job."

"Would you do that? But they've gone."

"I'll go after them. Who's got a car?"

"Mrs Brown will know."

But when they return to the house, Mrs Brown has gone. Nancy bares her teeth, in rage, Ada thinks until she sees that she has been stung on the jaw and on the collarbone.

Ada grabs her handbag. "I'm going to need cash. Is there cash in the house?"

Nancy pulls a sheaf of notes from the housekeeping tin.

"Go. Get on, go."

"But where am I going? Exeter's a big place. Where will she take them? Which church rooms?"

She sees Nancy covering her face and slumping against the wall.

"I'll find out. Don't worry. I'll find them."

She hurries out of the front door just as Michael Brown's motorcycle pulls up by the gate. His mother climbs with unexpected agility out of the sidecar.

"In you get," she waves Ada into her place. "I'll keep an eye on them here. It'll be St Edmund's. Sylvia Morris is always going there for WVS business with the vicar's wife. Go there first."

"I'll pull the top over," says Michael, looking fierce behind his goggles. "We're going fast."

He waits while she lowers herself onto the leather seat, convinced that she will find herself sitting on the road with her knees round her ears. He pulls off a gauntlet and fixes the canopy round the windscreen. Nancy has emerged from the front door.

"I hear your hive has gone over," shouts Michael over the engine noise. "You'll be able to sort that yourself. They won't be very pleased with you!"

They're off. Ada feels a clatter of gravel against the floor of the sidecar.

The vibration, noise and motion is relentless and battering. The only steady thing in her vision is Michael's corduroyed leg by her right ear, glimpsed through one of the three little windows on that side. The windscreen in front of her is spattered with insect corpses. She worries that she didn't even say goodbye to Rufus or tell him where she was going. She feels an inner tug, as she always does when parted from him. He'll cope, she tells herself. And she realises that, in a cavity somewhere around the same part of herself, she is filling up with joy. And then, as if a plug has been pulled out, with fear. Suppose the children have been put on a train already. To London? Will she ever find them there? Nancy won't forgive her if she fails.

They swing round a bend, brake suddenly and she feels the wheel beside her losing its grip. Michael takes the machine up onto the verge, tipping her against the side of her little cabin. She thinks she hears him shouting an apology, whether to her or to the other driver she's not sure.

It starts to rain and with relief she gives up trying to see through the smudged and steamed up windows. She draws her knees back from the occasional splatters that come round the edge of the canopy. It is such a ridiculous situation to be in and she is so helpless that she starts to laugh. She should be reflecting seriously on the step she is about to take but she cannot. She laughs.

She knows they have reached the city. The red glare of a traffic light fills the sidecar. And then Michael is releasing the canopy, shaking a trickle of water into her lap. She unfolds herself and stands before a large maroon-painted door.

"The church rooms," says Michael, stepping back. "I'll be out here when you're ready." He pulls out a tin from his pocket and starts to roll a cigarette.

The door gives when she turns the handle and she steps inside. The same pot of paint has been used for the walls. It's a tunnel into a kidney, she thinks. She pushes open the next door onto a hall painted a gloomy yellow. There's a heap of equipment in the middle of the floor – kit bags, camp beds, possibly even tents. At the far end is a huddle of women and children. Ada can't see Dennis or Annie and she doesn't know Mrs Morris by sight.

"Now you each need a bed," instructs one of the women. "That's one of these with the thin poles. Can you each get yourself a bed from the pile there?"

"Excuse me," says Ada.

"Mumma!" exclaims a child's voice. It's not Rufus. Rufus isn't here. She turns and sees Dennis and Annie emerging from a side door. The woman with them looks exasperated and is practically pushing them with the hand that is not holding a clipboard.

"This little madam won't say a thing," she grumbles for her colleague to hear.

Dennis is staring at his sister. "But she did," he says, with a big grin on his face. "She just said something!"

He comes over to Ada. "Did you come for us? Can we go home now?"

He holds her hand, something she doesn't think he usually does, even with grown-ups he knows better, and grips Annie with the other. There's consternation among the women.

"You can't just take them. They're on the list."

"I would say *you* can't just take them," Ada says. "You don't seem to realise, I'm adopting them. I've spoken to the lawyer. We just need a bit of time for the process to go through."

She hopes that this will not be a moment when Dennis's pedantry results in awkward contradictions. She decides to put him off his stride by putting her arm around his shoulder and pulling Annie into a hug.

"Do you want to be Rufus's sister?" she whispers. "And Nancy's?"

Annie nods and giggles.

"Really and truly?" whispers Dennis. "And me, too? Brother, not sister I mean."

The woman with the clipboard is flipping through her sheaf of papers. "Didn't you get all the paperwork signed?" She addresses her colleague.

"It wasn't at all clear who should do it," says the other woman. "There didn't seem to be anybody with the requisite authority."

"We're straightening all that out now," says Ada firmly. "I really need to get them home now. It's been an upsetting day. We're getting ready for a funeral as I think some of you know."

They pack themselves into the sidecar. Dennis squeezes sideways into a space behind the seat that Ada had assumed was for a small piece of luggage. Annie crouches between Ada's knees. Michael has rolled up the canopy as the rain has stopped. "If I put that over you'll not have anything to breathe," he says. "Long as you don't jump out like the sheep try to."

Dennis whoops as they set off, rumbling over cobbles. As they leave the city behind he suddenly taps Ada on the shoulder and shouts, "We've not got our bags!"

"Too bad!" shouts Ada. "Mrs Morris can bring them."

"Have you really spoken to the lawyer?"

"Not about you two. But I will. If you want me to."

The words blow away but, as they slow down into the bends, Ada can hear a raucous sound that must be Dennis singing.

It's not until they are half way through the day before the funeral that Dennis suddenly says to Nancy, "Did she tell you we need to have a fire?"

338

"No. What do you mean?"

"She made us sort her papers, Mr Trench and me. And some of them say 'Burn'."

He stands in the bedroom doorway and points to a chest.

"In there. All those bundles."

There are stacks of manila folders with the word 'BURN' written in crayon in Dennis's handwriting on the front of each.

Nancy flips up the cover of the top folder.

"No," says Dennis sternly. "It's just papers from Josiah's work – that's Mr Mann. You're not to read it."

He ventures into the room, avoiding looking at the empty bed, picks up a stack of folders and sets off downstairs with them.

"You can bring some more," he says. "I'm going to make a bonfire."

There's a cobbled area beyond the woodshed and before the gate to the Lea where Dennis gathers a pile of hedge-trimmings, the bits of an old ladder and the parts of a hive that was consumed by woodworm. He tucks sheaves of paper in amongst them. But when he runs into the kitchen for matches, Nancy stops him.

"Wait. Let's do it when it's getting dark. Let's make a beautiful fire and sit out there and watch the sparks."

Annie's eyes widen and her face settles into a grin.

So Dennis scuttles around the outbuildings collecting dry wood, and then logs and stools and buckets, and anything else that could be sat on and places them in a circle around the heap.

Ada has walked to the church with an armful of asters and, as she leaves the churchyard, she passes a man who is, without doubt, staring at her.

"It's you!" he says, "Ada Henry!" He thrusts out a hand and as she grasps it she recognises Ian Pavey. The soft mousey hair has mostly melted away and what's left is silvered. His gaze seems more direct than she remembers, but the appealingly apologetic way he gathers his upper lip after speaking is still the same.

He waves an arm towards the church.

"Last time I was here I walked up to church on the Sunday morning with Frank and his mother. It was our last day before the ship.

"She didn't think much of me, I fear, though you have to forgive her making unfavourable comparisons with her fine son! I should apologise for being sensitive about it after all these years. She must have had some very hard years after that. She was still standing tall when I met her, but had something about the legs that encumbered her walking. It was about a year after that, I think, her eyesight started to fade. In fact, it may have started before. I had a strange feeling that there was a bit of a veil hanging between us."

He gives a little laugh. "She was still writing letters a few months after. I couldn't help – you know we shared the table in the Bike Shed, Frank and I, and I was sitting there writing when I caught a glimpse of the corner of a letter written in such large handwriting that I couldn't help reading it – 'your rather uninspiring colleague' she had written. It could only have been me." He shrugs.

Ada learns that he has travelled from Salisbury where he works as a geography teacher.

"It was good of you to come, if she was so brusque with you."

"And I rather dread funerals, the space they make for memory. The living step forward, leaving the dead behind. It can't be helped. I suppose I am here partly as a very late arrival at Frank's funeral. And I had hopes of meeting old colleagues."

Ian has booked in at the Webbern Hall Hotel a few miles away, but Ada invites him to Moorside for a cup of tea. She can see he is puzzled to see such a haphazard group of people at home in Mrs Mann's house. She introduces Nancy as Mrs Mann's granddaughter. She still doesn't feel entitled to claim her out loud as her own daughter but can see Nancy wondering if this is someone with whom she can claim Frank as her father, and ask about him.

When the sky begins to fade, Dennis rounds them up for the bonfire, and they sit, eating cider cake and watching the sparks flicking upwards in wavering lines. There's wax on the pieces of hive and they sizzle and flare and send out a delicious scent.

"Church," says Dennis, when he notices Annie sniffing.

"We should have songs round the fire," says Ian
Pavey. "Like at church camp. Have you ever been to a
church camp, Dennis?"

"I did," says Ada. "I remember lying in the tent,
staring up at the stars."

Nancy looks disbelieving. "If you were in a tent, how
could you be staring at the stars?"

"The sides were sloping, you know, a bell tent, and
we had the top of the door flap tied back. I thought I was
the only one awake, and the sea was shushing just over
the dunes."

They all listen, and it's not the sea this time, but the
wind in a pair of ash trees on the other side of the road.

Ian starts to sing.

"I'm just a poor, wayfaring stranger,
A-wandering through this world of woe.
And there's no sickness, toil or danger,
In that fair land to which I go.
I'm going there to see my Father
I'm going there no more to roam.
I'm just a-going over Jordan
I'm just a-going over home."

Scraps of charred paper rise with the sparks and
descend to become dust. A corner of a page takes
flight, flapping wings of flame, brushes against one of
the windows of the cottage and slips down to the sill

as a fragile black triangle. Nancy leaps up to stamp on another tiny flame establishing itself in a clump of dry grass between the cobbles.

"We're a bit near the house. I'm getting some water."

"There's a book on the fire!" says Rufus. Dennis pokes with a stick.

"It's a passport; Mr Mann's passports. He won't need them anymore."

"Let's see," says Ada and grabs Dennis's stick to hook the end in the little window at the front of the passport and pull it free of the fire. "That's not his. It's Ivy's! Ivy Smith, see."

"Auntie Ivy's? But she's Mrs Mann."

"Is that what she said?" Ada laughs. "Oh dear!" She meets Ian's eye.

She flaps the passport to cool it.

Nancy returns with a bucket of water and wets the ground around the fire. Dennis soon becomes as keen to quench the remains of the fire as he was to start it.

18

Ivy

June 1948

Ivy knows that Moorside House will be full so she has booked a room at the Webbern Hall Hotel. She has her trusty suitcase in one hand and wrestles with the front door. Then she freezes, staring at an object on the hall table.

"Excuse me," says a voice.

The woman behind her looks faintly familiar, smiles with recognition and even puts down her own bag ready to shake hands.

"I know you, don't I?"

"Er, Smith," says Ivy, sticking out her hand. "Ivy Smith."

"Edith Chancellor. You'll probably have met me at Meredith Hall now the SPMS offices are there. So we're both here for the funeral."

Their host ushers them across the draughty hall to the reception desk to begin the ponderous process of taking down their names and addresses. Guests are coming and going, and every time the front door is opened and bangs, his papers fly up and he loses his place. When he leads the way to the stairs to guide them

343

to their rooms, Ivy hangs back, continuing to glance at the side-table where there is now just a hat, a gentleman's hat.

"There was something there, just now, a little ..."

"May I take your case, Madam?"

Alone behind the heavy oak door of her room, Ivy stands, turns, turns again.

She throws herself on her knees beside the bed. Then, impulsively, she jumps up again, pulls the door open and, without a pause, knocks firmly on Edith Chancellor's door.

Edith is sitting on her bed, with her hat beside her and looks startled to see Ivy marching into the room.

"Was it you who sent the daughter here to Middlecombe?" Edith is frowning, wondering what she is being accused of.

"She gave me such a fright. To see Frank's child, like a ghost, on the doorstep. It was too much for me, overwhelmed me. I couldn't stay. I couldn't bear it. I even left those poor children for her to look after."

"I don't understand. You brought Frank back, didn't you? And then you were still there when the daughter came?"

"His mother, she needed me. She needed someone, a housekeeper. You could say I drudged for her. Particularly once we had the evacuees. But when the girl came, it was impossible. I wasn't her mother. She was looking for her mother."

"I sent her to her grandmother. She knew her mother wasn't there. It was right they should meet, wasn't it?"

"Oh yes. It was right. It was me who was wrong. The wrong person in the wrong place."

She's grinding the heels of her hands together.

"My dear girl, do sit down." Edith indicates the stool by the dressing table and Ivy sits. "You helped Frank, you helped his mother. What was wrong with that?"

Ivy is looking at Edith's reflection in the dressing table mirror.

"I wasn't her - Ada. At the very end, even he probably thought I was."

"Was it that you – loved him?"

"Jealousy, you mean? There may have been a bit of that. He was a very fine man. He responded so well, so powerfully, to spiritual need, such a natural missionary. But I had never understood Ada or how she could be right for him. Did she really know what we were confronting out there? Frank, now, he was strong, despite his illness, and he guided her. He might have been ill but he insisted on the wedding even when she was hanging back and weak. He knew she was grieving so he organized everything, even though it meant Andrew changing the dates of his trip down south."

Edith leans forward. "You can tell me, can't you, what happened to her there? I have wondered for so long. She was my dear friend. You were there. You were at their wedding. How was it that he couldn't help her?

And why did she abandon him when he was so ill? She didn't shy away from taking on a burden of that kind. So why then? Why could he not replace the family she had lost? Why was she fleeing from him?"

"That morning, after the wedding..." Ivy interrupts herself: "You've never been somewhere like that, have you? You people from Meredith Hall send girls out there to the field, but you don't know what it's like."

It seems to Ivy that Edith flinches at this accusation, so she explains:

"You get such a sense of evil. There are all these cheerful people living their lives, just like the village here at Middlecombe. But then, all of a sudden it seems, they are giving themselves over to hidden powers, passionate, crazy trances or slaughtering animals, drunkenly gathering round huge fires with tiny children tottering round ready to fall into the embers. I knew I should wrap myself in Christ's mantle but at such moments I would actually doubt my faith – not doubting that God was there, nothing like that, but I'd doubt that I could call upon his strength when I needed it."

Edith is gazing at her sympathetically.

"And then once you'd seen them in that state, you'd see how they'd be giving themselves to that same overwhelming power of evil in tiny ways all the time. Little tiny gifts perhaps, but like leaks in a vessel. They let that dark, overwhelming thing in."

"Tell me what happened. What did that have to do with Ada?"

"The night after the wedding, I was alone in the hut for the first time. Before, when Rachel Burstow was ill and dying, I had gone down to the compound with her and shared a room in case she needed anything. But with Ada and Frank using the Sinclairs' room and Andrew and Diana in the guest room, I was alone in the hut. Of course, I didn't like it. I kept imagining I could hear movement at the other end, in Ada's room or on the ladder at the back. After a dreadful night, I went through to go down and get myself a cup of water. The door to Ada's room was ajar and I saw a thing on a little shelf that was hooked into the weave of the wall. At first I thought, someone had been in there, someone had made one of their little spirit altars and put it there like they do in their own houses. But then I saw that it was bound about with the red string that I had seen Ada gather up just a day or two before. The thing was bits of bamboo and reed, all carefully woven and strapped together, I thought it was like a little boat or a chair. She'd been learning how to make little things - tiny little baskets, with one of the old ladies. So of course it was her, she'd made it.

"I felt then that the house was contaminated, as if one of their nasty little spirits had been sucked in. The thing was, she always seemed a bit too curious about what they were doing. She would talk for hours with this funny little crippled man, supposedly getting her language up to scratch. I sometimes went past and she was always listening, not talking, just listening."

"I know who you mean. She wrote about him."

"So I saw this object and I thought - how could she do such a thing? I wrapped it in a scarf and took it down to the compound. 'What has she done?' Diana said. 'She's not one of us, not one of us at all.' She actually fell to her knees. We prayed together, Andrew and Diana and I, while Ada and poor Frank went off to catch their train."

Ivy stands. "Could we perhaps get something, a cup of tea ...?"

Edith gathers her handbag. "Let me get you a drink. Come down to the bar."

They find a quiet corner and when two sherries, one very sweet and one very dry, have been delivered to their table, Ivy picks up her thread.

"Many years later when I had settled here at Middlecombe – if you can call it settled – I found a notebook. We all used them, grey with lined paper, and Burmese script on one cover and Exercise Book in English on the other. I'd thought it was mine, with my lists for packing and so forth and popped it in a drawer. But then, at the other end I saw that Ada had been keeping a journal. Not systematic with dates and so on. Just a jumble of thoughts, grieving thoughts. Maybe I shouldn't have read it. She wrote about her poor sister

and how she would rock her in a chair, a rocking chair...
A chair with red string to damp the rockers.

"But, you must understand, when I heard that day, the day after their wedding, that she had abandoned Frank on the train and disappeared, I was sure that she had given herself over to a kind of madness. Could she have leapt off the bridge, even?"

"Oh my," breathes Edith.

"We didn't know for some days what had become of her until the story got back to us that she had somehow got herself to the sugar factory and was recovering from an injury there.

"That didn't explain anything. Then just a few weeks ago, I read this."

She pulls a sheaf of flimsy paper out of her bag.

"One of her letters," says Edith.

"She sent it to Frank. It was too late by the time it got here. I only read it a couple of weeks ago."

She reaches across the space between them.

"I can't read someone else's letter," says Edith, pushing it back.

"Huh! I've done that, and worse." She takes the letter back with one hand and clutches at Edith's sleeve with the other, suddenly desperate. "You must hear me. Because of me a child was born and abandoned. Ada sought forgiveness from him, he couldn't give it and so she closed her heart to the child. His child! Like a ghost, just like him."

As she sits back, she catches her sherry glass with her elbow so a sticky puddle spreads across the table. She stares at it.

"No use crying," she says.

Edith smiles ruefully. "If it helps at all, I believe the girl's life with her adoptive parents was perfectly happy except that they both unfortunately died rather soon. And she did find her grandmother – just in time."

19

Nancy

June 1948

Pegging the washing, Nancy watches the two boys – her brothers! – in the garden. Dennis is showing Rufus the place under the bushes where they buried a blackbird. Dennis had found a split stick, whittled the face of it smooth and pencilled the date – 16th February 1948. But now after several months of nature's many little touches, there seems to be nothing but the blank grey space where the writing had been.

"We didn't know its name," Dennis says, shaking his head sadly.

"Are we digging it up?" asks Rufus.

"Of course not. It stays there for hundreds of years. Like all the people in the churchyard."

Nancy remembers the hand washing after the burial and her own disgust that Dennis and Annie had handled the dead bird so freely. How *do* you prepare children for a funeral?

She thinks of Annie's hand in Mrs Mann's and the way she'd stand at the side of the bed or chair, just leaning a little to make her presence felt to the blind woman. She decides. She won't ask them to go to the funeral, to sit in church staring at the glossy sides of a coffin, knowing and not knowing what is inside, to stand by the grave watching the polished wood gliding past the rough walls of the grave. Rufus, in any case, is too young. Mrs Brown has asked if she can help. She can mind all the children together, or the two little ones if Dennis wants to come.

Despite having a certain amount of expertise on the subject, Nancy was relieved to find that Mr Cartwright, the vicar, had a sheaf of instructions, prepared almost a year ago, covering the funeral arrangements. There was a list of places to send notifications – the *Times*, the *Scripture Pathway Messenger*, the *Western Morning News* – and some addresses of distant relatives to be notified. There was even a sheet of stamps tucked in with the list, which Nancy now remembers being sent to buy.

On the day of the funeral they are to expect the hearse at 12 o'clock. When it comes, somewhat earlier than that, Nancy sees that there is a formal sheaf of white lilies laid on top of the coffin, just like the last coffin she followed.

She calls Dennis to bring the stepladder and grabs a huge pair of kitchen scissors. Dressed as she is in a slim black jacket and skirt that must once have fitted Esme, she attacks the thorny white rose that climbs up to Esme's window, tossing the flowers into a heap on the mossy grass below. Then she reaches across and tugs lengths of the honeysuckle that grows beside it, nutmeg-scented, bruise-coloured flowers, and heaps them on top of the roses. With yelps, Dennis gathers up the prickly branches and carries them to the kitchen where they tie them into a huge bunch of drooping white heads and spurts of soft colour. They look at each other, knowing that the undertaker will object to this wild bouquet.

"It's all right," says Dennis. "Annie! Take this."

When she shrinks from the thorny stems, he makes a hammock from the hem of her skirt balances the bunch on it.

"Take them to the man out there," he says. "The one with the hat."

She hesitates and he frowns.

"Do it," he says, pushing her. "Do it for Mrs Mann."

At the second push her eyes start to fill with tears. By the time she arrives in front of the man with the top hat she is a picture of grief. He takes the bunch in his gloved hands and lays it so it droops over the foot end of the coffin.

"Do you want to come?" Nancy asks Dennis. "Quick, jacket and cap. The others can stay with Mrs Brown."

At the door of the church Mr Cartwright intones: "And though after my skin worms destroy this body, yet in my flesh shall I see God."

There's a clattering of feet, the brushing sounds of clothing, some small human noises, and now the old lady lies where the heart of the church should be, under her flowers, the sleek lilies over her breast and the wild and thorny bouquet at her feet.

20

June 1948

Ada

One of the church bells tolls. The chiming of the hour, perhaps – but the bell goes on. Time is stuck.

Lying there in her box, Esme Mann awaits the attention of the people who knew her – but none of those who knew her very well, as they have all gone. Even so, she is at the centre of a network of relationships. Who owes her an apology? To whom does she owe thanks? Is her finger pointing in accusation at Ivy? Ada suspects that Ivy thinks so. But she has at least as much justification for bearing a grudge against Ada herself, who has done so little for her. And what of her circulates in the blood of her granddaughter who hunches there in the front pew with poor puzzled Dennis beside her? She won't like it, Dennis had said, if we don't do things properly - she planned it all to be proper. Is her tongue arched to tut disapprovingly?

Or is she emptied of all of that? A box within a box? The bell ceases.

The organ squeezes out a line of tune and obediently the congregation draws breath and sings. As Esme knew they would. She chose the hymn.

Nancy keeps glancing round, no doubt wondering who all these people are, poor child. Could it be that the local people she has become accustomed to seeing in workaday clothes are transformed, the women with black hats, the men with balding crowns where their flat caps should be? Or are they all relatives from afar? Ada knows that Nancy had to lick stamps and send a set of envelopes left ready with the funeral instructions. Mr and Mrs Eric Hobday; Miss Selina Carter; Mrs Pheobe Tholey.

The psalm is not soothing: "Take thy plague away from me ... I am even consumed by means of thy heavy hand ... thou with rebukes dost chasten man for sin, thou makest his beauty to consume away, like as it were a moth fretting a garment ..."

Fretting, fretting, like Esme's restless fingers plucking at the bedclothes as she drifted ever further away. Ada had seen Nancy attempting, once, to still them and had murmured discouragement. No doubt the poor child's dying mother's blue-veined hand had done the same. So many do.

"For I am a stranger with thee, and a sojourner, as all my fathers were. Spare me a little that I may recover my strength, before I go hence ..."

The words lift to the rafters.

I go hence, I go hence.

I go hence. Esme could have been sure that Ivy – faithful Ivy, if a liar - would be there, and would be listening intently to the words; perhaps she might not have known that her eyes would be clenched shut: she always worked so hard at her prayers, Ada knew. Esme must have seen little of her, knew her by sound, by what she said, by what they shared in that house together. What had Esme shared with Ivy in the last days before her sight faded? They would both have had the memory of Frank's head rolling from side to side on the pillow, eyes closed, forehead glazed with sweat. He would have been lost and confused, peering at Ivy out of one eye. Did I marry you? Was it you I married? I shouldn't have married; I have to go. How could I think God wouldn't take me? He must have realised at the end, what a bad idea it was. Neither he nor she, it turned out, had the strength to look after the other.

Eventually he would have stopped shaking; she remembers him seeming to sink into his bed in the Bike Shed, embedded like a solid object sinking into wet sand. But finally, back in the bed in his childhood room, he must have sunk into fidgety silence, as Ivy muttered prayers, hoping that he could hear - over and over, the same words. She'd have used the words of Evensong whose comfort she tried to depend on but which, too often, seemed to flail like a curtain in front of a night-dark window. Dark like those jungle nights.

Poor Ivy, searching for God in that dark place.

Ada remembers the insects flitting into the light of a paraffin lamp. Smoke drifting past. The fearful words of Psalm 22 pulling fear from the air: "Many oxen are come about me; fat bulls of Basan close me in on every side. They gape upon me with their mouths: as it were a ramping and a roaring lion." Ripples of yellow and orange light dancing from side to side as the fire across the clearing was replenished. Tall headdresses, the long feathers the witchdoctors wear, moving among the shifting people.

Strong words, fearful words. "I am poured out like water, and all my bones are out of joint; my heart also in the midst of my body is even like melting wax. My strength is dried up like a potsherd, and my tongue cleaveth to my gums; and thou shalt bring me into the dust of death. For many dogs have come about me ..."

The congregation sits for the lesson and there's an accidental squeal from the organ. Ada remembers the animal sounds of terror on that fire-lit night and Ivy's clinging fingers digging into her leg. "Deliver my soul from the sword ..." They had heard the sound of sacrifice – terror brought to sudden silence. Why did they do that? Death as a relinquishment, celebrated. Something about the moment of death.

Ada hears a rough and heavy sigh from the pew behind. Ian Pavey. Poor man, he has passed through a valley of death – or several valleys. Pursued by death, fleeing before the threat of it like a building wave, audible in cruel tales dropped by the light-footed who floated past.

"Behold, the celestial city!" Frank had said, when a journey's end came in sight. What a relief, to end a journey. Could death be like that? Dropping burdens, shedding the filth of the trek. A homecoming.

Under where the coffin is resting on its trestles is a gathering of foot-worn names. Sacred to the memory of Henry Youngman: and his wife Rebecca; a sooty-looking stone in loving memory of Walter Wise. For each stone, a name, sometimes two. For each name, a person, in a web of people, joined by repeated actions, by shared plates and cups, hand-me-down clothes, facial features, arguments and even tears. Near them, immediately in front of Ada, sits Nancy. Frances. She, poor child, was given a name and then thrust away to the other side of the country. Whatever was held together by the first name bestowed on her ended up dismissed and ignored. There was a new set of people, things and even purposes to become part of.

Can she expect her name to be etched in stone here, in this village? Is that what Esme hoped for, for her son's child? The solicitor had visited, making sure that the instructions for the funeral were found and followed, the notices sent out to relatives and newspapers. He made them aware that they did not need to search for a will – it was in his care – but he gave no inkling of what was in it. He seemed quite brusque with Nancy – a so-called relative, so recently discovered.

Mr Cartwright pauses in the middle of a long reading and clears his throat. "Evil communications corrupt good manners," he reads. Ada remembers her mother saying that though she didn't know at the time that it was part of the long explanation of how the dead are raised up. She knows now you have to wait to make any sense of it. "Thou fool, that which thou sowest is not quickened, except it die". Then the bit about seeds and celestial bodies. And then, finally, very finally, "in the twinkling of an eye, at the last trump ... the dead shall be raised incorruptible, the mortal shall have put on immortality." Such a long argument, such an unlikely outcome.

Ada feels herself open up to the high space of the church, whitewashed, striped with dusty sunbeams, not unlike the church of her childhood where she used to sit very still, letting the words ring through her.

Her eye rests on the gleaming wood of the coffin and she thinks of Frank's mother bundled up in the elaborate shroud she had helped Nancy to choose. All in white petticoats, there wherever the dead go.

The funeral director gathers up his hat and stick and the bearers line up on either side of the coffin. The bunch of roses and honeysuckle slithers off the foot of it as they make their turn. Nancy, in the front pew, fields it and walks from the church clutching it like an anguished bride.

They move into the churchyard and stand not far from the stone with the name so like Nancy's original one. Francis Mann's mother is to be buried a little to the north of him.

Northwards. That's what Mahgawng Kajee said. "They go northwards."

Sitting with Ada on the veranda of the half-built church, he had asked her, in one of her first conversations with him, "Do you have a father? Do you have a mother?" These were standard questions she had learned to answer and it was easy because at that point she had both. Then, "Is your father a lord?"

She had laughed. "He makes things from wood. And he sends dead people on their journey. In their coffins."

That had excited Mahgawng Kajee. "A *dumsa*?"

"What does a *dumsa* do?"

"He tells them where to go."

"No! Not a *dumsa*. Not a *dumsa*. He doesn't know where they go."

That hadn't helped to teach Mahgawng Kajee the way to Paradise. So, the next time, she had asked him, "Is it good, where the soul goes when you die?"

"We go to the land of our ancestors. A long journey. We see them again, our parents. They are happy to see us. We are happy to see them."

Ada wondered how that worked for Mahgawng Kajee who, so far as she knew, was abandoned by his parents.

"If you follow Jesus," Ada had begun again, "you go to a very good place."

"My ancestors are not there. *Your* ancestors are there."

"There is a place for you. Jesus welcomes everybody who follows him."

But she saw it through his eyes – a crowded place full of strangers. Foreign strangers. Scores of them gabbling in the dark; like it was for her on her journey to the mission, when she got off the train at Sagaing, just west of Mandalay, and had to find a way to cross the great black river and continue northwards.

She sees her own mother, thin and hunched with her arm round plump Louise, the pair of them toiling up a rocky path. Trudging towards the bridge of snakes and the bridge of bamboos.

The poor, weary soul travels so far and still has mistakes to make.

21

June 1948

Dennis

Leaving the graveside, Dennis wonders what he is going to say to the other children. As far as he knows, almost all his relatives are dead, yet he has never been at a funeral before and is wondering what it has been for. It seemed to have little to do with Mrs Mann and has left him with a sense of uncertainty. She has to wait for the resurrection, but when will that be? She has to rest, but for how long? And are they just saying that because it's better to be asleep than dead? He trails along the lane behind Nancy, Rufus's mum and Auntie Ivy.

Mr Trench, who had nodded to him in church, hurries up behind him with a briefcase under his arm.

"I need to talk to the ladies. Do you think they can give me a moment?" he asks.

Dennis nods and ushers him through the front door.

"Mr Trench is here."

The door to the dining room is open and Mr Trench rests his briefcase on the table. The three women, still with hats and bags, line up behind the chairs on the other side while Dennis hovers by the door.

"I cannot delay this afternoon, but I should inform the three of you, in outline, of the terms of Mrs Mann's will. This has not been straightforward as there are a number of problems to do with identity."

Dennis hears the chair in front of Nancy jarring against the floor but Ada is between her and the door so she can't run away.

"The adult beneficiary is Miss Smith."

"One of the cousins," mutters Nancy. "Was there a Smith?"

Ivy shifts uneasily. "How could she do that?"

"She knew all along," says Ada. "And of course she was grateful. You did so much for her."

"But not to say a word!"

"You, Miss Smith," continues the lawyer, "are to receive an annuity of two hundred and fifty pounds per annum for as long as you live."

"No!" says Ivy. "How can I take it?"

"Shall I go on?" says Mr Trench. "With the exception of two charitable donations, the remainder of the estate, this house, all investments and some woodland where I believe beehives were once kept, are to go to Miss Frances Mann who, being not yet of age, will receive them in trust in the first instance, until January next year whereupon they become entirely yours." He nods at Nancy.

"But can you be sure that's right?"

Everybody's got the wrong name, thinks Dennis. Perhaps I'll have to change mine if I'm adopted.

"We will have to examine documents, but a birth is registered in the name of Frances Mann and I believe you are the rightful holder of that birth certificate. I have to hurry away now, but I will return on Thursday."

The solicitor emerges from the dining room and gives Dennis a nod as he passes to the front door, then steps back and holds out a hand for Dennis to shake.

"I think we will be able to solve your problem now," he says. "Just so long as everybody agrees."

Ivy, Ada and Nancy emerge into the hall. Ivy is shaking her head and pushing her fingers up her sleeve where she keeps her handkerchief. Is she about to cry?

"Was it all right?" Dennis asks Nancy. "It's yours, this house? Can we stay here?"

"I think," says Ada, "that this means there is no rush. You won't kick us out, will you, Nancy?"

They're making their way to the kitchen when there's a thump on the front door – the side of someone's fist. Dennis opens it. There's a tall man with floppy hair and a scruffy tweed jacket.

"Oh," says Dennis, unable to decide who this may be.

"Don't open the door, Dennis," calls Nancy from the kitchen.

He's forgotten that they are still hiding from Mrs Morris until they have officially started the adoption.

"It's all right, he's here for me," says Ivy, "That is, he'll give me a lift. Come in, do. This is Mr Warren. He's been at an auction and, I think, can take me back to Bournemouth... "

She stops suddenly and Mr Warren just stares at her.

Dennis reaches out a hand. "Good afternoon Mr Warren. Would you like ...?" He's not sure what he can offer "... a glass of water?"

Mr Warren smiles but is still staring at Ivy who has shut her eyes and seems to be groping for an invisible thing in front of her.

"Is everything all right?" he asks.

Ivy clearly, for some reason, cannot speak. He takes her hand, lays it on his forearm and pats it. Ivy pulls it back and sends it up her sleeve instead to where she perhaps hopes there's a second handkerchief.

"She knew! She knew. And yet she put me in her will. For my lifetime! And she knew all along! Can we go? My bag is here."

"Oh dear, oh dear." He picks up the bag and pats it comfortingly. "We can go. Good afternoon to you all."

A large brown van is parked awkwardly across the road. They watch him shutting the passenger door for Ivy and giving it another comforting pat.

"I did know there was something she wasn't telling us," Dennis says.

22

June 1948

Ada

It was only when she turned to leave the church to follow the coffin to the grave that Ada realised Edith was there in the church. They reached out to clutch each other's hands.

"Come to the house," Ada said, hastily. "When people have gone. There's someone I want you to meet."

So, later in the afternoon Ada and Edith sit on the bit of brick terrace that faces westwards from the French doors at the end of the sitting room where a rough lawn turns gradually into orchard. Edith sits in a chair with a tasselled canopy but Ada brings out a stool carved in the shape of an elephant for herself. As soon as she sees that Edith and Nancy have met before, she realises that Edith's summons to her had not been as straightforward as it seemed. Nancy, in the role of hostess, disappears into the kitchen and leaves them to remember their relationship and accommodate Edith's well-meant intervention.

The children are playing in a tattered string hammock slung between two apple trees.

"I wudna do that," says Rufus. "You'll fall out."

"*You'll* fall out," says Annie.

"Listen to her. She's talking!"

"Is that surprising?" asks Edith.

"She's apparently not spoken since she came here to Devon. Not even to Dennis."

"Do you remember," asks Edith then, "what it was like to be a child? Or Nancy's age? We were there at Meredith Hall at Nancy's age, asking ourselves again and again what the purpose of our lives was. Are we any wiser now?"

"No," says Ada bluntly. "Sometimes I think we should pay more attention to the little things and forget the big things. The little bumps and scratches we get and give in passing. But not the grand idea of where we are going and who we think we are."

"Why? I love to see a young woman who has a sense of where she's going."

"But it's not our ideas that make us who we are. Haven't you noticed, that's what's so lovely about children?"

"Ah, there aren't many children in my life. When she came to see me, she was so frantic. I kept myself from telling her where you were. But then when she wrote to me, struggling with the situation here, I thought, I'm her godmother; I have a job to do." Edith slips her fingers into the side pocket of her handbag. "I've brought this."

It's a photograph. "It was in the SPMS album for Burma and India but nobody's going to miss it."

Ada sees a young woman in a pale dress – very pale green it had been, with soft raised dots in the fabric. She's holding a trailing bunch of jasmine and white gardenias. The scent had filled her head, it would have filled the church. She must have blinked - her eyes are a blur. Frank, beside her, is staring steadily at the lens. Around them are their colleagues: Ian Pavey peering round Maud Bennett's shoulder, the Sinclair children in neat white socks.

"Poor Frank," says Ada. "He thought he was building me into his life, his very fine life."

"I thought I might give it to Nancy," says Edith, "If you don't particularly want it."

The hammock twists upside down and there's a row of three reversed heads, hair brushing the ground.

"You'll get ants in your hair!" calls Ada.

Nancy has arrived with a tray of tea, which she puts down abruptly.

"They're all going to fall on their heads!" She strides across the lawn to unwind the hammock but finds herself sitting beneath it with her arms full of children's limbs.

"What you can't see," says Ada, handing the photograph back, "is that she was there. Nancy. She had begun."

When Edith has gone and the evening meal is over and done with, Nancy, with the photograph in her hand, confronts Ada.

"So why did you abandon him? He was *dying*. What kind of a wife leaves a husband who's dying?"

"An entirely inadequate one. I had answered him too easily. He was so sure that it was God's plan. I very quickly knew it wasn't that."

"Is that why you gave me up? Why did you do it? You lost your mother and your sister but you could have had me. You could have loved me. I was just a baby."

"Of course I could. I could if I'd been in my right mind. I was lost, Nancy. I was poisoned by guilt."

"But didn't it make you more guilty, abandoning me as well?"

"Of course it did. It does now if I let it. I feel sadness that my mother's life was so shrunken and crippled. I feel sadness that my father lost track of who he was, who I was, and couldn't be helped. I feel sadness that I never cuddled the daughter I gave away – and when I realised the beauty and terror of caring for a new baby, I felt such a loss. It swept through me, tremendous sadness. Rufus was more or less blond when he was born; I almost feel that his hair changed to auburn because of the tears that streamed over him."

Nancy won't pause to take that in. She accuses: "Is that why you want to save the children, to make up for it?"

"No, I don't think so. That's quite different. I think I'm happy now to be someone with softer edges, someone who can take on new shapes when needed. Like unbaked dough, still rising."

Nancy is listening now but she says, "Mummy used to grumble about people who'd make out they were ready to do anything for anybody, but really they're manipulating other people and trying to make them feel guilty. Because you should look after your own and leave others alone was what she said."

"But ... she looked after you, she took you on. I mean, when you were tiny. Of course you soon became hers, her family," she adds hurriedly.

Ada feels she deserves the suspicious look Nancy is giving her, as well as the pang of loss that surfaces.

"One thing I've learnt is that the end of possibility doesn't just come with death. It's with us all the time. My father, he didn't know me for years before he died – his memory was quite gone. And before he forgot entirely who I was, he couldn't bear the sight of me. I could try and try to be who he wanted, who I was for him in the past, but all he had hold of was the person he was angry with. It was like pushing against some kind of armour; I couldn't get any closer to him, something had crusted over."

"I tried to find him. I went to Norfolk. I was too late."

"That's so sad."

There's a rap on the front door.

Ian Pavey had gone to eat the meal he had ordered at his hotel but asked if he might return later in the evening. "I have something to give you."

He's brought a bottle of port but doesn't appear to be carrying anything else. He invites both Nancy and Ada to drink with him. As he arranges three glasses in a row Ada sees that he has lost the top joints of three fingers on his left hand.

"What happened there?" she asks, and then wonders if she shouldn't have done.

"My war wound," he says. "It wasn't easy getting out of Burma in the end...when the Japs were coming roaring up from the south."

"I read a bit about it, what they put in the Messenger."

"I tell the boys I teach that it was an elephant that did it and they never believe me. But it's true."

"What were you doing with an elephant?" asks Nancy, as sceptical as the schoolboys.

"We had to walk out of Burma. We'd almost left it too late. There'd been instructions to get the women and children out – there were flights arranged from Shwebo, to the south of us – and once they'd gone, the rest of us were rushing around trying to set up our compound as a hospital for the retreating military who we knew were heading our way."

He fills the glasses with blood-dark port.

"That Good Friday we did a service by lantern light and came out from the church into the dark and heard that Mandalay had been bombed - razed to the ground.

"I lost track of Easter after that. There was a flood of sick people, whole hospitals, officers who had fled north by train and were exhausted or hurt and could only just walk and we were rushing around finding food and space to lay yet another mattress – or something that would do instead of a mattress. And then the order came for all British personnel to get out to India as best we could. We had bicycles and our two ponies and some of the military had jeeps. But we were all burdened down with all the things that seemed most useful to us and the transport was basically best used to carry the gear. It all gave up on us: bicycles first, then we became unable to find forage for the ponies, the jeeps got bogged down and in the end it was just us on our own feet carrying what we could."

"Lydia had gone, hadn't she? I know they stayed on, but she evacuated safely, didn't she?"

"They had two children by then. She'd left with them. Our little band depended on Hocknell as we made our way out. He made the decisions about when to stop and how to manage the stores and so on. And then we found an elephant abandoned by the forestry company, just left with her mahout. That's her driver," he adds for Nancy's benefit. "And he, the mahout, had nothing to do except make sure she got the food she needed. When we said there was work for him and her to do because the Japanese were coming he made off, back to his village, I suppose, and we were left with an elephant to manage. She was such a nightmare, roaming at night despite her hobbles and pretending to be dim when we knew she was cunning. I was undoing the hobbles one morning and she crossed her legs and launched herself forward and crushed my hand with the chain. My hand was ripped to bits and she was looking at me with an evil glint."

"So did you leave her behind?" Nancy asks.

"Oh no! We needed her when we came to the rivers. You could put two or three people and lots of gear in the baskets on her back.

He turns to Ada. "We were crossing one of the rivers, I forget the name of it now. The rains had started in the mountains so it was getting stronger and wider every hour. We fretted on the bank for half a day trying to decide whether we could make rafts or get all our party across on the elephant in about ten trips, and one of the soldiers wanted to build a bridge of rafts – he'd seen the engineers do it. And all the time Hocknell sat with a heap of palm fibre, plaiting it together until eventually he'd actually made a rope that would be long enough."

"Frank said that was his gift, making things soundly."

"The rope did give way in the end but he couldn't be blamed for that. We had four weeks of it, crossing that landscape that was scored through with deep valleys. As if some fiend had dragged great claws through it, determined that we would not pass.

"You could only tell where the path was by the trail of dropped possessions, ever more valuable as their owners became ever more desperate.

"Everything was against us - the incline, the stones on the track, the tangles of creepers and thorns – and then the rain came and what wasn't clinging mud was a glissade of rock coated with clay and grit and trampled stems. We had to fight for each step, trying not to think of food, everybody having to ignore a throbbing wound or a gripe in the belly. And this was the thing. This is why I hate funerals. At the beginning, a fallen traveller collapsed beside the route would become the focus of a cluster of helpers. Soon it became difficult to tell which were still living.

"And then there was one, a young woman. Her eyes were half open so I called out to her but there was no doubt she was dead. Her expression was one of endurance, hopeless waiting, patiently expecting that somebody would do something, but at the same time knowing that they wouldn't. Could she be a Christian, I wondered? Did she need my prayers? Was I just to keep going, leave her body behind? So I grabbed a handful of leaves from a nearby sapling to lay over her face. They had a fresh, beautiful smell like fine leather. A bit later I was horrified to see my hand streaked red – another injury, both hands ruined – but it was the stain of the sap. Just like blood.

"After that there were so many bodies alongside the road, they became so frequent that if there were none, we'd think we had lost the way."

He puts his head in his hands.

"I'm so sorry. Funerals always do this to me. They take me right back there. We're all trudging along, abandoning the dead, decomposing as we go."

He pulls out a handkerchief, mops his face and blows his nose.

Ada replenishes his glass, and when he has taken a large gulp, refills it again.

"Anyway, what I am getting round to explaining is this. By the time we crossed the border, a completely invisible border that meant we'd got into India, what we were carrying were the things that randomly survived – the things we didn't have to eat, or wrap around a wound, or give away to gain a favour. I had a small package of Frank's papers that I delivered here a couple of years ago. There was his marriage certificate that was left on our desk when you set off together. I also had an odd little thing belonging to you, Ada. You will think me foolish, keeping this, but it was light and tucked into the package with my papers."

He pulls out from his jacket pocket a handful of tangled lengths of split bamboo. "I've squashed it a bit. I had it all in order at the hotel. Except I nearly left it behind when I was putting my hat on. After it travelled all that way."

With a tweak or two the chaotic skeleton takes shape as a rocking chair, just the size to sit in the palm of a hand. Strips of palm fibre are knotted to hold the rockers in tension with the arms and there's a wind of red string round each of the rockers.

Nancy, who has been lying on her side the length of the sofa, sits up and peers at the thing in his hands. Ada reaches for it and takes it to her face, sniffing, passing it to and fro under her nose. Her eyes are closed but tears leak out.

"But why did you bring it?"

"I suppose I saw that it mattered. It was made with such care. I tried to find you at your father's address, almost as soon as I got off the ship. Maybe he told you. I got shouted off the premises. This little thing does seem to carry turbulence of spirit with it. There was a terrible fuss, that morning after your wedding and it was all about this. Did you know? That it was a bit too much like the things the Jinghpaw made for their spirits."

Ada feels understanding wash over her like a wave.

"Was that it?" she says. "Was that why Diana was so angry? As if I had betrayed everything any of us had believed in. As if I had cursed God."

Ian frowns uncomfortably but she continues, "I was wrong. I know I was wrong. You could say I should never have been there. I wonder now how much I was ever part of the work of the mission."

She trails off, then flicks the little chair with her finger.

"But this, this little object was never my betrayal. We hurried the wedding. I wasn't fit to marry at that point. I couldn't join any kind of new effort just then."

She sees him hesitate.

"I thought perhaps he rushed you. You know he insisted on the date. He made Andrew delay one of his trips down south. I wondered why he was being so insistent, and his illness coming and going made it odder in a way. There was a day when I was going off on a tour, I'd packed up and gone but after I'd gone nearly a mile I came back for my little kit bag with books and things. I'd left it hanging on the outside wall of the Bike Shed. And I heard you were in there together."

Ada flushes and flicks a glance at Nancy, who appears to be dozing. There were two times Frank had invited her into the Bike Shed. The first time she had simply sat on a stool by the writing table while he stood with a hand on her shoulder and showed her the photographs he was going to send to his mother. The second time she had sat on his bed – it was the only place to sit side by side – and he had enclosed her with the mosquito net, held her close, laid her down. What had Ian heard?

"He didn't think much of me, you know," says Ian. "He was such a pillar of a man, strong but with a strength that held him apart from others' frailty. You could see it in his work with converts. He would be their example but he wouldn't let them give any weight at all to their old feelings, the things they feared, the people they cared about. They had to step away and be like him."

"I know what you mean. Was I meant to be one of his converts? A failed one? He said he'd give me his strength. But I'm not sure it was his kind of strength I needed."

Ian watches the rocking chair until it stills. "In many ways I prefer objects to words, when I'm trying to understand someone. We can't know, can we, what things mean for others. But that doesn't mean we give up on understanding. We don't have to construct a scheme of our own to describe what's going on. We can just watch."

"Oh yes. Oh yes." Ada feels a rush of gratitude. "Words fly in and take shape inside our own heads. Whereas objects are hard and resistant and we cannot distort them. Or we know it's us doing it if we do."

She has a sudden memory of a tall moonlit figure against a fire-reddened sky transforming itself into an assemblage of battered weaponry.

"I've come to think we have to accept that we can only catch glimpses. But we can notice the place things have in other people's lives, the tears they shed over them, how close they hold them, how much they avoid them. And then what we know of them is true, even if it is only part of it all."

Ian puts down his glass and leans forward. "Do you know why I joined the Scripture Pathway rather than any other mission group? We didn't build schools. We weren't there to be part of any project to wipe out the local culture. We respected their ways of doing things. We thought we could add to their lives, strengthen their sense of purpose, bring a better rhythm to their lives."

"Do you think that's what we did?"

"We gave them aspirin and iodine and a bit of minor surgery. And we told them a story that gives them a moral foothold, somewhere to move on from. Not to be stuck in weakness and fear."

Ada picks up the rocking chair.

"When I made this it was because I was plunged into grief and guilt for my sister. I felt I should have been there, that I had been wilful in coming away. She needed care, all the time. And my mother couldn't manage. I knew she couldn't manage – not that she couldn't do what needed doing, but she couldn't keep cheerful and purposeful while she did it. It was all a punishment as far as she was concerned. And then I went away."

"My other grandmother," murmurs Nancy, opening her eyes.

"When I heard about the fire, I blamed her. I was so angry. Her weakness destroyed my family. But now I know better. Once we are bound to others, and we always are, we are bound to let them down."

She sees Nancy's anxious frown.

"But even so there is always something to hold on to, new ways of understanding each other. The chair, our rocking chair at home, that was how Louise and I moved together, working together, you could say, to share an understanding. I only understood what a miracle that was when both the chair and Louise were gone."

She tweaks the joints and straightens the way the chair sits. It is fully three-dimensional, standing a hand's breadth from the table-top.

380

After a moment, Nancy picks it up. "Can I keep it?"

She yawns until her jaw creaks, then carries it on her palm to the door, turns and bids them goodnight.

Ian stands and says he'd better not drink any more or his car will be bouncing off the hedgerows. The house is quiet when he's gone. Ada creeps upstairs to look into the children's room. Rufus is head-to-toe with Annie. Ada considers lifting him out in case he regresses and wets the bed – it hasn't happened for many months, but you can't be certain. The children's feet just overlap under the sheet, with Annie's heels gently hooked behind Rufus's. She leaves them be.

Printed in Great Britain
by Amazon

32822967R00219